Totally Bound Publishing books by Rosanna Leo

Handymen
A Good Man
An Irresistible Force
A Reluctant Attraction

Dark Paranormal Investigations
Darke Passion

I0607647

Darke Paranormal Investigations

DARKE PASSION

ROSANNA LEO

Darke Passion
ISBN # 978-1-80250-517-7
©Copyright Rosanna Leo 2023
Cover Art by Kelly Martin ©Copyright March 2023
Interior text design by Claire Siemaszkiewicz
Totally Bound Publishing

DARKE PASSION

Dedication

For my husband Doug, my ghost tour companion
and fellow graveyard explorer.

Acknowledgements

Thank you to the wonderful team at Totally Bound Publishing for all the support and enthusiasm. To my editor Rebecca Baker, in particular, thank you for always guiding me in the right direction and for being such a great cheerleader.

I am absolutely in love with my cover for *Darke Passion*, and I send heartfelt thanks to artist Kelly Martin, for bringing not only my characters to life, but also the unique creepiness of the King Street Bed & Breakfast.

I was fortunate to have a special team of early readers who helped me shape this story. They are all fabulous authors themselves, and I'm honored to call them friends. Thank you, Anise Eden, Sarah Smith, Kat Turner and Sheri Williams.

Author's Note

Darke Passion was born on a visit to Niagara-on-the-Lake, Ontario. My husband and I visit the picturesque town regularly, and I have long been interested in its history. Although my story is fictional, it touches upon some real people, places and events. If you read about Upper Canada's involvement in the War of 1812, you will recognize the names I mention in the book: Major-General Isaac Brock and the 49th Regiment of Foot, the Mohawk chiefs John Norton and John Brant, and Joseph Willcocks and the rebel Canadian Volunteers. Of course, the Battle of Queenston Heights and the burning of Newark in 1813 are both real events that impacted our country's sense of nationhood. However, the characters of Ann Forbes, Captain James Kingston and Reginald Perry are completely fictional.

Nonetheless, my ghost story was inspired by what some believe to be a real star-crossed love. There is a charming B&B in Niagara-on-the-Lake that once belonged to the Powell family. General Isaac Brock himself was apparently secretly engaged to Sophia Shaw, Mrs. Powell's sister. Sophia was staying with them at the time of the war. It has even been said that Brock rode out to see Sophia one last time before the Battle of Queenston Heights, a battle that would claim his life and cement his reputation as a Canadian hero. Family lore states that Sophia offered him a cup of coffee to keep him warm, then bade the dashing officer farewell. Not every historian believes this account to be true, but I couldn't help but be fascinated by the thought of a soldier paying one last visit to his true love. I decided to make James Kingston an aide to General Brock, and to create a ghost story that originates with his final visit to his beloved Ann.

Prologue

Newark (Niagara), Province of Upper Canada, 1812

Ann Forbes padded through the dark house, clinging to the shadows. She hoped to avoid disturbing her father and sisters. They had all retired for the night, but it wasn't uncommon for her father to awaken in need of relief. The girls, at least, would be asleep. Grace and Amelia had long since ceased their giggling and gossiping, and although Fanny would have stayed up late into the night reading by tallow candlelight, she would be in bed by now.

As Ann passed through the kitchen, the various smells from their earlier labors triggered her senses. She and her sisters had had a busy day. Her body still ached from retrieving the last of the garden's herbs. Sweet basil, thyme and sage now hung from a rack, drying for the approaching winter. They'd also done some baking today, and the house still smelled like buttery apple cake and the dying embers in the fire.

She slipped out of the house and into the night, where October's chill greeted her. It draped a cloak of coldness about her shoulders as she took her first steps outside. Her skin tingled and froze at once, as if touched by a heartless lover. The sun was setting so much earlier these days, and the garden bore no memory of its beams. Instead, it was dark and somehow foreboding. Dry leaves crunched underfoot and a stale sweetness permeated the garden, a mere memory of the roses that had grown there in the summer. Even now, a lone rose trailed on the ground, the last bloom of the season. Soon, it would die too and the snow would come, blanketing the bush in frost. Ann pulled her shawl tighter, but it was no match for the fierce wind. It whipped through her, lifting and tangling her unbound hair.

She hadn't bothered to change back into her muslin, but wore her nightdress so that her father wouldn't suspect anything. After telling him she would retire early, she'd waited for him to fall asleep in his chair. Thankfully, he was a deep sleeper. He slept so much more lately, now that the illness was making him forget himself and those he loved.

Ann swallowed past the scratch in her throat. Father had insisted on calling her by Grace's name several times today, and he'd looked astonished when she'd gently reminded him of her own.

At least he found peace in his slumber. If only Ann could find such rest. When she closed her eyes, terrors appeared, so she kept them open every night as long as she could. Her nightmares, frightening and disjointed, tinted in garish red, all centered on James.

Stop it. There was no reason to allow fantasy to overwhelm her. James was fine and on his way to meet her now. A messenger from the fort had assured her of that.

How she yearned for a time when she could meet James without having to resort to such subterfuge. She shivered as the wind cut through her again, but she dismissed her discomfort.

If her dear James could endure the horrors of battle, she could endure a breeze.

Passing through the vegetable garden at the back of the house, she continued toward the forested area that bordered their land. Father had always warned her not to linger in the "wilderness" beyond their home, but Ann loved sitting amongst the mature sycamores and maples. Father had no idea that this wilderness was her sanctuary.

But that sanctuary was transformed by night. Although the thick line of trees shielded her from prying eyes, it created frightening shadows where there normally were none. With each step that she took, the shadows seemed to follow.

"Be sensible," she murmured. She clutched her shawl even harder, needing to hold onto something.

James would be there soon. That was, as long as he could get away. Major-General Brock kept his aides busy. James had often remarked about his commander's tendency to work into the early morning hours, and he expected such stamina of his men.

A rustling in the trees made Ann bristle, but her eyes had already adjusted to the night. She peered between the tree trunks, hungry for a glimpse of the man she loved. Although she could not make out the familiar scarlet of his uniform, almost black in the darkness, she knew the curves of his strong shoulders. James appeared beneath the branches of an overhanging willow, their usual rendezvous. He brushed aside the drooping branches and called her name.

She flew to him. "You came."

"Nothing could keep me away, my dearest Ann." Captain James Kingston of the 49th Foot Regiment cut a dashing figure. Ann had never considered herself prone to romantic notions, but every time she spotted him in his uniform, his blue eyes twinkling, he took her breath away.

Sheltered in her wilderness, they embraced. She lay a hand on the Field Officers Gold Medal at his chest, awarded to him after the capture of Detroit, only two months ago. He held her close, stroking her hair as if it might be the last time.

Would it be? She never knew.

This was the only way they could meet—under cover of darkness. When they did see each other in public, such as at the recent church tea and banner presentation to the regiment, they could not acknowledge each other with anything other than banal niceties. Ann's father, when he was lucid, would not listen to talk about the regiment. He didn't care that James was a lawyer by trade, and an honorable man. Her father had come from humble Yorkshire stock, but had made his wealth as a wine merchant after settling in Newark. He always said he remembered how it felt to go hungry, and he was determined to see her marry a man who would keep her in pretty ribbons and bows, her pantry stocked with good food and her table set with fine silverware and pewter.

Her father didn't trust Major-General Brock, or anyone in uniform. He didn't trust the Americans either, for all their bluster. His distrust extended to anyone who presented a threat to his livelihood, and his opinion was shared by many in Newark. The townspeople wanted to be able to go about their lives unmolested. Ann understood the sentiment, but she trusted James.

As the eldest of four daughters, it was important for Ann to make a good match. Her father would have her marry a man with initiative, a man with a head for business.

In fact, he had chosen someone for her. Unfortunately, that man made her stomach turn.

Reginald Perry was her father's assistant, and he planned to open his own shop one day. Father had recognized a ruthless streak in Mr. Perry's dealings, and he respected his calculating ways. Not a day went by that her father didn't thrust them together in some way. He often brought him home for the evening meal, and Mr. Perry's presence never failed to sour the occasion.

Ann had glimpsed a coldness in Mr. Perry's eyes. She'd heard the rumors of how he drank himself into stupors at the local tavern, maligning those in power in his drunken rants. She'd heard a great deal, in particular, of his dealings with women and of the brute force he'd sometimes employed to have his way with them. Ann knew of two servant girls in Newark who had been turned out into the cold for having babes in their bellies, and everyone knew who'd put them there.

Lately, Reginald Perry had turned his eye toward Ann. She despised his covetous glare and his curled lip. In all honesty, she wasn't sure why she fascinated him so. At one-and-twenty, she was already a few years older than the girls who normally received his attentions.

That didn't stop her skin from pricking whenever he turned his horrid gaze upon her.

James stroked her cheek. "So quiet, my love?"

Something rustled in the bushes. "Did you hear that?"

"It's nothing. Just an animal in the undergrowth."

Then why did she feel eyes upon her, even now?

She'd never told James about Mr. Perry, and the knowledge festered in her stomach. He had enough to worry about, and she didn't want to add to his troubles. She prayed that she'd somehow convince her father that Mr. Perry was the last man on earth for her, but Father's illness had made him stubborn.

"I don't have much time," said James. "The general believes an attack from the Americans is imminent."

"James, no!"

"We've received word from Major Evans this evening. He was sent to reconnoiter with the enemy about releasing prisoners, and caught wind of their plans. I was in the officers' dining room when he told the general, and heard it all myself. He's been ordered to make all the necessary preparations for an assault."

The hand that covered her mouth trembled. Surely it couldn't be her own?

James pried her hand from her face and kissed it. "We'll be ready for them. General Brock has positioned over a thousand men at Fort George. We are allied with the Mohawk chiefs John Norton and John Brant. Our numbers are strong. Mark my words. I shall return to you in no time, and we'll make our engagement public. I'll speak to your father. Surely, he'll see sense."

"But…" She couldn't find the right words, and her eyes filled with tears as he spoke. *Foolish creature! You must be strong for him.*

"Ann. Do not cry, my love."

She was trying to be brave, but the most horrid sensation gripped her. A ball of discomfort churned in her stomach, and bile climbed up her throat.

Somewhere along her peripheral vision, shadows gathered and lengthened, taking the shape of clawed wraiths. The figures crept into her forest sanctuary, defiling it. They skulked and threatened, their shoulders hunched in warning. By degrees, they slithered toward her and James.

No!

It had been years since she'd seen the shadow people. In fact, she hadn't seen them since right before her mother died, but there had been a time when their appearance was a common occurrence. Frankly, she'd hoped she'd grown out of them.

Ever since she was a little girl, she'd been able to see the troubling specters. Her mother used to tell Ann she had the "sight." It was a trait she apparently shared with her grandmother. She, too, had been full of strange tales, none of which had given Ann any sort of comfort.

Only, in Ann's case, the figures only ever appeared before someone was about to die.

"James." She gripped his coatee so hard that one of the shiny buttons fell off in her hand. "Don't go."

"I must. I need you to be brave, my love."

"Come back to me, James. I will not rest until you come back to me. I swear it." She bit her lip, trying not to cry, and tasted blood.

The shadows teased, pulling at her hair. She twitched, trying to shake them off. Did he not see them? No, of course not. She was the only one who ever did. They clawed at her, scratching her skin. One of the creatures clutched at James' shoulders in an attempt to separate them. But if he felt anything, he did not show it.

"I will always come for you, my darling Ann, whether in this life or the next. I am yours, and you are mine, and no one shall ever part us."

They clung to one another, until James finally pulled away. "I must leave." His tender smile was meant to encourage, but she felt no such consolation. "Go back to the house, my sweet. You'll catch a chill."

She wanted to shout, to scream, *'Stay with me!'* And yet, her tongue would not form the words. They were stuck in her throat, frozen like the last of the summer's roses, trapped in a flash of ice.

With a last kiss, James walked away from their willow. He then slipped into the shadows and became one with them. There was some rustling beyond the line of trees as he headed back to the spot where he would have tied up his horse. Within minutes, he would be back at Fort George.

Ann was all alone with the shadow wraiths now, but their torment ceased. One by one, forming a terrible parade, they followed James out of the ravine and into the night.

They didn't want her.

"Dear God," she whispered into the wind. "Keep him safe, I beg of you."

Then, clutching the 49th Regiment button, she hurried back toward the house.

Chapter One

Toronto, present day

Edwina Darke clicked her keyboard with the fury of an avenging angel, removing yet another crude comment from her YouTube post. She called to her sisters in the other room. "Hey, listen to this one. 'Cute video, girlies. Now show us your tits!' Gross. Delete, delete, delete."

Her sister Susannah brought her a coffee. "Ed, you need to stop worrying about comments from random dudes. They're like the Hydra. You can delete one, and two more will pop up." She peered over Edwina's shoulder at the screen. "Besides, I'm pretty sure 'Gary69lover' is no authority on paranormal research, or anything else for that matter."

Their other sister, Adelaide, sat in the plush corner chair and nursed her coffee. "Methinks Gary doesn't get to see a lot of tits. He has to go online and beg."

Adelaide's evil chuckle soothed Edwina's temper, but only a little bit. "I hate these guys. Every time we upload a new video, the comments start. I bet you any money that 'Gary' is a cover for Walter Tipton. He's exactly the sort of person who would set up fake accounts to harass us. Tipton's pissed because we've captured more credible anomalies on camera in one year than he ever has."

Susannah pulled one of the kitchen chairs into the living room and sat opposite Edwina. "You really think Tipton's trolling us?"

"Who else could it be?" said Edwina. "I could understand a few random trolls popping in here and there, but this Gary dude seems to have made it his mission to discredit us. Plus, he keeps posting links to Tipton's site in the comments. Walter's got, maybe, seventeen subscribers on YouTube, and he's a dinosaur. Somehow, I just don't think his followers are all that keen. It's him, all right."

"I don't think so. The last time we ran into him, I asked Maria to tell me what she sees," Adelaide said. "She says his left knee is causing him a lot of pain right now, which puts him in a bad mood. Also, his wife has begun divorce proceedings. He's got other things on his mind."

Edwina and Susannah traded looks. There were many things that set Adelaide apart, but her references to her spirit guide Maria still managed to throw her sisters off kilter. It wasn't so much that she had a spirit guide — Maria had been clinging to Adelaide ever since they were kids. It was more the fact that Adelaide constantly referred to her as if she were an invisible fourth sister.

Even though it wasn't new, it still made Edwina uncomfortable. She always felt like she was being watched by some creepy Edwardian-era kid. She dismissed her misgivings about Maria. "Darke

Paranormal Investigations is my baby. We can't afford to have someone fucking with our reputation. It's hard enough being women in a field dominated by men. I want DPI to be a success."

"We all do." Susannah checked out her polished nails. "But you stress out about this stuff too much. Paranormal investigation is our hobby. We all have careers."

"I still want us to be seen as the best. When people in Ontario think of paranormal investigators, I want them to think of us. You know, instead of all those jacked-up guys on the TV shows, running around cold cellars, chasing orbs and shouting at each other." Edwina couldn't help feeling competitive. She was in every other area of her life. Why not this one?

"DPI's reputation is solid, and it's only going to get better." Adelaide's tone was calm and assured.

"You don't know that," Edwina argued.

"Yes, I do know it. Besides, Maria said so." Adelaide's shoulders slumped. "I really thought that by now you would be more inclined to believe what I see. I haven't been wrong yet. But that's Edwina Darke for you, always a skeptic."

"Someone on our team has to be skeptical. I don't doubt your abilities, Addy, but you know as well as I do that not every anomaly is supernatural. Sometimes it really is just dust on a camera lens."

Edwina's kneejerk reaction was always to play devil's advocate, which sometimes came across as not trusting Addy. She did trust her. After all, in being her sister for thirty-odd years, she'd seen some freaky shit. It had been Adelaide's psychic talents that had allowed them to capture the phenomena they had. She always seemed to know just where to look, enabling Edwina and Susannah to document the hauntings. Thanks to those videos, they'd snagged their first grateful clients and their YouTube subscriptions had skyrocketed. DPI had only been operating for a year, but they'd already cleared several properties of unwanted spirits, while debunking other manifestations.

But Adelaide was right. Edwina was a proud skeptic. Although their mom's side of the family was "sensitive," she tended to align with her dad's way of thinking. A math teacher, he'd taught her to question everything. Although she'd always been fascinated with the world of the paranormal, she also believed most "hauntings" could be explained.

Her real job also played a part in her beliefs. Her BFA in Stage Management had allowed her to work for the past few years in the Toronto theater scene. She worked backstage for local opera and ballet productions, numerous musicals and even some work at the Stratford Festival. As a theater tech, she'd learned how to create illusions with light and sound. She was familiar with all the tricks, and she knew how easily and how effectively a haunting could be staged.

So, an anomaly had to be spectacular to impress her.

If only her own sister wasn't a spectacular anomaly.

Adelaide was part of the reason Edwina and Susannah had developed an interest in the spirit world. Edwina's fascination went down a different path, though. At around the age of seven, Edwina had seen something in her bedroom that had disturbed her so much, something for which she had no explanation, that she'd made it her mission to learn everything she could about the paranormal world.

Now, at age thirty-five, there was nothing she liked more than being able to debunk unnatural phenomena. Every time they heard of a new haunting, it reminded Edwina of the terror she'd experienced as a child. The feelings of fear and anxiety would return, as well as horrible nightmares. Each time they managed to unshroud a supposed ghost, she was able to regroup a little. Finding explanations restored balance and peace to her life, and to the lives of the people they helped.

Was it possible she'd never really confronted what she'd seen in her bedroom all those years ago? Absolutely, but she sure as hell wasn't ready to do it yet.

So, yeah. She took their business seriously, even though they never charged for their services. No legitimate ghost hunter would. Most of them were in it for the thrill and for the purpose of acquiring knowledge. The women of Darke Paranormal Investigations simply wanted to help people feel at ease in their own homes. And if they could document compelling anomalies for the internet crowd while they were at it? Even better.

Edwina was the techie of the group, and she was never happier than when fiddling with K2 meters and spirit boxes—the tools of the trade. As a historian, Susannah provided the background information they needed for each investigation. And Adelaide…well, she talked to ghosts. She had from a young age, and while the others did their best to take it in stride, it certainly made life interesting.

As a team, they worked well together, except for those moments when Adelaide and Edwina butted heads about the authenticity of a haunting. It happened often, and had resulted in several heated conversations.

Susannah commandeered Edwina's laptop. When her eyebrows danced, Edwina thought another comment from 'Gary69lover' had come in. "What is it now?"

"I think we might have a new assignment," said Susannah. "There's an email from some guy in Niagara-on-the-Lake. Does the name Simon Teal mean anything to you?"

"Simon Teal," repeated Adelaide, drawling. "He sounds dreamy, like he could be the hero of a romance novel. A highwayman, maybe! No, a roguish duke with a terrible secret."

Edwina rolled her eyes. "Or another of Walter Tipton's aliases? Maybe Gary wasn't flowery enough. Let me see."

The email read:

Hello DPI.

I'm the co-owner of the historic King Street Bed and Breakfast in Niagara-on-the-Lake. It's a beautiful property in the heart of the tourist district. For the last few months, my partner and I have been dealing with strange phenomena at the property. Doors slamming, unexplained noises, that sort of thing. Some of my guests have experienced much worse. There have been reports of shadow figures, faces appearing in mirrors and voices coming from empty rooms. Our last few guests all complained of "feeling watched" when they were alone. Several said the covers were pulled off them in the middle of the night. One couple claimed they were touched and shoved. It's affecting our reservations and has become a concern for our dwindling staff. We need to get to the bottom of this as soon as possible.

My partner Connie is more open-minded, but to be honest, I've never believed in ghosts. That being said, I have no explanation for what's happening. Something here is just not right. Can you please let me know if you can help us?

Sincerely,
Simon Teal

Edwina was just about to open up another tab on her laptop when Susannah spoke. "I'm already googling it on my phone. Ooh, it's a nice bed and breakfast. Very swanky."

Before Susannah held up her phone, Adelaide put her hands over her ears and stood. "La la la la la la la la. I don't want to know anything about the place before I step foot inside it. Tell me when it's safe to come out." Adelaide raced off to Edwina's bedroom and shut the door. A moment later, they heard tinny music coming from her phone.

Adelaide made it a practice to know as little as possible about each location before they conducted any vigils. There would always be those who questioned her credibility, but the chances lessened if she went in unaware of the history.

Susannah lowered her voice. She held up her phone so Edwina could see the display. "Lots of history in Niagara-on-the-Lake. Fort George is nearby, as well as Fort Mississauga. And from what I can see here, the old barracks aren't far away from the property either. This sounds promising."

The hairs on Edwina's arms bristled. This was exactly the sort of case they loved. Because they were dealing with a house, the square footage wouldn't be huge, and it wouldn't be hard to test for drafts and creaky floors and all the other common occurrences that led homeowners to think they were haunted. It probably wouldn't take them long to debunk all those slamming doors and weird noises. They'd certainly dealt with larger properties.

She quickly reread the email.

Simon Teal. He really did sound like he belonged in a Regency romance. A picture of the bed and breakfast owner formed in her head, one of him wearing pantaloons and a cravat.

Niagara-on-the-Lake wasn't far from Toronto, and she happened to love the place. Maybe they could book one of the cute boutique hotels in town as their base. An excited shiver danced down her spine.

Something here is just not right. Teal's words of concern repeated in her head.

From deep in her consciousness, a dark memory teased. Once again, the image of the terrible apparition from her childhood appeared in her mind. Gnarled and growling, it reached for her.

She blinked a few times to banish it.

She had never been able to debunk that anomaly, and it haunted her. She'd have to settle for debunking as many of the others as she could.

Resolved to silence the demons that had plagued her since she was seven, Edwina sent Simon Teal a reply.

Chapter Two

"Please don't leave," said Simon. "I can put you in a different room. In fact, I can give you the honeymoon suite at no additional cost." Why the hell not? No one else was using it.

But Mr. and Mrs. Ortega were already packed. He was fighting a losing battle here.

"You're very kind," said Mrs. Ortega. "But I don't think my nerves can take much more, dear."

"You should try to attract the younger crowd," agreed Mr. Ortega. "You know, people who don't need as much sleep. In fact, I read an article in my travel magazine just the other day that said there are people who *want* to stay in haunted hotels! Imagine that." He pointed at Simon. "Now, *those* are the customers you want."

At this point, Simon had half a mind to try it. Although he suspected the ghost lovers were a niche group. He might get a few reservations at Halloween, but other than that? Somehow, he just didn't see the coffers overflowing with that scheme.

Besides, he hated the idea of labeling the King Street Bed and Breakfast as "haunted." He didn't get into this business to run a damn fun house. His expertise was in hospitality, making people feel welcome, not scaring them away. "I appreciate your feedback, and I'm sorry you've had to cut your getaway short. Of course, I'll refund you for the night you've had to miss." Heck, he might have to refund their entire stay to ensure they didn't leave a bad review. He eyeballed them, wondering if they were the type to want to destroy him from behind their keyboard.

Nah, they were too sweet.

Mrs. Ortega patted his hand. "You and Connie really do have a very nice place, Simon. If you ever get rid of the ghost, let us know. We wish you lots of luck." The old couple glanced around the reception area before walking out of the door. It broke Simon's heart that they were so clearly worried that a few creepy entities might be following them out.

It took all of Simon's energy not to lay his head on the reception counter and leave it there for good.

Connie Willard, his business partner, popped out of the back office where she had been going through the books again. She still had a pencil tucked behind her ear, nestled in her thick braids. "The Ortegas finally gave up the ghost."

"Too soon, Connie. Too soon."

"I know. Just trying to maintain some levity."

"That was our last booking. They've officially dried up." He shook his head. "Summer is the busiest season in Niagara-on-the-Lake. We should be turning people away because there's no room at the inn. Instead, we've got an inn with nothing but room."

"Which is why we're doing something about it. I'm glad you agreed to call in those ghost hunters. Seeing as we have no customers right now, they'll have the run of the house."

"I don't know."

"This is a good thing," said Connie. "We have to stay positive."

Positive. Simon couldn't remember the last time he'd been positive about anything. It was pathetic.

He'd used to be a glass-half-full kind of person, but after the shambles of the last couple of years, it had been hard to see things through the same filter. He was thirty-six years old, and his business was failing. His father had told him he was making a mistake in leaving the Toronto hospitality scene, repeatedly in fact, and he didn't want to give the miserable old coot the satisfaction of being right.

He and Connie had invested so much time and money in the bed and breakfast. This should not have been a risky venture. He'd been in hospitality for years, had managed large hotels in downtown Toronto. In fact, that was how he'd met Connie. They'd been managers at the same large, soulless property, and had learned the ropes together. When they'd decided to go into business together, they'd agreed a charming Niagara-on-the-Lake bed and breakfast would be a sure bet. With so many international visitors every summer, they should have been making money hand over fist.

Instead, their fists were employed fighting poltergeists or demons or…whatever the hell was occupying this house.

What a load of rubbish.

"I guess this is just hard to swallow because I've never seen the '*ghost*,'" said Simon, curling his hands into a couple of very annoyed air quotes. "I'm not convinced that's what we're dealing with. It's an old house with a lot of history. Imaginations go wild. People get carried away."

"Simon." Connie's left eye twitched. "I've witnessed it myself. I've heard the moans. I've seen the shadows. I've been touched when I was all alone. So has Margie." There had been a few evening shifts a while back when Connie's wife Margie had kept her company because Connie had been spooked. Margie had worked in the back room while Connie handled the desk, but both women had had experiences that had left them unsettled. "You know me as a level-headed person. Same with Margie. Are you saying *our* imaginations got carried away?"

"No. I'm sorry. There must be a part of you that wishes you'd packed it in when George left. Frankly, I wondered if you might hitch a ride with him."

When they'd first opened the place, they'd been so busy they'd had to hire a few additional staff members. George's help as a cleaner had been invaluable, but because George had often been alone while cleaning the rooms, he'd experienced some unpleasant phenomena as well. Things had been thrown at him and he'd apparently heard so many disembodied voices they could have formed an otherworldly choir. Being a religious sort, he'd handed in his resignation, convinced there was something demonic at play.

So why did it never happen when Simon was around? Dealing with the fallout from an invisible foe had been nothing short of maddening.

"Look," said Connie, "I'm not going anywhere. I have just as much invested in this place as you do. And even though I know you'd like to stiff-upper-lip your way through this, that doesn't always work. Keep an open mind with DPI. I'm sure they'll get to the bottom of it." She straightened out the edges of her shirt. It almost disguised her shiver, but he caught it. "I'm going to pop out for a coffee. Can I bring you one?"

"Yes, thanks. You're an angel."

"I know."

As Connie headed out, Simon fiddled around on his laptop, unsure of what else to do. Once again, he found himself clicking on the link for Darke Paranormal Investigations. It wasn't as if he'd spent a lot of time researching paranormal investigators, but he had to admit DPI had an excellent website. It was full of testimonials, flashy graphics and actual footage of some very weird things that they called "anomalies."

In the About Us section, there was a photo of three white women standing in front of an old warehouse. The image of the sisters was professional and slick. In fact, he'd been taken aback when he first saw the photo.

For some reason, he'd expected the women to look a bit like Elvira, Mistress of the Dark. In reality, DPI consisted of three normal women.

Okay, three good-looking, normal women.

He could admit he'd done a double take upon first seeing them. Who wouldn't? Susannah, the historian of the group, had an ethereal vibe with her long blonde curls and pale complexion. Adelaide, the so-called psychic medium, was just as striking with her shorter chestnut hair and expressive eyes.

But it was Edwina who kept drawing Simon's attention. The proclaimed tech expert of the group oozed self-assurance in her photo, maybe even a bit of bravado. With her arms crossed over her chest and one eyebrow quirked, Edwina looked like someone who took no bullshit.

She had shoulder-length auburn hair and full lips, and could grace the cover of a magazine, but that wasn't what kept him coming back to her picture. He much preferred the "don't even try it" attitude in that arched eyebrow. She had a Lara Croft vibe—part adventurer, part ball breaker.

He liked it.

"Oh, for fuck's sake." Simon really did put his head on the desk this time. He had no business fantasizing about a ghost hunter, or anyone else, for that matter. His livelihood was at stake.

Besides, given his comically tragic history with women, the last thing he needed right now was another entanglement.

Still, there was definitely something about Edwina Darke that made him want to indulge in a few choice fantasies. It didn't matter. The important thing was the Darke sisters seemed to have the chops to do the job. He hadn't just gazed at their photo, he'd read their impressive biographies as well. He was hopeful they'd help him eradicate his pest, whatever it might be. They would be here at the end of the week. In truth, they couldn't come quickly enough.

As he studied the cute dimple in Edwina Darke's raised chin, a banging noise made him jump. Simon raced into the office, half hoping and partly dreading that he might finally encounter the King Street ghost.

The small office space had once been part of the large kitchen, but over the years it had been renovated and a wall now separated it from the cooking area. It looked out over the backyard garden.

After a quick search, he located the source of the banging noise. The metal receptacle that held his pens was now on the floor, the pens scattered. Although the window was open, it wasn't a breezy day. Even if a strong gust had come through, he had a hard time believing it would be enough to knock over a metal desk accessory.

As Simon picked up the pens, the hairs at the back of his neck rose. Being a take-charge kind of person, and at the end of his wits, he decided to put it all out there. "Look, you little shit disturber. You might be able to scare our customers away with your parlor tricks, but you're going to have to try harder with me. Consider this your invitation. I would *love* to have it out with you." He clenched his jaw as he stared around the room.

But there was no response, worldly or otherwise. No moans, no creaks, no floating severed heads.

Feeling like a gullible ass, he went back to reception and waited for Connie to return with his coffee.

He clearly needed some caffeine. And maybe a tequila chaser.

Chapter Three

This was a house that had seen things.

At first, Edwina would have sworn that the King Street Bed and Breakfast was as benign as any other well-maintained historic house. With its white-painted brick exterior, clean windows and established garden, it had plenty of curb appeal.

But there was something beneath its pristine surface, something that beckoned. It was one of those houses that had its own personality. Its quirks gave it life. They drew her in and made her want to explore.

Although the original building was symmetrical, there were some modern additions around the back and side of the structure. It now boasted a couple of bay windows and what looked like a breakfast nook. In front, there was a series of older, smaller windows. These were clearly part of the original architecture, and Edwina could almost imagine the faces of long-dead inhabitants pressed up against them.

It was clear that a lot of money had been spent to keep the exterior of the building tidy and fresh. The paint on the black shutters was new, as were the roof shingles, and there was an inviting wraparound porch. In the front garden, a rainbow flag flew proudly. Several ferns hung around the porch, creating a sense of privacy and balance.

And yet, something had disturbed the equilibrium here.

Edwina knew from experience that appearances could be deceiving. Even the coziest homes could make one feel ill at ease. Conversely, she'd been inside buildings that frightened neighborhood children, and hadn't found any evidence of spirit activity at all. She knew to keep an open mind.

She glanced around the corner at one of the additions. According to Adelaide — and her weird pal, Maria — construction projects often upset spirit people. Indeed, Edwina had often read accounts of hauntings that had occurred as the result of a renovation.

Ghosts didn't always appreciate people coming into their spaces and changing things around. Was that the case in Simon Teal's situation?

She doubted it. These additions weren't brand-new and might have even been added by a previous owner.

She peeked around the side of the house. It opened into a spacious back garden, one with many healthy perennial plants, but the most striking feature of the garden was that it backed onto a wooded ravine. She imagined that one could feel somewhat intimidated standing in that green space. The massive trees provided a wide canopy, and although it was beautiful, there was something wild about it as well. The canopy blocked out any view of the nearby homes, adding a touch of primeval atmosphere.

A low ringing began in Edwina's ears. No, a hum.

She walked back to where Susannah stood in front, but the hum didn't go away. There was a voice-like quality to the sound, and she glanced at Susannah to see if she was making the noise. However, her sister was quietly checking out the house.

"You okay?" asked Susannah.

"Yeah." Edwina rubbed her ear. "Just a weird ringing sensation. It started a second ago."

"Hmm. Well, you know what they say. Someone's talking about you."

"Right."

When Simon Teal opened the door, Edwina forgot about the clamor in her ear. She glanced up, and her breath caught in her throat.

Whoa. Their client was hot.

Not, like, hockey player hot or bodybuilder hot. She'd dated plenty of those dudes, and unfortunately, many of them had proven disappointing beyond the first titillating glance. No, Teal had a quieter appeal, but it appealed nonetheless. His blond hair was short, but long enough to run one's fingers through, and judging from his uneven part, he'd been running his own fingers through it a lot. He wore nerd glasses with thick black frames, nice jeans and a gray polo shirt. Edwina couldn't help noticing the style of shirt because it highlighted his intriguing biceps. He resembled the sexy professor character on her favorite nighttime drama. A scholarly sort who was hiding a devilish side.

Christ. She sounded like Adelaide now. She was already inventing his backstory.

And inserting herself into it, in a variety of lascivious ways.

Um, Ed. Not appropriate at all. The guy's your client and he has a partner. Down, girl.

Susannah elbowed Edwina. "Hungry? You're nibbling your lip."

"Shut up." Edwina pasted on a smile as they walked the remaining steps toward the door. She held out her hand. "Simon? I'm Edwina Darke. This is my sister Susannah."

He shook their hands in turn. "Nice to meet you both. I appreciate you coming." There was a wariness in his tone, but his hands were nice and warm, and they gave her a pleasant sort of tingle. So pleasant, Edwina was reluctant to let him go. He gestured at the house. "Welcome to the King Street B&B. Come on in."

With its large foyer and grand wooden staircase, the bed and breakfast was definitely not the average nineteenth-century house. Even before the additions had been built, it must have been a fine property. Original hardwood stretched from the foyer into the other rooms. It had a gorgeous floor—polished and maintained, but full of charm with its nicks and dents.

How many people would have walked on those planks of wood? How many would have held that handrail as they headed upstairs? Susannah was usually the sort to gush about these things, but there was a bit of history geek in Edwina as well, and that geek was jumping for joy. She'd always gotten a thrill in old homes, from being able to touch the surfaces so many others had touched.

This property wasn't decorated like other old houses that she'd seen, though. She'd been inside plenty that were embellished with lots of chintz and fussy wallpapers, so much so that one would think Laura Ashley had self-combusted in them. This bed and breakfast had more of a modern aesthetic. Although there were period features like intricate moldings and some antique furniture, it had been decorated with the modern guest in mind. There were a lot of sleek lines, and a neutral color palette helped the vintage features shine.

"You have a beautiful place." Edwina knew she was gawking, but it was hard not to be impressed.

He ran his hand through his hair, which drew her attention back to those distracting biceps. "Thanks. It was full of florals and flock wallpaper when we bought it. Not really our thing."

"You and your partner live on the property?" asked Susannah.

"Yeah. I mean, I do. My business partner lives offsite."

Ah, a business partner. A happy little flutter struck the underside of Edwina's ribs.

"There's a small addition next to the office area that I've reserved for myself," continued Simon. "More of a studio apartment than anything else, but it's enough space for me for now, and it allows me to keep an eye on the place. My plan is to eventually purchase another property nearby so I don't have to be onsite all the time. But right now, there's just not enough money coming in."

"Because of your ghost issue," said Edwina.

"Yup. Because of…whatever this is." He waved toward the parlor. "Come on in. Have a seat."

Although the parlor was painted in steel gray tones, it was warm and cozy, thanks to a fireplace and leather chairs in the seating area. A gorgeous blue billiards table and a library nook with built-in bookshelves made up the rest of the room. They sat on the leather chairs and Edwina had to a stifle a sigh, they were so comfortable. Simon and his partner had definitely put a lot of money into this property. No wonder they were eager to resume business.

Frankly, if she'd been looking for a place to stay, she would have booked it in a heartbeat. It was full of charm. It felt like a home.

"Can I get you a drink? I have coffee, tea or sparkling water," offered Simon.

"We're fine," Edwina said. "We just had coffee."

"Okay." He looked between them nervously. "I thought there were three of you."

"Adelaide will join us soon," explained Susannah. "She's a psychic medium, and she prefers to come in cold, with no background information to influence her readings. You can rest assured whatever you communicate to us today will not be shared with our sister until after she does her walk-through. That's when she takes the pulse of the place, so to speak."

"Makes sense."

Footsteps sounded just outside the parlor door. A Black woman joined them, her face lighting up as she greeted them. She looked to be about forty years old, had shoulder-length braids and pretty eyes that were made even prettier by the laugh lines around them. Although she was dressed in business-casual attire, trousers and a classic white blouse, her smile held the promise of mischief. Edwina liked her right away.

Simon introduced her. "This is Connie Willard, my business partner. She was the one who suggested I reach out to DPI."

Connie pumped their hands. "I'm so excited to meet real ghost hunters! I have so much to tell you."

"And we want to hear it all." Edwina cast a glance at Simon. Based on the stiffness of his spine as he sat, he didn't seem to share Connie's bubbly energy. That was typical. In most of their investigations, they encountered clients who were relieved to have them on board, and others who regarded the proceedings with a healthy measure of uncertainty. "How many staff members did you have before?"

"Just a couple," said Simon. "We had a gentleman who came in to do the cleaning. His wife sometimes joined him. And in our first summer, a local student helped us out a bit on the desk. Within weeks, they were gone. They found the atmosphere too oppressive."

Edwina soaked in the vibe in the pleasant room. Nothing set her on edge. Of course, Adelaide was much better at that sort of thing. She could walk into a room and immediately feel that something was "off."

"Could we get their details?" asked Susannah. "I'd love to speak to them too."

Connie jumped up. "You bet. I've compiled their contact info and some eyewitness accounts from customers. I've already given everyone the heads up, so they're expecting your call. I'll be back shortly with their info."

"So." Edwina's gaze cycled back to Simon. *Wow.* Were his eyes periwinkle blue or more of a cornflower? She cleared her throat. "Could you begin by telling us a bit about the house?"

He glanced her way, doing a subtle doubletake. Had he noticed her checking him out? Or was he checking her out? "Sure. I freely admit I haven't done a deep dive into the history, but I can tell you it's one of the oldest homes in Niagara-on-the-Lake. The original part of the house dates from around 1815, but the foundation is even older."

"So it was torched by the Americans in 1813 like the rest of the town?" asked Susannah.

"Right," said Simon. "I just remembered you're the historian of the group. Yes, from what I've read, the entire town was basically destroyed. This property was originally owned by the Forbes family, but I don't know anything about them, other than the fact that they rebuilt the house after it was burned down. The place remained in the Forbes family for many years, but it's changed hands a few times over the last few decades, and Connie and I bought it a couple of years ago. I assume the 1812 period will be of most interest to you?"

"Not necessarily," said Susannah. "Niagara-on-the-Lake is famous for its connection to the war, but that's really just scratching the surface as far as its history. There's an incredible wealth of Indigenous histories in this area, going back to 100 AD. The first Europeans started to show up in the early 1600s. Of course, we know there were many Loyalist families in this area, people who fled the American Revolution, but that's certainly not all. Much has been written about Niagara's role in the Underground Railroad, but it's important to remember there were families here who took part in African enslavement. This area was built on the backs of those enslaved people. Niagara-on-the-Lake might be considered a sleepy little theater town by some, but its history is anything but."

"Sometimes, it seems all anyone knows about this place is the Shaw Festival and General Brock," commented Simon.

"Right?" Susannah's voice rose in excitement. "Brock was turned into this mythological figure by the British. Very few people talk about how Indigenous warriors saved the day at Queenston Heights, to say nothing of the company of Black soldiers who helped recapture the Redan Battery after Brock died in his reckless charge." She blushed. "Sorry. I could go on and on."

"No, I appreciate what you're saying," said Simon. "I guess, from a possible haunting point of view, we have a lot to consider."

"We do."

"Did you grow up around here, Simon?" asked Edwina.

"No, as much as I love the Niagara area, I'm a Toronto boy. I grew up on the Danforth, and I really miss the energy of Greektown sometimes. That, and the souvlaki. I didn't like how busy and congested it was becoming, but I'll always think of Toronto as my home. Go, Raptors!"

Edwina was pleased to hear him mention her favorite team, especially in that warm, snuggle-under-your-favorite-blanket type of voice. Between the twinkle in his eye and that smooth baritone, it was easy to picture him indulging in some dirty talk.

Again, girl, whoa. Keep it in your pants. She cleared her throat.

"It was only recently that I considered moving," he continued, frowning. "I, uh, guess you could say I needed a change."

There was something sad behind the slash of his brows, and it scattered all her naughty thoughts. The snoop in Edwina was dying to know what it was.

Stay on track. If it doesn't affect the investigation, it's none of your business.

Susannah scratched a few notes in her notepad. Edwina knew the way her sister's mind worked. No doubt, one of her aims would be to see if the Forbes family had any remaining descendants in the area. It was entirely possible that they might be familiar with the alleged ghost, and that they might have theories as to its identity.

As Susannah made her notes, Simon turned to Edwina. An appealing pinkness spread across his cheeks. "I read that you're the tech person, Edwina."

"Call me Ed." Her cheeks heated when he smiled, in response to his own blush. *Damn. He has dimples too?* She was such a sucker for dimples. "And yeah, I'll be setting up the equipment before Adelaide joins us later in the week. Actually, I'd love to get a tour of the place, if that's okay with you."

"Of course." His gaze strayed to her lips. "Follow me."

As they walked out of the parlor, Susannah nudged her.

Sheesh.

There were times when Edwina appreciated having a sister who was so detail-oriented that she didn't miss a trick.

This was not one of those times.

As Simon toured them around, she realized just how spacious and elegant the place was. The dining room took her breath away, with its crystal chandelier and marble mantelpiece. A wall must have been knocked down at one time to make the room so large. As a result, guests could spread out while they ate their meals. Next on the tour was a smaller study that had been converted into a business center for guests, and it was equipped with a couple of desks, laptops and printers.

As they walked upstairs, the floorboards creaked. Edwina mentally made note of exactly where the creaks seemed loudest. The flooring on the second level was not as highly polished as the beautiful dark hardwood below, but it had just as much antique character. Simon showed them into a series of bedrooms. There was a gorgeous honeymoon suite with white draperies and linens and an ensuite bathroom. The remaining bedrooms were named after some of the varieties of wine that had made Niagara-on-the-Lake famous — Riesling, Chardonnay, Pinot Noir and Merlot. They all had luxurious private baths, the kind that would make one want to take a long, hot soak in the tub, probably with a companion.

They ended the tour downstairs where Simon showed them the professional-grade kitchen. There was also a basement, where they stowed bits of unused furniture, and a small cold cellar.

The King Street Bed and Breakfast was definitely full of interesting features, but nothing seemed to be in disrepair. As Simon toured them around, Edwina made sure to flick on all the lights and open any closet doors. Upon first inspection, she noted new windows everywhere, and she didn't anticipate drafts. Nothing was out of alignment, and there were no rusty hinges. There didn't appear to be any leaky faucets or faulty electrical work, at least from what she could see. Of course, they would have a chance to check things out in greater detail on their vigils. Because the house was old, there were some slightly uneven floors, but nothing bad enough to cause objects to slide off furniture or down the hall.

Still, she had seen stranger things happen.

The sisters had been in homes that had initially felt light and pleasant, only to be overwhelmed by dark auras as their vigils wore on. Edwina didn't always credit the phenomena to paranormal activity. That being said, they had run into some spirit people. Sometimes, those phantoms kept to the dark, hiding in corners until the time was right.

They returned to the parlor and had a seat again. "So," Simon said. "First thoughts? Notice any goblins peeking out from behind the dressers?"

"No goblins." Edwina didn't mind his sardonic tone because it was delivered with a charming smile. Besides, she understood. "I know you mentioned in your email that you're not a believer in the supernatural."

Before he could comment, Connie returned to the room and handed Susannah a folder. "Simon doesn't believe in the ghost. He's never seen it, although pretty much everyone else has."

"Full body apparitions?" asked Edwina.

"No," said Connie. "More like impressions. I can *feel* someone around me. I've been working alone and have suddenly felt breath on the back of my neck. It makes every hair stand on end. But I've seen things moving by themselves, and I've heard voices when no one else is around." She shivered. "And I've been touched. You can't make that shit up, although Simon just thinks we all have wild imaginations."

"Busted," he replied. "I mean no offense. This is just hard to swallow."

Edwina smiled. "I get it. Would it help if I told you I'm a fellow skeptic?"

"You are?"

"Yeah. I usually don't believe in anything unless I've touched it or seen it myself. It's important for me to have proof. It doesn't mean I don't acknowledge when something abnormal is happening. I just like to keep my feet firmly planted on the ground."

"Of course, sometimes the spirits pull the rugs out from under us," Susannah countered. "That's where Adelaide and I come in. We provide a different perspective. Addy gets messages from the dead, and we validate those messages through my historical research."

Simon nodded, then made eye contact with Edwina again. He held her gaze, a bit longer than necessary. For a split second, she forgot there were others in the room with them, but when he spoke, it brought her back to reality. "It sounds as if we're in good hands, then. Will you help us?"

Edwina shook his hand, then Connie's. "We will. DPI is officially on the job."

"All right." He relaxed into his chair a bit more.

"Over the next few days, I'd like to get my equipment set up," said Edwina. "Susannah and Adelaide have their own preparations to do, so I'll hang out on my own and get a feel for the place. It'll give me a chance to take some preliminary video, and I wouldn't mind getting some footage of you and Connie just going about your day. I'd like to do some on-camera interviews, too."

"Sure," said Simon. "And if there's a simple explanation for all of this?"

"If we can locate a cause for the phenomena, then we'll make recommendations on how to fix it." Edwina considered all the various factors they'd encountered on previous investigations. "Sometimes, it's just a matter of bringing in an electrician or a plumber. And other times, it's psychological. Stress can manifest in bizarre ways. As humans, we fall prey to suggestion here and there. You'd be surprised how many people think they can see things in the dark that weren't there in the light."

Simon gnawed on the inside of his lip. "Okay, and if there is no explanation?"

"Then we'll deal with that too," said Edwina. "Either way, we'll get to the bottom of it. If there happens to be a ghost, or ghosts, they're about to learn this bed and breakfast has new owners. And we won't stop until they're moved on to a better place."

Connie let out a cheer. "Yeah! Did you hear that, ghost? Your days are numbered."

When laughter erupted throughout the little group, Edwina got the sense it was a much-needed release. Connie was clearly nervous about the activity. As for Simon, Edwina could tell he hadn't laughed in a while, and that made her sad.

Oh boy. Here we go.

She'd always had a thing for guys who were a little bit broken inside, and her addiction to trying to cobble them back together had led her down some frustrating paths.

She would not go there again, no matter how much Simon Teal's eyes sparkled or how earnestly his dimples relayed his gratitude. She knew nothing about him. For all she knew, he could be a total prick, like Gary69lover.

She already had more than enough of that energy in her life.

Chapter Four

It had been suspiciously quiet around the house since the Darke sisters left. Of course, Simon had to keep reminding himself that it would seem quiet without any guests, but it wasn't just that.

There was a new stillness throughout the rooms, a sense that the entire house had taken a breath and was waiting to exhale. Simon wasn't the sort to get caught up in those types of notions, but even he had to admit it was eerie. There was a different energy in the house, and the place almost crackled with it.

For the first time since buying the property, he'd been uneasy going to bed in his studio apartment. He found himself turning on a lot more lights than usual, and couldn't shake the sensation that someone, *something*, was watching.

It was as if the Darke sisters had created a disturbance in the force. He repeated that line to himself, forcing a chuckle, anytime his hackles went up.

It was, therefore, with a mixture of emotions that he welcomed Edwina Darke back to the bed and breakfast the next day, so she could start setting up. When Simon opened the door to her, bright and early that morning, he felt equal parts trepidation and excitement. Trepidation, because he couldn't believe he was going to be partaking in this bananapants exercise. Excitement, because it was Edwina Darke, and he was more curious about her than he'd been about anything for quite some time.

"Edwina, hi. Thanks for coming."

"Thanks for having me."

He opened the door wide so she could enter. "Do you need help with any of your equipment?"

"Maybe in a bit. Right now, I just want to wander and have another look. Feel free to do whatever you need to do. I won't get in your way. I promise, you won't even know I'm here."

Simon did his best Vincent Price impression, which, frankly, wasn't great. "And so she wandered, as silent as the grave."

She narrowed her eyes, but some amusement shone through. "You might want to practice your Vincent Price. It sounds more like William Shatner."

He scratched his head. "Not my best work, admittedly. Look, I don't want to get in your way. Just let me know if you need me for anything. I have some very stimulating work to do, in the shape of some overdue accounting, so I'll be in my office. Connie's around today too. She's just out right now, haggling with our linen supplier. She's a much better haggler than I am."

"Gotcha." She glanced out through the foyer window. "The light's really good right now. I think I'll start by doing some filming outside. We usually do a little video montage at the start of each YouTube episode, and I like to have a variety of shots for atmosphere."

"Great. What are your sisters up to?"

"Susannah's interviewing your former employees today, and Adelaide's doing some of her own work until we bring her in."

"Okay. There's a fresh pot of coffee in the kitchen, and some croissants. Help yourself."

"Hmm. You're the first client who's ever fed me. Keep it up, Simon. You might just become my favorite."

He kept his response to a smile. The idea of being Edwina's favorite anything was altogether too appealing, and he didn't trust himself to comment on it appropriately.

Simon let her get to work, and he busied himself in the office for a time. However, the accounting only held his attention for so long. It wasn't every day that he had a paranormal investigator in his house, and his curiosity was growing by the minute.

Besides, it had been about an hour and Edwina still hadn't come in for croissants. She must have been getting hungry.

He saved his work and headed into the kitchen to gather up a few things. He poured her a travel mug full of coffee, including sugar and cream on the side on a plate. Then, he collected two of the biggest croissants from the box. He wrapped them up in one of the takeaway bags that they used for customers. Not every visitor to the place wanted to sit down for breakfast. So, for the ones who wanted to eat on the run, they'd printed up cute takeaway bags, ones with the bed and breakfast's logo on them.

He sighed as he headed outside. He'd thought the bags were a nice touch, but when he looked at them now, he just saw money going down the tubes.

Hopefully, Edwina and her sisters would fix whatever was ailing the property.

He found her in the backyard, taking some long shots of the house. "There you are. I thought you could use some sustenance."

She set her camera down on the edge of the porch and accepted the goodies, her brown eyes lighting up. "Thanks. When I get going, I sometimes forget to eat."

"I wasn't sure how you took your coffee, so I brought cream and sugar. If you're not into almond croissants, I have a couple of other flavors in the kitchen."

"Thank you. This is perfect." She took a bite of croissant, and her eyes rolled back up into her head. "Oh my gosh, this is so good. I love croissants."

Noted. He'd have to make sure they had a fresh supply whenever she was around. "Who doesn't love flaky pastry, right?" He indulged in a quick fantasy of feeding her one of the croissants and offering to wipe up the crumbs that fell about her cleavage. "So, how's it going?"

She washed down her second bite with a sip of coffee, and he couldn't help but admire the way her lips moved against the edge of the travel mug. She was wearing a reddish lipstick, and it left a faint stain on the cup.

For some reason, that stain fascinated the hell out of him.

He had friends who complained when their partners left lipstick marks on their clothes or dishes, but he would be happy for Edwina to leave her mark on every mug in his kitchen. Or on him, for that matter. It was sexy as hell.

It occurred to him that maybe he shouldn't be staring so intently at her lips while she was talking.

"Do you know much about the architecture of the house?" she asked.

"I'm told it's neoclassical, the oldest part anyway. Apparently, the symmetrical layout and decorative front entry are a dead giveaway. I know the modern additions kind of take away from the effect, but I like them. It's got a mishmash of styles and I like houses that are a bit quirky. It's just one of the things that drew Connie and I when we started our search for a property."

"You seem to make a great team."

"Yeah. Connie's awesome. We worked together at a big hotel chain for years. I managed the front desk, and she managed catering. Our work threw us together a lot, and we hit it off. We realized we had the same vision as far as hospitality is concerned. One day, we worked our asses off to make this huge event a success, and for a dipshit VP who'd only landed in the role because his daddy put him there. We got no credit, no thanks. After that grueling shift, Connie and I looked at each other, and said, 'Let's do it.' We handed in our resignations within minutes of each other, and became partners."

"I'm glad it worked out for you." She was staring at one of the upper windows. "Is Connie back? Because I was hoping to ask her a couple of questions about her experiences here."

"Nope. I just got a text from her. She's still at the supplier."

"Are you sure?"

"Yeah. Her car's not here, and the appointment is in St. Catharines. It usually takes her a couple of hours."

"It's just...I thought I saw someone looking out of one of the bedroom windows."

"Oh." Even though it creeped him out a little to do it, he glanced at the window.

There was no one there.

"I'm sure it was just a trick of the light," said Edwina. She bit into her croissant and swallowed. "Thanks for breakfast, Simon. When Connie gets back, could you let her know I'd like to chat with her? If she has the time, of course."

"Of course."

As he walked back into the house, his gaze strayed toward the same window.

Sheesh, dude. Relax.

Like Edwina said, it was probably just a trick of the light.

Nevertheless, as Simon got back to work, he had to fight the urge to keep looking over his shoulder.

See what the power of suggestion will do?

Power of suggestion or not, he was much more at ease when both Connie and Edwina joined him inside the house later.

* * * *

The peculiar feeling lasted over the next couple of days. He had to keep reminding himself to get a grip, and to relax his jaw and neck. His posture had become tense all of a sudden. There was no need to be nervous. The shadow in the corner of his room was nothing more than that—a shadow. The creaking floor upstairs was just Edwina moving around.

At least, he really hoped so.

Susannah had been in touch in the meantime. She had interviewed their former employees, and had documented their bizarre experiences, but was hesitant to draw any official conclusions. She'd also continued her research of the property and the area.

As for Edwina, she'd been in and out several times, and had set up all their equipment. Every time she'd walked through the door, he'd had to stop himself from giggling like a schoolkid. He'd kept all their interactions friendly and professional, but there was just something about her that he found so attractive.

"I've set up a few motion detectors around the location," she'd said during another visit. "I like this model because it has a range of up to twenty feet and it alerts you with a light as well as a gentle chime. You know, so you don't jump out of your shoes when you hear it. There are also video recorders watching the sensors to make sure nothing natural triggers them. Everything is battery-powered, and I've put in fresh batteries." Hands on hips, she'd admired her work. "Oh, yeah. We're ready."

Simon had learned something about himself in that moment. Listening to Edwina talk about motion detectors and video recorders gave him a serious boner. He'd had to walk away, muttering some nonsense about having to "count towels."

That didn't mean he hadn't indulged in a couple of fantasies. In fact, in the shower that morning, as he'd lathered up, he'd envisioned Edwina in a sort of BDSM dungeon, only it was filled with ghost-hunting equipment, as well as whips and nipple clamps. In his fantasy, she'd been wearing high-heeled boots and a corset, and her amazing lips had been rouged red.

She'd ordered him to remove his clothes and get on the bed, then she'd done nasty things to him.

"Get it together, Si." Today, Adelaide would be coming over with her sisters for her first walk-through. The last thing Edwina needed was for him to be trailing her like a starving puppy after a bone.

Besides, although he'd done his best to create a romantic atmosphere at the King Street Bed and Breakfast, it didn't feel that way anymore. In preparation for Adelaide's walk-through, Edwina had draped all the artwork in black cloths. Because it was a business, he didn't have any personal photos hanging around the place. However, he had invested in some amazing old maps of Niagara-on-the-Lake and had framed them and hung them in many of the rooms. But, with all the black draperies, the place resembled a house in preparation for a wake. He kept expecting to walk into one of the rooms and find a body in a coffin.

"It's so that Adelaide won't be influenced," Edwina had explained. "If she sees photos or certain kinds of art, it can interfere with her impressions."

He supposed that sounded fair enough. What did he know?

Connie arrived before the sisters did, with a full tray of coffees. God bless her. Once she handed the tray to Simon, she clapped her hands in excitement. "Are you ready to de-ghost our property, Simon?"

"Ready as I'll ever be."

Soon afterward, the Darke sisters arrived in Edwina's black Jeep. Because neither he nor Connie knew what to do or where to stand, they waited for them outside on the porch.

Edwina led the way. "Simon, Connie, this is our sister, Adelaide."

Simon wasn't sure what he'd expected in meeting the psychic Adelaide for the first time, but it was not the vision before him. Her bobbed brown hair was caught up in a series of sparkly flower barrettes, and she had a sprinkling of freckles over her nose and cheeks. She wore jeans, as well as a Luke Skywalker T-shirt under a baggy cardigan. On her feet, she wore pink Converse sneakers, and had a small purse slung across her body. It was pink and sparkly too. All in all, she portrayed a youthful image, although he suspected she wasn't as young as she appeared. He extended his hand. "Nice to meet you, Adelaide."

"Nice to meet you too." She shook his hand. "Wow. Simon, I don't normally do impromptu readings, but I'm getting a lot of energy coming from you. Would you be open to me giving you some information?"

"Sure. I guess so."

She clasped both her hands around his. "Your grandmother is here, and she really wants to communicate."

"*Here*, here?" He gestured back at the house. "Like, haunting the B&B?"

"No. Just around you. Protecting you. She wants you to stop worrying, to trust in what's happening here," said Adelaide.

"Okay." *How convenient*. Simon swallowed the suspicious huff at the back of his throat.

Adelaide continued to stare at him in that unnerving way. "She tells me you were always a suspicious kid, that you used to argue with your teachers a lot. She says you were especially trying to Mr. Dooley, your history teacher. If he told you something was in the history books, you'd say, 'Where's the proof?'" She released his hands. "That's okay, Sybil. I'm used to skeptics."

"Sybil's my grandmother's name."

Adelaide smiled. "I know. She just told me not to get offended if you become prickly, that you're really a sweet boy at heart. Her sweet little monkey."

Hold on. Simon stepped back. His grandmother used to call him her sweet little monkey all the time, on account of how often he got into scrapes while climbing trees. There was every possibility Adelaide had researched his family online. It was easy enough to do, but there was no way she'd know about his grandmother's pet name for him, or about the Mr. Dooley story.

Simon had indeed gone through a tricky time when life at home was getting to him. As a result, he'd turned into a little shit in the classroom. Adelaide couldn't have known that. Although, just hearing his grandmother's name was enough to rattle him. "Interesting. I'll just take my prickly energy over here."

Connie thrust out her hand. "I don't suppose you might be able to do an impromptu reading for me?"

"I think that can be arranged." Adelaide held Connie's hand for a few moments, then frowned. "There are a few people around you, but one of them is really eager to talk to you. He's an elderly white man. He has a full head of bushy white hair and is wearing a brown sweater vest. He says his name is Jim. He keeps saying, 'Tell Margie I'm sorry.'"

Connie gasped. "Oh my God."

"He wishes he'd told you more about his illness, but it came on so quickly. He kept asking you to delay your visit because he just didn't want his daughter and her partner to remember him that way." Adelaide nodded. "Thank you for sharing that, Jim."

"Oh, Jimmy. We understand, honey." Connie's eyes teared up. She took a few deep breaths. "He was always a good father-in-law to me. We never had anything but love and support from that man."

Simon, eyes stinging too, put his arm around Connie's shoulders. "Jesus. We haven't even gone inside the house yet, and we're all in bits."

"She's good, isn't she?" asked Susannah.

"She's something else," said Simon.

Edwina leaned closer to him. "Don't be too spooked. I know Addy's talents are unnerving. She says she sees spirits hovering all over the place. Apparently, we all have them around us."

"Great." Simon looked over his shoulder, wondering if he'd catch a glimpse of Grandma Sybil. She'd always been his favorite grandparent. Although his family was a dysfunctional one, she'd always been kind. She did, however, speak her mind. For instance, she'd recognized early on that Simon's parents spoiled his brother Rupert, and she'd called them out on it several times. Of course, it hadn't improved the situation, but it had helped Simon to know he had an ally. So, whenever Rupert acted up, Grandma Sybil would pull Simon aside and fill his pockets with hard butterscotch candies.

He still couldn't look at butterscotch candies without developing a thick throat.

Adelaide turned to the others. "Before we head in, I'd like to say a prayer of protection." She grabbed her sisters' hands, and they brought Simon and Connie into the circle. Adelaide closed her eyes. "To the earth and those who lie beneath. To the paths we are about to walk and to those who tread them before us. To the homes we will enter and to whom they once housed, know we come in peace."

She opened her eyes. "Simon, Connie, I'd like to explain a bit about my process. When I enter the house, I will ask permission of the spirits gathered there. After all, I wouldn't just barge into anyone's home, and I want to make sure the spirits are comfortable with us."

"Sure," said Simon, even though it really didn't make any sense to him at all. As far as he could tell, he and Connie were the only owners of this property. He was fairly certain the "spirits" had never made a mortgage payment. Frankly, if they were planning on sticking around, they could help out a bit more.

"As I do the walk-through, I'll be inviting them to communicate with us, and hopefully they will." Adelaide angled her head as if she was listening to someone speak over her shoulder. "Yes, Maria, I'll tell them." She grinned. "I have a spirit guide named Maria. She wants me to let you know she's here. She's protective of me and will sometimes make her presence known in interesting ways, so please don't be concerned if you see me talking to her."

Connie waved at nothing in particular. "Hi, Maria. You're welcome here."

Simon, on the other hand, did not wave or extend a greeting to the mysterious Maria. This weird exercise was already freaking him the fuck out.

It was much easier believing ghosts didn't exist at all. Frankly, it was more convenient chalking up the strange occurrences to a rash of rodents and a need for pest control.

Adelaide took a deep breath. "All right. Let's begin. Ed, your stuff's all good to go?"

Edwina nodded. "Baseline readings have been established. Susannah and I are both recording, and I'll be monitoring the temperature once we're inside. I can't wait to use my new ranged thermometer."

Simon suppressed the ripple of excitement that tore through him upon hearing Edwina discuss her gadgets again. He was still giddy from when she'd described her EMF meter the other day, although for the life of him, he couldn't remember what it was supposed to do. Something about measuring electromagnetic fields. He'd thought it was an expensive walkie talkie. All he really knew was he liked the way Ed held it, all firm and authoritative-like. *Jesus, calm down.*

There was a distinct chance that it had been too long since he'd been laid.

"We're going to let Adelaide do her thing today," explained Edwina. "When we return for the first nighttime vigil, Susannah and I will take the lead, and we'll try to capture some anomalies. Hopefully, even some good EVP."

"EVP?" asked Simon.

"Electronic voice phenomena," replied Edwina. "We scour the audio after these sessions. Sometimes messages are recorded, ones we didn't hear during the vigil. Of course, in most cases, it's just a snippet from one of our conversations, or interference from radio transmissions or a noise outside."

Adelaide adjusted one of her sparkly barrettes. "And sometimes, it's actually a spirit message."

Edwina shrugged. "Sure, but we always need to rule out any other possible explanation before making that leap."

Simon noticed how Adelaide, and to some extent Susannah, bristled when Edwina talked about needing proof. There was definitely some tension between the women, although he didn't suspect it was more than a difference in approach. They were siblings who worked together. Some annoyance was to be expected.

There was no way in hell he could ever work with Rupert. They were in the same business as well, but Simon could never be tempted to partner with him. He'd rather gouge his own eyes out.

As Edwina continued the discussion with her sisters, he took a moment to check her out. She looked badass as usual in form-fitting jeans, a black T-shirt that hugged her torso, and black Converse sneakers. Her auburn hair was up in a ponytail, a silky cascade. Although she didn't seem to wear a lot of makeup in general, there was a bit of sparkle about her eyelids and lips.

Hmm, shimmery.

The woman got sexier every single time he saw her.

When the others all turned to stare at him, he realized they were waiting. "Oh, right. Let's do this." Simon opened the door and led them all inside. Once they were all in the foyer, he and Connie stepped aside to let them do their work.

Adelaide stood in the foyer, and slowly circled the space. She walked up to the bottom of the staircase and glanced toward the second floor. "Hello. My name is Adelaide, and I'm here with my sisters Edwina and Susannah. We've come tonight in the hopes of making the acquaintance of any spirit people gathered here. We're not here to harm you. We just want to help you be at peace. I hope you don't mind us coming inside."

During the short pause in her speech, the other Darke sisters stood still, poised for action. Adelaide continued to glance around the area, while Susannah took random photos.

Edwina had a small thermometer in one hand, and easily balanced a video camera in the other. She shot Simon the odd glance. His nerves must have been etched on his face, because she quirked her lips in a half-smile.

Just like that, some of his jitters faded.

This was definitely one weird-ass situation, but her smile did wonders for his peace of mind.

Adelaide craned her neck to look upstairs, a gesture that Simon found unnerving because it was as if someone stood at the top of the stairs, waiting for at them. "We've brought a lot of equipment here with us, but I want to assure you none of it will hurt you. It just helps us communicate. So, if you'd like to use the devices to speak to us, we'd appreciate it. Or, if you prefer, you can talk to me."

"Any first thoughts, Addy?" asked Edwina.

The medium nodded. "The first thing I felt as we walked inside was worry, a huge wave of anxiety. This house, this land, has seen its share of upheaval. Some happiness, too, but it's the fear that has remained, like a red wine stain on a white carpet."

Simon had to hand it to Adelaide. She told a good story.

Connie was completely immersed in it too. "See? That's exactly how I described it to Margie. This house has a stain on it, and no amount of scrubbing is going to take it away." She sighed. "How are we supposed to make it welcoming to visitors if that anxiety brushes off on them?"

"Part of my job," said Adelaide, "is to figure out if we're dealing with simple residual energy or an actual haunting. Residual energy is like a spiritual echo. It's a moment, caught in a loop. And even though it's unsettling, you can learn to live with it because it's not there to interact with the living. It's the real hauntings that concern me, because they seek to interact. At the end of the day, my aim is to help any spirit people here go into the light. Unfortunately, they don't all go willingly, or they get stuck somehow. It's a scary transition."

She moved down the hallway and back again, peering into each doorway. She touched a hand to her forehead. "I'm getting a feeling around my head. It's heavy, like the foggy state at the start of a migraine. This person is worried, so worried, and they're drawing me to the windows. I believe someone spent a lot of time staring out of these windows, waiting, hoping to see a particular face. Someone connected to this house was very much loved and missed. Unfortunately, I think this person waited in vain for their loved one to return."

A thumping noise sounded in one of the upstairs bedrooms.

Simon had been so wrapped up in Adelaide's tale that he almost jumped out of his skin. Connie did too. She grabbed his arm.

Like a shot, Edwina tore up the stairs.

Simon was amazed. He'd never seen anyone move so quickly, and toward a potentially frightening situation. He roused himself and hurried up behind her, and the others followed.

She waited at the top of the stairs. "Do you feel that?"

As Simon hit the top step, an undeniable blast of cold air wafted toward him. "What the hell?"

"Right? A whole fifteen degrees colder." Edwina immediately walked off to check the window in the hallway. "Still closed and locked. No drafts coming from here, and the vent for the A/C isn't blowing in this direction."

Simon moved aside so the other women had room to gather at the top of the stairs. As Connie reached the top step, her eyes widened. "I've felt cold spots in this exact same place."

Once again, Simon was left wondering why he'd never experienced any of the phenomena. There was no mistaking the temperature drop, and he didn't need to consult any of Edwina's fancy devices to know it was damn cold.

Had he just been willfully ignorant? He felt bad for doubting Connie and the others.

Susannah said, "I'm going to search for the source of that noise."

"It sounded like it was coming from the Merlot room. I can tell you if anything looks wrong in there," said Connie. Together, the two women headed toward the bedroom at the end of the hall.

Meanwhile, Simon remained on the chilly upper landing with Edwina and Adelaide. "What now?"

"I want to check the other bedroom windows, in case there's a broken seal I might have missed in the earlier inspection," said Edwina.

"There's no broken seal." Adelaide held on to the banister. "There's a spirit here. A young woman. She's white, has dark hair and is wearing a nightgown and a shawl. She's curious but doesn't want to get too close. She's showing me that she keeps to the bedrooms a lot because she doesn't like it downstairs. She was watching from upstairs when we came in. Now she's moving down the hall."

Sure enough, the cloud of cold air around Simon dissipated. The urge to shiver went away.

Edwina checked her infrared thermometer. "The temperature has gone back up."

Adelaide's gaze was focused on the hallway. "You're safe with us," she said to the spirit. "We want to help you. Tell me your name."

"Why doesn't she like it downstairs, Addy?" asked Edwina.

"'Because *he's* there.' That's what she keeps telling me," Adelaide replied.

"Who?" Edwina pressed.

Adelaide shook her head after a moment. "She's gone. Hopefully, I can reconnect with her later."

"Wow," said Simon. "We're off with a bang, aren't we?"

Edwina smirked. "Don't get your hopes up. Those paranormal investigation shows on TV make it seem like the investigators are bombarded by spirit activity all in one evening. It's good theater and it's great for ratings. The truth is it takes a lot longer than that to capture credible evidence. That's why we're going to be in your hair for a while. There are going to be nights when nothing happens at all. It could get boring."

Boring? Simon was pretty sure he could never be bored while the Darke sisters were around. Especially Edwina.

"She'll be back," said Adelaide, in that weird and quietly assured way of hers. "She wants to communicate. She's just afraid. Someone made her afraid."

"Guys!" Susannah called from the Merlot room.

They walked toward the bedroom and found Susannah and Connie in the corner.

"We just noticed this on the floor." Susannah indicated the item.

They all gathered around. It was one of the bookends from a low shelf that Simon had placed in that corner. He'd bought the pair of bookends from a local antiques dealer because they were in the shape of boats. They'd reminded him of the boats used in a local reenactment of the War of 1812 done a couple of years ago.

"I was telling Susannah that this bookend has never just fallen off the shelf." Connie picked it up and passed it around. "See? It's heavy. Why would it fall off?"

They all looked to Edwina.

"It's still possible," replied Edwina. "The floors in this place are old. As we ran up the stairs, there might have been enough of a reverberation to nudge it off the shelf."

Simon couldn't miss the way Adelaide rolled her eyes, even though she didn't make a show of it.

"I'm going to continue my walk-through," said the medium. "I need to find the spirit woman. She's hiding and I want to convince her to come forward."

As they followed her out of the Merlot room, Simon hung back with the older sister. He would never have outwardly scoffed at what Adelaide did, but he was definitely Team Edwina on this one. Connie was correct in saying that bookends didn't just leap off the shelves around here, but it was still possible the heavy item had been moving by degrees for a while. Maybe it had already been hovering near the edge of the shelf, and the movement tonight finally caused it to fall.

As they meandered through the various rooms, he took the opportunity to chat with Edwina. "It must be hard being the one who always has to call 'bullshit.'"

She chuckled. "Yeah, but someone's got to do it. If we're going to put our evidence out there into the world, we need to make sure it's rock solid. What Addy does…it's remarkable, but there will always be people who say they just don't believe her, that she's feeding off people's emotions. It's important to me that she appears credible."

"I realize I don't know your sister well, but I get the sense she doesn't care what people think. Maybe it's just you?" Simon suggested gently

"Maybe it is." Her tone was clipped, missing its normal alto warmth. "Still, we have a reputation to consider."

"I'm sure you do." Had he annoyed her? That bothered him. He'd have to keep his mouth shut from here on in. He wasn't qualified to make those kinds of judgments.

And he understood what Edwina was saying. He appreciated proof, too.

One need only ask Mr. Dooley, that poor, patient man.

As a group, they traveled through the house, visiting each room. Each of the Darke sisters continued to call upon any lingering souls, while recording the proceedings on their individual phones and devices. Adelaide called on the woman in the nightgown several times, but claimed the ghost remained hidden.

"Addy, are you able to make a guess as to when the spirit woman lived here?" Susannah asked.

"She didn't reveal much at all, and because she was wearing a nightgown and had her hair down, it was hard to tell the time period. But I'm sure I saw some hand stitching on that gown. I think we're looking at the nineteenth century."

The walk-through continued in a fairly uneventful manner, although Simon heard a few odd creaks from the floor. Still, no disembodied voices, no more ominous thuds. Just a lot of standing around while the Darkes appeared to speak to walls.

At one point, he wondered about the sisters' endgame. Could they be running some kind of scam? *Nah.* For a scam to take place, they would have to have asked for payment. If anything, they were spending money to come to him. They would have already racked up expenses for gas, for fresh batteries and new equipment, and even for their hotel stay. And, despite his skepticism, he didn't get the sense that Adelaide was putting on an act. If she had been, he assumed she would have laid it on thickly. She didn't, though, and mostly gave impressions of how the house "felt" in places.

Besides, every time Adelaide or Susannah questioned as much as a flickering lightbulb, Edwina was right there to cast doubt on it. If they were out to take advantage of their clients in some way, surely they'd be on the same page.

An hour later, they ended up in the kitchen. As they approached the entrance, Adelaide stopped in her tracks. Simon hadn't noticed her gold necklace earlier, but she touched it now, fingering the pendant. "There's another presence in this house. A man."

She tipped her head toward the fridge. "He's there, watching us. I'm getting waves of animosity washing off him. He had a real sense of entitlement in life, and that hasn't changed. He goes wherever he wants in this house. He wants me to know that. He's saying, 'Tell them. This is *my* house now.'" She shook her head slowly. "Oh, he does not like us being here."

Susannah aimed her phone toward the fridge. "Tell us your name"

Adelaide continued to play with her pendant. "He's stopped talking, but he's curious. And's he's coming closer." She moved her head in the slightest of flinches. "Maria, can you ask him to identify himself?"

From out of nowhere, a child's cough sounded in the room. It was raw and pained, and it sounded as if the little one was gasping for air.

Simon jumped back. "What the fuck was that? Is there a kid in here?"

Adelaide held up a trembling hand. "It's Maria. She died of whooping cough. She coughs when she's trying to warn the living."

"But that's not possible," Simon argued.

"Okay." Connie started to back out of the room. "Things are getting a bit too creepy for me now."

The cough manifested again. Simon looked quickly at all his companions. Had one of them thrown their voice? No. There was no way any of them could have made that prolonged sound without him noticing. Besides, it was clearly the voice of a child, high and hiccuping and desperate, and it wasn't coming from anywhere in particular. It was just...there, all around them.

"Maria says he's a bad man. He doesn't like women." Adelaide closed her eyes and leaned against the kitchen island.

"Doesn't like women, huh?" Edwina let out a bitter laugh. "Well, buddy, you are going to have three very determined women crawling over every inch of this house. Hopefully, you'll be a good boy and play nice."

"He called us dirty bitches." Adelaide sank against the island.

"Addy?" Edwina touched her sister's shoulder. "Are you okay?"

"He doesn't like women," she repeated. "He hurts women. He's showing me images of how he's done it in the past, and he wants to hurt us too."

"What does he look like?" Susannah pressed. "Can you get a name?"

"Too close." Adelaide wrapped her arms around her chest. "Get him off me, Maria! Get him off!"

"Jesus Christ." Simon didn't know what to do.

Edwina and Susannah had obviously seen this phenomenon before. Without even consulting each other, they encircled their sister, wrapping her in a group hug. They spoke in unison. "In the name of all that is goodness and light, surround our sister in the white light of protection."

"You're safe, Addy," said Edwina. "We've got you."

Susannah joined in. "He can't hurt you. We won't let him."

Adelaide continued to implore Maria to remove the unwanted spirit, but her voice grew quieter by the moment, and she stopped shaking.

Simon glanced at Connie, who shook her head, clearly as flabbergasted as he was.

Eventually, the Darke sisters let go of each other. Adelaide opened her eyes. "I'm okay. He tried to jump me, but I'm okay."

"What does that mean, he tried to *jump you*?" asked Simon.

"She means possession." Edwina faced Adelaide, defiance shining in her eyes. "But to do that, he'll have to go through us."

"He likes scaring people," said Adelaide. "Pinching and pushing them, pulling their hair. He especially loves hurting the women. It makes him feel strong. He's proud of himself when he can frighten someone away. The spirit woman usually keeps to the upstairs, as I mentioned, but this man wanders. He's hungry for power, and he'll do whatever it takes to get it." On her next breath, her shoulders drooped. "I need some fresh air."

"Of course. I think we've done enough for today." Susannah grabbed her sister by the arm and led her outside.

Connie brought a hand to her mouth and shook her head. "I think I need some air too." She headed outside with the others.

Simon was left alone with Edwina. "What the hell just happened?"

"It sounds like we might be dealing with a couple of entities, one of them definitely hostile."

"Isn't this the part where you're supposed to tell me this can be explained through rational means?"

"What can I say?" said Edwina. "I don't have an explanation for everything. I should warn you, Simon. Sometimes when we begin a new investigation, the activity increases. Addy is a beacon to these spirits. They're drawn to her light, and they see it as an opportunity to get their stories out."

"That sounds, frankly, exhausting for Addy."

"It is." Edwina turned her worried face toward the door. "What I'd like to do later today is comb through the recordings we made, to see if I can find any sort of evidence. But as for what Addy saw, I can't explain that. Hopefully, once she's had a chance to regroup, she can offer up some details that might allow us to identify the spirits here."

"Was that whole whooping cough thing for real?"

"Try as I might, I can't debunk it." Edwina shook her head in amazement. "I don't even try anymore. Maria has been with Addy for years. She's talked about her since she was a little girl and has given us details about her. Susannah was able to use that information to find the death record of a toddler named Maria Slater, who died of whooping cough in Toronto in 1907."

"That's wild."

"Yeah. Although she manifests with that childish cough, she apparently appears to Addy as a young woman. We've heard her cough out loud before, but it's only ever happened in moments of real danger."

"What kind of danger?"

"Something demonic."

"Oh." Suddenly, he wasn't so keen on hanging around in his own house. *Get a grip. A lot of this can probably be chalked up to the power of suggestion.* "Is she going to be okay?"

"Sure. Other ghosts have tried to jump her before. She's stronger than she looks."

Simon touched Edwina's elbow. "What about you? Are you all right?"

"Me?" She grinned. "Yeah. It takes a lot to scare me, certainly more than a dead misogynist. Truth be told, I love provoking those sons of bitches. Besides, I'm tougher than old leather."

Funny. Her skin didn't feel that way at all. It was soft and silky and all too distracting.

Realizing he was still touching her, he stepped back.

"How about you, Simon? You're the one who has to stick around."

"I'm tough too. At least, that's what I'm telling myself. Besides, Connie will be here to keep me company for a while longer. That is, unless she's cut her losses and run."

"Well, you've got our numbers. Feel free to call during the night if anything feels off. I'm hoping Addy's suspicions are wrong, but if we are dealing an evil entity, I don't want you to confront anything. If it becomes oppressive, just leave."

An evil entity. Wasn't that peachy? Maybe he should lock up and check into a hotel. If he wasn't already bleeding money, he would. "I've got your numbers. I'll be fine."

Susannah came back inside and the two sisters went around the house, collecting a few of their various devices. They left most of the items where they were but brought a few of them into the Jeep so they could review their recordings.

When they were ready to leave, he followed them outside. Adelaide was sitting in the backseat, drinking from a water bottle. Simon waved, and she nodded in acknowledgment.

"Okay," said Edwina. "I guess that's it for now. Tomorrow evening, we'll do the first nighttime vigil. I suggest everyone get a good night's sleep tonight."

Edwina got in the driver's seat, and Susannah slipped into the passenger seat. Simon watched them drive away, then turned toward the house.

Something demonic.

Connie tapped her foot next to him. "I think I'm going to catch up on some paperwork. Anything but work in the kitchen."

"Listen, Connie. Just because Adelaide had some sort of episode in the house doesn't mean it's haunted. I'm sure the sisters mean well, but this could very well be an Adelaide thing."

"You think she faked that? Because if that was an act, Meryl Streep will need to watch her back."

"I don't think it was an act, but maybe she's just... I don't know. I have no words for what happened. That whole coughing thing? I've never seen anything like it."

"I get it. It was your first time experiencing the haunting. The first time I sensed a presence, I doubted my senses too."

"I just hesitate to label this a haunting."

"Right. You do you, Simon." Her arms crossed over her chest, she walked back into the house.

Taking a deep breath, Simon marched up the porch steps and followed her.

Chapter Five

The day of the vigil, Edwina decided she needed to get out on her own for a while. She'd spent the remainder of the previous day reviewing footage from the walk-through, to the point where her eyes had started to hurt. Despite the thump in the bedroom and the incident in the kitchen, she and Susannah hadn't recorded any visible or audible anomalies.

She had a suspicion they'd have better luck at the vigil tonight. If Edwina knew anything about darker entities, it was that they liked to play at night.

Over a quick breakfast, she checked in with her sisters.

"Niagara-on-the-Lake has a small history museum," said Susannah. "I've set up an appointment with the curator to see if they have any other info on the property."

"Sounds good." Edwina polished off her croissant. It was a nice croissant, but not as tasty as the ones Simon had offered her.

Mmm. She lost herself in a fantasy of Simon feeding her one of his delicious croissants. The flaky crumbs would probably drop into her cleavage, and he'd have to fish them out for her.

Okay, stop it. If you told him about your pastry-inspired delusions, he'd run for the hills.

"You won't find anything about the spirit man at the museum." Adelaide's comment scattered Edwina's perverted daydreams. "I don't think his ties to the property are in any sort of record. He has a different sort of connection. He was there often in life. At one point, he said, 'All this *should* have been mine, but it's mine now.'"

"What the hell does that mean?" Edwina brushed pastry flakes from her shirt.

"I'm not sure." Adelaide rubbed her temple.

"Let's not press Addy for any more details right now," said Susannah. "She'll let us know when she finds out."

"Of course," said Edwina. "You doing okay, Addy?"

"Yup." Their younger sister had been quiet but calm last night. She remained detached this morning. Edwina wasn't concerned though. They all had their own methods for coping, and sometimes Addy kept her thoughts to herself.

"I'm going to grab a latte and go for a walk," said Edwina. "Want to join me?"

"No, thanks. I want to clear my head before the vigil. I'm going to head over to St. Mark's and sit in the old churchyard."

"Are you sure you want to hang out in a churchyard after what happened yesterday?" Edwina asked.

"You know what I always say about burial grounds."

Edwina and Susannah answered together. "The dead don't haunt graveyards. They haunt the living."

"Exactly."

Edwina wasn't alarmed by her sister wanting to be alone among the graves. Given their favorite pastime, they'd all spent a fair bit of time in cemeteries. If Adelaide was after some peace and quiet, she couldn't get any more peaceful or quiet than the town graveyard.

They set out on their own for the day. After buying a latte from the coffee shop across from their hotel, Edwina strolled up Queen Street, the main drag in Niagara-on-the-Lake. Although new buildings had gone up over the decades, it wasn't hard to envision what the town might have looked like in the old days.

Thanks to the presence of a number of well-kept historic buildings, it was easy to look beyond the façade of gelato shops and clothing stores and see the layers underneath. The town had done an excellent job of preserving its vintage features. There was even an old apothecary on the same corner as her hotel, one that was now set up as a museum.

If Edwina allowed herself to tune out the throng of international tourists and visitors to the Shaw Festival Theatre, she could imagine soldiers in red coats crowding the taverns, and townspeople selling their wares and performing chores. It would probably be very interesting to stroll these streets at night, when it was quiet and hushed. She'd bet her last dollar that the atmosphere would change then, taking on an eerie sort of stillness.

As she walked by the apothecary, Edwina's ears began to ring again. Like a faraway clarion call, it was out of place yet hard to ignore. Was she coming down with something? Hopefully, this wasn't the start of a nasty inner ear infection.

Listen.

The thought came to her out of nowhere.

"Listen to what, exactly?" she murmured.

The curious alarm echoed in her brain, growing in intensity. She rubbed her ear but it didn't do anything to disperse the annoying sensation. It hammered at her, less than gently and insistent. She stopped walking and turned away from the intersection, trying to focus more on the ringing than on the cars a few feet away. If she had some sort of inner ear problem, she wanted to be able to describe it to her doctor.

A man's voice came through. *Can you see me? I'm here.*

There was kindness in the voice, but also desperation.

Edwina looked around. There were a couple of pedestrians on the same corner, but both were women, and they were facing away from her.

Maybe she'd overheard a snippet of another passing conversation.

Troubled, she tugged on her earlobe.

Turning away from the main street, Edwina walked toward the Niagara River. There were a few residential blocks between Queen Street and the waterfront, mostly filled with lovely historical homes bearing dated plaques. There were some new builds as well, but for the most part, the town retained the quaint atmosphere that made it such a hit with tourists. Everywhere one looked, there was history. Simon and Connie's place wasn't the only bed and breakfast, either. There had to be at least one every couple of blocks.

Lots of competition.

Edwina felt for them. Here they were during the busiest season, unable to keep guests under their roof. In a business like theirs, so much relied on word of mouth. They had to be stressed out.

They were nice people. It made her even more determined to help them.

She recalled the way Simon had touched her elbow yesterday. There had been something considerate in the way his fingers grazed her skin. Even though he'd pulled his hand away quickly enough, she'd been tempted to drag it back.

The last guy she'd dated had thought it was okay to pat her ass on the first date. Needless to say, that date had been cut extremely short. Edwina wasn't opposed to hooking up, but people needed to be on the same page. That guy had been in another book altogether.

There was a park up ahead. If she recalled correctly from her last visit to Niagara-on-the-Lake, there was a pretty gazebo overlooking the river, a perfect place to breathe in the air. Sure enough, the white wooden structure still stood there. There were a few families nearby, and a couple of kids kicked a soccer ball around. However, the area around the gazebo was quiet. There was only one person there, and she could make out his profile.

He had blond hair, cute nerd glasses and nice biceps. Simon.

She sucked in a breath and held it as she approached. He leaned on the railing, staring out over the water. She couldn't help noticing the pleasing curve of his ass. *Settle down. It's not the first ass you've seen.*

Although, it was a good one, nice and firm.

"Simon, hey."

He stood and a pleasant smile washed over his face. "Ed. Hi." He pushed his glasses up his nose.

Okay. Adorable. "Please don't tell me that you had to escape your own house."

"No." He chuckled. "It's been quiet since you all left. Thank God for that, or, you know, whoever was responsible. How was your evening?"

"Fine. What about you, though?"

"If I'm honest, I didn't have the greatest sleep of my life. I seem to have suddenly developed an overactive imagination. You know, the same thing I accused everyone else of having? I kept replaying everything that happened in the kitchen, trying to make sense of it all. I finally managed to drown out my thoughts by turning the TV on. It stayed on all night."

"Oh, I'm sorry." He did have dark circles under his eyes. Not that they made them twinkle any less.

"Any luck with the footage?"

"Nah. Like I said, it might take a while to capture something compelling."

"That's okay. Yesterday was compelling enough."

She joined him at the railing, and they stood quietly for a few moments, admiring the view. There was a bit of a breeze, and it carried Simon's scent toward her. It was a nice soapy scent, lemony and fresh. She resisted the urge to press her nose against his neck. "It's beautiful here. I've always found it interesting that the United States is right there, within swimming distance."

"Yeah. That's Old Fort Niagara across the way. I think this must have been a tense place to live back in 1812, with the Americans just over the river."

"It's a good thing we're all friends now."

His eyes crinkled with amusement. "I was going to go for a walk. Want to join me?"

"Yeah, sure. Why not?" They walked along Ricardo Street, a quiet road with lots of cute little bungalows. It took them behind St. Mark's Church and its neighboring graveyard. Edwina pointed her thumb toward the gate. "My sister's in there somewhere, communing with nature."

"Adelaide?"

"Yeah."

"Boy, she must be really comfortable with death."

"I don't know if it's comfort, so much as not having a choice. Addy's been talking to dead people since she was a baby. My mom said she used to catch her gurgling happily in her crib, as if someone was holding a toy for her, or tickling her tummy. We all knew there was something different about her, but for many years, our parents just chalked up her weird conversations to invisible friends."

"It must have been a shock for them to realize that wasn't exactly the case."

"Yes and no. My mom's always been sensitive. So was my grandmother, but neither of them could do what Addy does." Her gaze shifted to the nearest grouping of headstones. "I think it must be an awful burden sometimes."

"I never really thought about it, but I guess you're right."

"I mean, she's learned to live with it. She makes her living doing readings."

"Really?" he asked. "Does she have a curtain-draped salon and a crystal ball?"

"It's nothing like that. She actually goes to people's houses. And, let me tell you, her clients are devoted to her because of her accuracy."

"You mean, like how she told me my grandmother was watching?"

"Exactly, you sweet little monkey," she teased.

"I'm never going to live that down, am I?" His gaze narrowed and focused on her lips.

"Nope." As he gazed at her, her tongue slipped out to lick at the edge of her mouth as if it had a mind of its own.

His flustered huff was extremely cute. "I'm impressed," he said, his voice a bit rough. "She's turned what could be perceived as a problem into success."

"It wasn't always that way, though." Edwina sipped her latte. "Addy was bullied in school. Quite badly, actually."

Simon stopped walking. "I'm sorry to hear it. That sucks."

"Yeah. I think that's why I sometimes feel the need to validate her messages with tangible proof. You were right. She doesn't look for validation, and she never has. I think it's my bizarre way of trying to protect her. If I can provide evidence, people will be less likely to call her names."

"I hear you."

"It's bad enough that she never gets any peace because someone's dead uncle needs her to deliver a message. Having to deal with that as a kid had to be hard. I worry about her sometimes. I try to talk to her, but she doesn't like to upset us, and sometimes I end up saying the wrong thing anyway." She shook her head. "Whew! I didn't mean to spill my guts like that."

"You're a good big sister." He sighed and started walking again. "I wish I'd had someone like you in my corner when I was growing up."

"No siblings?"

"Oh, I've got a brother. Rupert. He's just a jackass."

"Sorry about that. I guess you can take comfort in the fact that he got saddled with the name Rupert?" Edwina pulled a face, hoping he'd laugh.

To her relief and delight, Simon cackled. "Yes! I take immense comfort in that. I like how you think, Ms. Darke."

She tipped her coffee toward him in a salute.

"Of course," he continued, "with my name, I can't be too smug. Honest to God, Simon and Rupert. Our parents must have really wanted everyone to think we were pompous shitheads. Actually, I believe 'Pompous Shithead' is our family motto. If we had a crest, it would be on it."

Strong words about his own family. There was a story there, but she wasn't sure if she should ask about it. "Simon's a much better name than Rupert. You lucked out, I swear. Rupert sounds like a crotchety old guy who shakes his fist at passing teenagers. Simon sounds like the hot nerd you used to lust over in English class."

He turned to her, one eyebrow quirked. "I'm sorry, did you say 'hot?'"

"Yeah," she said, smiling. "But I also said 'nerd.'"

"You're not wrong, you know." He gave her a playful once-over. "And if you ever give me ten minutes to talk about the extensive graphica collection that I have in storage, I'll prove it."

"I'd be into that." She probably shouldn't say anything about how she found nerds incredibly sexy.

"So, what's Rupert's story, then? Why's he such a jackass?"

His face tightened around the eyes and mouth. "Hey, did you know they do jet boat tours down at the marina here? It's a blast. You should check them out when you have some spare time."

"Uh, okay. Sounds fun."

In her mind's eye, a tiny red flag began to wave.

Declan used to avoid her questions too. Hell, he'd made it a sport.

Forget Declan. He's history.

She'd wasted plenty of time dealing with his antics, enough time that she'd learned how to recognize them in others.

She was getting ahead of herself. This was not the same situation at all. Declan had been her boyfriend for the better part of a year. She'd made plans with him, had envisioned a future with him.

Simon was just a client.

A really cute client who smelled like lemon squares. *Don't go there.*

She probably shouldn't judge him for wanting to change the topic. After all, Simon barely knew her, and most people didn't like getting into the inner workings of their families with near strangers.

This was not a *thing*. She would just take note.

They continued walking along Ricardo Street until they reached the marina. With moored boats and an old lighthouse, it made for a picturesque spot. There was another gazebo on the waterfront trail, and they meandered there toward it. Edwina's latte had long since grown cold, but she continued to sip it, just happy to be out and about.

With Simon, specifically.

She liked being out and about with him.

There was definitely something intriguing about him. As he launched into a funny story about one of his customers, she realized what it was. He made conversation so effortless. There were no awkward lulls and she enjoyed listening to him. It must be all that hospitality work. It had no doubt given him a chance to hone his conversational skills.

As they took their spots in the second gazebo, he turned the spotlight back on her. "I bet you get a lot of looks when you tell people what you do. It must make dating interesting."

Was he fishing for her status? "It does, I won't lie. I mean, I do have a real job too. I work in theater."

"Ah! Leading actress?"

She snorted out a laugh. "Hardly. I'm a theater tech. I handle all the behind-the-scenes wizardry."

"Of course you do, Inspector Gadget."

She'd never heard anyone purr those two words before. Did he think her tech knowledge was hot in some way?

"So," Simon continued, "how on earth do you squeeze in all those paranormal investigations around production schedules?"

"I found a way to make it work. There are a few theater companies that I work with regularly, and sometimes I take on odd jobs, if a show comes to town for a limited run. I've made a name for myself, and luckily, I can pick and choose which productions I do. It allows me to conduct investigations on my off time. My sisters and I are fortunate that way. Susannah is a regular contributor to a couple of local history magazines and she does a bit of teaching. She can be flexible with her time too, and Addy just reschedules her appointments when we have a case."

"What a fascinating trio."

"Not everyone thinks so. In fact, I don't always bring up the paranormal investigations to guys I'm seeing. It's been my experience that most of them don't know what to do with that information."

"Let me guess. They're intimidated by a strong woman who battles demons in her spare time?"

"It's not always that dramatic, I promise you. I don't know. I guess toxic masculinity runs deep. For the most part, though, most of them just make fun of me when they hear about it for the first time. You know, calling me Daphne. Which is ridiculous because I'm more of a Velma."

"Amazing." He leaned back against the railing. "Are you seeing anyone now?"

"Are you just making small talk, or are you interested?"

Simon's eyes widened, but never lost that sparkle. "Edwina Darke, you just say whatever's on your mind, don't you?"

"Pretty much." She sipped the last of her coffee. "Unless I'm in the midst of an exciting round of Scrabble, I don't play games."

"Refreshing. Well, then yeah. I'm asking because I'm interested."

"In that case, I'll answer. I'm not seeing anyone right now." Edwina allowed her gaze to drop toward Simon's chest and back up again. "And I might be interested too."

His lips spread in a smile as he maintained eye contact. Edwina wasn't the sort of person to get flutters in her chest easily, but there was something about that luxurious grin that caused a commotion in her core. It was as if a thousand chrysalides had been suspended from her ribs, and they'd all just emerged as butterflies.

"Good to know."

Dammit. She'd established a "no dating the clients" rule some time ago. Dating made things awkward.

It seemed she was willing to break a rule or two for Simon Teal. It made her wonder what other rules she'd break for him.

"*But* we're in the middle of an investigation, and I want to get you some answers, first and foremost. I pride myself on my professionalism."

"Of course. I get it. We can talk later."

Okay, good. He understood.

Only, he was still smiling. To make matters worse, he gnawed on his bottom lip while doing so.

Shoot. That move always made her weak in the knees. She needed to put the focus back on him. "What about you? It must be tricky having a relationship in your business as well. What you do is very demanding."

"Fair enough, but you can make anything work if you want it badly enough." His expression darkened. "Although it's been a while since I dated. The last relationship left a few scars."

"Battle wounds, huh?" she gently teased. "We all have some of those. Want to talk about it?"

He turned toward the marina. "Hey, did you notice the lighthouse over there? It's a landmark."

And just like that, the little red flag returned. Only this time, it flapped in her face.

Simon had deflected a second inquiry, and she wasn't in the habit of offering third chances.

Edwina's red flag system rarely failed.

Correction.

It had failed before, with Declan, and horribly so. Her flags had waved at her then, but she'd tossed them to the ground and had stomped on them. That decision had led to months of heartache and regret.

Since then, she'd made herself a promise to always listen to her inner voice.

Right now, her inner voice was shouting, *Nope, nope, nope!*

Unfortunately, her libido was screaming, *He's hot as fuck and he's into you. Jump his bones!*

"Want to walk a bit closer to the lighthouse?" he asked.

"Um, you know what? Maybe another time. It's going to be a long night with the vigil ahead. I'm going to head back to the hotel for forty winks. You should probably rest up too."

"I'm fine. I don't need a lot of sleep. Having been in the hospitality business all these years, I got used to working god-awful hours."

"Sure. Well, I'll see you tonight, Simon. Thanks for the walk."

"No problem." He ran a hand through his hair. "Edwina, um…"

"Yeah?"

"Never mind." This time, the smile didn't reach his eyes. "See you later."

As Edwina walked away, she hoped she hadn't sounded abrupt. It couldn't be helped. She'd grown gun-shy of men who couldn't be honest.

He did tell you he was interested. He just didn't want to divulge all his secrets. It doesn't mean he's untrustworthy. Cut him some slack. You've only known him for five minutes. You don't know what's in his past. It could be painful.

She understood not everyone was as forthright as she was. It was hard for some people. But she'd been clear about not playing games, and after Declan, she had no time for people who couldn't be real.

Did that mean she sometimes made snap judgments? Sure.

Still, she barely knew Simon. That didn't mean her bruised heart hadn't already put her on alert. She knew she had a tendency to erect walls early. Few people got past them nowadays. Anyone who knew her history with Declan wouldn't blame her. The man knew how to play mind games.

Once again, she reminded herself she wasn't dealing with Declan anymore. Simon was a completely different person.

And he did smell really good. Like, steal-his-shirt-and-hide-it-under-the-pillow-so-she-could-sniff-it-later good.

But if he wanted to get to know her, he'd have to be honest with her, and right from the start. She wouldn't settle for less.

She had once. Never again.

Chapter Six

"You sure you're not tempted to break your plans and stick around for the nighttime vigil?" Simon asked Connie as she prepared to leave.

"Hmm, let's see." Connie pretended to weigh her options via an invisible scale. "Join my gorgeous wife for a fancy night of schmoozing and gourmet treats, or stay here and get scared out of my boy shorts?"

"There's something to be said for getting scared. Margie could join us," he suggested weakly. "It would be like a slumber party where someone smuggled in a Ouija board. It'll be...fun."

"Sorry, Simon. We R.S.V.P'd weeks ago. I can't let Margie down." Connie's wife worked for a local bus tour company, the type that carted tourists around to tastings at Niagara wineries. Margie had been invited to the grand opening of a new local winery, and it promised to be a ritzy evening. It was rumored there might even be some celebrity guests. If nothing else, the wine would flow. Connie and Margie were true aficionados of fine wine. They swirled it around in their glasses and everything. Simon usually just threw his right down his gullet.

"I get it. Of course, I want you to get wined and dined. Have one for me, a tall one. I think I'll need it."

"That was some weird shit yesterday. I didn't sleep a wink last night." Connie patted his arm. "You know you don't have to go through with this, right?"

"I know. I just wouldn't feel right canceling on the Darkes. They've already done a lot of work. The least I can do is allow them to capture some of that weird shit on camera. Go, enjoy yourself. Just promise me you'll notify my next of kin if I die of a heart attack tonight."

"You'll be fine, Simon." Connie arched an eyebrow. "That nasty kitchen ghost doesn't seem to have a problem with men."

"Fair enough. So, you're saying it's up to me to protect the womenfolk?"

"*Those* women? They'll be protecting you." Connie laughed, a little too heartily in his opinion. "See you soon."

Standing at the door, he watched her get into her car and drive away. In those quiet moments before Edwina and her sisters arrived, Simon walked the length of the porch. He'd never really noticed how dark the garden was at night, but it struck him now. There was a thick hedge of evergreen shrubs that bordered the side of the yard next to the sidewalk. At the far end of his property, a wooded area led into a ravine. Huge sycamore trees with wide trunks dotted the landscape. There were even a couple of ancient willows. Some of the trees were so big, they must have been around for centuries.

Aside from its historical charms, he'd fallen in love with the property because it felt so private. It was a quiet sanctuary in the midst of a tourist town.

Tonight, it just felt gloomy and vague, like anything could be hiding in those far corners of the yard. He should pick up some solar lights to illuminate those pitch-black nooks.

Then again, perhaps he didn't want to see what was in those corners.

Something shifted in his periphery. He turned his head toward the far end of the garden and stared.

But there was nothing there. Of course.

Or was it possible that he was being watched in ways he couldn't comprehend?

"Sheesh," he muttered. "You sound like Adelaide now."

This stuff was rubbing off on him.

Maybe, just maybe, it was conceivable that there were forces out there that defied understanding. Simon had been born Anglican, but had never been a spiritual sort. Tonight, he found himself wondering if he'd been wrong all these years, and just how wrong he might have been.

"Well, Grandma Sybil. Adelaide says you're kicking around, protecting me. If that's the case, I want you to know it's appreciated."

The sound of a car coming around the corner roused him from his metaphysical contemplations. He walked back toward the entrance. The Darke sisters piled out of Edwina's Jeep, looking like a group of hot cat burglars. No Converse shoes and sparkly barrettes tonight. Instead, they all wore dark cargo pants, Doc Marten boots, and black shirts with the DPI logo. As they sorted themselves out at the car, grabbing some of their tech devices, they each put on a headlamp.

Edwina came up the walkway first. Although she wore a polite smile, it lacked its usual warmth. "Hey. Nice night for a vigil."

"Sure is." Simon adjusted his glasses, even though they hadn't fallen down his nose. *Stop fidgeting*.

He'd been a bit evasive in speaking to Edwina earlier, and it had clearly hit a nerve with both of them. It wasn't that he'd wanted to change the subject. He just hadn't wanted her to judge him for his fucked-up family dynamic. He'd already let on that his family was peopled mostly by assholes. That was probably enough to send her running right there, and for some reason, the last thing he wanted was her running from him. After all, she was Edwina Darke, the baddest thing in cargo pants.

He wished he could pull her aside and explain. Heck, he wished he could shut the world out and give her all his attention. She impressed the hell out of him.

He didn't want to be any less impressive in her eyes, especially seeing as they'd both admitted their interest — the single most exciting moment in his recent memory.

She handed him a spare headlamp. "For you. I figured you wouldn't have one lying around."

"You figured right. Thanks." He slid the headband over his head, but it caught in his glasses. Convinced he was putting his best dorky foot forward, he struggled to free his glasses arm.

"Here, let me." Edwina stepped forward. "Do you mind?"

"Not at all."

Her touch gentle, she reached for his glasses and slowly pulled them away from his face and the headlamp straps. Once they were free, she fixed the straps and made sure the small lamp was facing forward. Only then did she raise her eyes to his. Her lips parted, and a puff of minty breath hit his face.

Nice. Would her lips taste cool and minty too?

"Definitely periwinkle," she whispered.

"Pardon?"

"Oh, nothing." She stepped back and handed him his glasses. "There you go. You should just be able to slide those on around the straps now."

"Thanks." He permitted himself a quick glance at the logo on her chest. "I like the uniform. Totally kickass."

"Thanks. Most of our footage comes from the vigils and we wanted a cohesive look. Glad you, um, like it."

Like it? He'd be dreaming of it later.

She turned back toward her sisters, both of whom were standing still at the bottom of the walkway, watching them. Susannah had a shit-eating grin on her face, while Adelaide whispered something in her ear.

"Uh, what are you waiting for?" Edwina huffed and marched into the house. "I guess I have to set everything up myself."

Once Susannah and Adelaide reached the porch, Simon pulled them aside. "Is she okay?"

"Yup," said Susannah, in noncommittal fashion, before moving past him into the house.

Of course. Why did he think her sisters would give up her secrets?

Too bad. Because, all of a sudden, he wanted to know every last one of Edwina's secrets. He wanted to know if she dreamed of him the way he dreamed of her.

Once they were all inside, the sisters doublechecked all their various devices to make sure they were ready to go.

Edwina was all business. "Okay. For our first night vigil, we're going to be doing our best to get something on camera. We will likely break into teams as the night goes on, but for now, I think it's best we stick together." She turned to him. "Simon, Susannah has found some info on the history of the house, but we're going to hold off on sharing it until after the vigil. We want to see if Addy can come up with some details first. Then, we can try and match it up with the historical record."

"Okay."

"Everyone ready?" asked Edwina. They all nodded and switched on their headlamps and recorders. "Simon, could you cut the lights, please?"

He'd already turned off most of the lights in the building earlier, so he flipped the switches in the office, the kitchen and in the foyer. Because their only light sources were now coming from their headlamps and their cameras, the house was cast in shadow. Those shadows moved, following them down the hall as the group took their first steps around the bed and breakfast.

Edwina focused her camera on herself. "We're here at the King Street Bed and Breakfast, a location that has already proven intriguing because of the variety of activity. I have a feeling this vigil will be a memorable one." She panned her camera around the foyer.

Remembering that they had told him to act natural, Simon asked, "Where to first?"

Edwina focused her attention on the hallway leading to the kitchen, a great cat zeroing in on its prey. "How about we pay Mr. Misogyny a visit?"

"No." Adelaide walked toward the stairs. "The woman's back. She wants us to go upstairs."

Susannah and Edwina aimed their cameras at the stairs and they all followed Adelaide as she slowly climbed them.

Adelaide addressed the spirit as they all got to the top of the stairs and situated themselves in the hallway. "Thank you for coming back. I want to help you, but for that, I need to know your name."

As she spoke to the spirit woman, she explained what she saw to the others. "She's wringing her hands and seems upset. She spent some of her last days crying, in mourning, but never told her family of her pain. She kept it to herself, and it grew and grew, so much so that when death finally came for her, she welcomed it."

Susannah's eyes were bright with interest. "Addy, ask her when she lived."

The medium's gaze was pinned on the far end of the hallway. "She says it was cold when she died, so cold. The militia came and showed no mercy. She's showing me an image of people, women and children, old people too, being driven from their homes. Some had babies. Some of them didn't even have a chance to put on their shoes. They were made to watch as their homes and belongings were burned to the ground."

"Jesus," Susannah whispered to Simon. "That sounds like the winter of 1813, when American soldiers torched the town." She once again appealed to her sister. "Addy, get me a name. Please."

Adelaide took a step down the hall, but then stopped. "She's worried we'll hurt her. Miss, I want to help you. What's your name?" She was quiet for a few moments. Finally, she nodded in acknowledgment and turned back to Susannah. "Her name is Ann."

Edwina and Susannah traded excited looks. Edwina slid forward slowly. "Ann, thank you for talking to my sister. Could you please tell her your surname as well? We would really appreciate it."

Adelaide continued staring at the same spot, nodding her head periodically, like someone listening to a friend's story. "She's talking about the cold again, the way it chilled her to the bone. I think she relives it lot."

"Poor thing," said Susannah.

"She's so upset, and she's a bit incoherent," explained Adelaide. "Ann, I'm so sorry you were treated that way. It must have been terrifying. I want to get to know you better. Could you please tell me your full name?" She fingered her necklace. "Her voice cuts in and out at times. I'm getting a name that starts with…S? No. It's an F. A bit clearer, please, Ann. Ford? No, she's shaking her head. Forbes? Yes, Forbes. Thank you so much, Ann."

Edwina quietly high-fived Susannah.

Only then did Simon remember. The Forbes family were the original inhabitants of the house.

But would Adelaide have figured that out on her own? She'd certainly had plenty of time to do her own research. Although he was inclined to be skeptical, he'd believed her sisters when they'd said Adelaide went in without knowing any details. They'd behaved with transparency and integrity so far.

The medium continued her odd conversation. "Ann, I know this is painful, but could you tell me how you died?" Adelaide gasped and shivered. "Oh, I'm so sorry."

Simon stared, aghast. Adelaide's breath was suddenly visible. Every time she exhaled, a silvery plume emanated from her nose and mouth. If someone had plucked her from the warmth of the house and set her down in the middle of a wintry landscape, it would have been more appropriate.

"She's showing me how cold she was." Adelaide held out a hand to Edwina. "Feel it."

Edwina took her sister's hand. "God, Addy. Your skin. It's frigid."

"May I?" asked Simon. When Adelaide nodded, he touched her hand. He'd touched blocks of ice that were warmer than she was right now. He withdrew his hand, not understanding. The house was set to a comfortable temperature. There was no way she could be so cold. His senses seemed determined to drive him around the bend.

Adelaide's teeth began to chatter. "Yes, I can see everything, Ann. Thank you for sharing that." She closed her eyes. "Maria, you can take it from me now. It's too cold. I'd like to be warm again." After a few breaths, Adelaide stopped shaking.

"Better?" Susannah rubbed her arm.

"Yeah," said Adelaide. "Ann showed me a barn, one the soldiers had missed when they were burning the town. Several of the women and children huddled there together. She left her younger sisters and her father there, but she stayed outside because she didn't want to take the place from someone more vulnerable. She thought she might be all right if she kept moving, but the cold took her. She wasn't thinking straight at the end. When she finally fell, she just didn't get back up again."

"What a horrible way to die," murmured Edwina.

Simon's throat thickened. He cleared it, swallowing past the unexpected lump of emotion. He couldn't help but be moved. Although he knew nothing about her, Ann Forbes had been an inhabitant of this house in its earlier form. The floorplan may have changed a bit over the decades, but for all intents and purposes, she'd walked the same halls and had slept under the same roof as him. He would have to be made of stone not to feel a sort of affinity with her.

"Did she say anything about why she was in mourning?" asked Edwina.

"Ann," prompted Adelaide, "I can feel your suffering. I can see you watching from the windows. Tell me, who do you mourn?"

Just then, one of the art prints fell from its spot on the wall. As it hit the floor with a resounding crash, they all jumped and there were a couple of cries of alarm. Simon was fairly sure his was the loudest.

The frame was completely smashed and so was all the glass. Shards had flown everywhere, scattering across the old hardwood like jagged diamonds. Simon looked to Edwina. She'd been standing closest to the print. Had she been hurt?

Edwina, however, appeared unscathed and in control. She shook some crumbs of glass off her kickass boots and continued filming, shifting her aim toward the wall.

She had nerves of steel.

He definitely wanted her on his zombie apocalypse team.

Simon reached for the black covering that the sisters had placed over the print. He extricated the picture from the broken frame and held it out. It was a historical image of Fort George.

"Did anyone get cut by the glass?" asked Susannah. They all shook their heads. Luckily, no one was hurt.

Edwina walked over to inspect the wall. Simon already knew the frame was a heavy one. When he'd originally hung it, he'd hung it from two points and on reinforced fasteners. Edwina picked at one of the fasteners, still holding her camera in the other hand as she filmed the proceedings. "These are solid. I'd like to state for the record that all the windows and doors in this house are shut, although it would take much more than a draft to move this print. There's no way that thing could have fallen off unless someone had lifted it off and dropped it."

"May I see that?" Susannah took the print from Simon. "Fort George. It's an artist's rendering from the 1812 period."

They all turned to Adelaide, who let out a heavy sigh. "Ann's gone. She didn't say anything else, but I think it's safe to say the person she mourned was someone connected to Fort George."

They were all quiet for a moment. Simon finally broke the ice. "Let me get a broom. I'll sweep up this glass." With only his headlamp lighting the way down the stairs, he went to the small utility room next to the office and retrieved a broom, dustpan and garbage bag. From what he could tell in the reduced light, the floor hadn't been scratched. As for the print, it could be framed again.

In truth, he'd been more worried in that moment about the glass shards hitting Edwina and her sisters.

He couldn't remember the last time his protective instincts had flared so quickly. It was probably back in his early days with Carly, although he barely remembered them now. When he thought back to that time, it was like trying to remember a passage from someone else's memoir.

Once the hallway was cleaned up, Susannah took charge. "I'd like to validate the details Addy gave us." Edwina aimed her camera at her. "As our viewers know, Addy always comes into these vigils without any sort of information to guide her. Of course, anyone coming to Niagara-on-the-Lake on a ghost hunt would likely expect to encounter spirits from the period of 1812. It was a time of incredible upheaval in this area. Even though I didn't want to assume the war would be the backdrop for this haunting, it's starting to look that way."

She took a breath. "Niagara-on-the-Lake was known as Newark back in 1812. This property was owned by George Forbes, a local wine merchant. He had four daughters. One of them, Ann, was unmarried at the time of her death. Their family lived here until the winter of 1813, when enemy militia burned the town to the ground. Unfortunately, Ann Forbes was one of the casualties of that terrible winter. Turned out into the cold on December tenth, along with many of the townspeople, she was forced to watch as the enemy destroyed her home. According to the records at St. Mark's Anglican Church, Ann died in December, although no exact date was listed. The record states she froze to death. She was only twenty-one at the time."

"She can't move on," said Adelaide. "She's searching for something, for someone, and it's left her in a state of confusion."

"We need to help her. She deserves peace." Edwina's voice sounded scratchy. "Let's split up now and see if we can shake off some more cobwebs from this place."

"Addy and I will take the bedrooms." Susannah led her younger sister down the hallway.

Edwina turned to Simon. "That leaves you with me. Feel like taking on the kitchen?"

"Oh, the place where we encountered Mr. Nasty last time?" He barked out a laugh. "Sure. I was hoping you would say that. The kitchen is now officially my favorite place in the house."

Edwina elbowed him as they made their way to the stairs. "Come on. It's just one terrifying little ghost. Nothing we can't handle. Watch your step on the stairs."

Watch his step? Simon could barely take his eyes off her.

She was a force of nature.

They headed toward the kitchen and Edwina cast her gaze around the room.

"You're not scared of anything, are you?" asked Simon.

She did a double take. "Um, I get scared, just like anyone else. But I guess I've also seen a lot more than the average person, so my tolerance is higher."

"Ed, a heavy art print literally jumped off the wall in front of us, and you barely flinched. Whereas I, I regret to inform you, just lost about five years off of my life."

"Like I said, I've seen worse."

He chuckled. "I'm honestly not even sure I want to know what you've seen." Only he did. He wanted to know everything about her.

Edwina continued walking around the kitchen, calling out to the spirit of the man who'd accosted Adelaide previously. "Come on, woman hater. I'm right here. Show yourself. Make the lights flicker. Turn off my headlamp. Addy tells me you like to touch women. Why don't you pull my hair? Pinch my arm. Go wild."

With every taunting word out of Edwina's mouth, Simon's body temperature rose. The very thought that she was offering herself up as some sort of guinea pig for a ghostly douchebag angered him. He braced himself, even though he had no idea what he was bracing himself for. He had an urge to throw himself in front of Edwina, to protect her from some sort of otherworldly assault. He had to keep reminding himself that she was the expert here, but he still wanted to keep her safe.

As time went on, it became clear the invisible man wasn't in the mood to play. He didn't show himself in any way. It hardly mattered. A chill of foreboding had settled in near the base of Simon's spine. He got the sense something would happen at some point, whether it would be during this vigil or the next. It left him with a bad taste in his mouth, and an urge to gargle.

"So, tell me," he babbled, in an attempt to distract himself, more than anything. "What *does* scare the all-powerful Edwina Darke?"

"I'm not all-powerful."

"You could have fooled me. Now spill. It'll make me feel better."

"Hmm, let's see," she said. "Shark movies. I have a thing about deep water. I just can't watch those movies."

"Nor should you. They're terrifying."

"Oh, and clowns. I hate those guys."

"Me too." He grimaced. "See how much we have in common? What else?"

"There's also... I mean, there was this one time, years ago." The headlamp caused shadows to flit across her face. "Never mind."

He touched her arm. "You can tell me."

Her gaze was full of questions, and he probably didn't have answers for them.

After all, he hadn't opened up to her earlier. It had clearly earned him her distrust. Why would she open up to him now?

He'd have to gain her trust, that much was obvious. Even though the knowledge disappointed him a little, he also respected her for it.

"Don't worry about it," said Simon. "I wasn't trying to put you on the spot. It was just a feeble attempt at getting to know you better."

Her face softened into a smile. "Maybe we can work our way up to deepest, darkest fears. We should start with the basics. Favorite movies and foods, and stuff like that."

Or perfumes? He leaned in toward her, trying to figure out her mouth-watering scent. Was that cinnamon? "I would love to know your favorite movies and foods." He was a pretty good cook. He could cook her something and maybe he could feed her.

Her lips parted in invitation.

Simon was just about to ask if he could kiss her, and whether or not they could do it successfully while they were both wearing headlamps, when a buzzer-like sound went off between them.

He jumped, as Connie would have said, out of his boy shorts. "Geez."

"The K2 meter," exclaimed Edwina, barely even shaken. The device was sitting on the island next to where they were standing. It emitted the buzzing noise, while its lights flashed.

"What does that mean?"

"The meter alerts us to changes in the electromagnetic frequencies. These devices are great at detecting issues with the wiring behind walls. They also tend to go off in the presence of ghosts."

"I see."

"If someone is here with us, we might be able to convince them to come forward." Edwina turned toward the fridge, where Adelaide claimed to have seen the man before. "Is that you? The man who tried to jump my sister?"

The lights flickered on the K2 meter.

"Show yourself. Do you like to push women around? Push *me* around."

"Ed, I don't think that's wise."

She ignored him and stepped forward. "Come on, dude. Give me something. Did you live here in life, or were you an enemy soldier? Is that your connection to this house? Are you the one who burned it to the ground, kicking Ann Forbes and her family out into the cold?"

At the mention of Ann's name, the light on the meter turned bright red.

"You did, didn't you?" Edwina's eyes widened. "I guess that makes you a total asshole. Or were you just following orders, unable to think for yourself? No backbone, no integrity."

The meter shook on the island, much like a cell phone might vibrate with an incoming call.

"Ed, be careful. We should stop."

But Edwina wouldn't stop. "You're a killer, aren't you? You killed Ann by sending her into the cold. You would have been kinder to strangle her in her sleep. Are you stuck here now, reliving all your evil deeds? Good. I hope you've been rotting away. Oh, by the way, before we're done, we're going to send you to hell where you belong."

The K2 meter sailed off the kitchen island and smashed against the opposite wall. It hit the wall hard enough to scratch the paint and dent the drywall.

Simon moved in front of Edwina. Because she was still trying to film everything, she stepped away and drew closer to the broken equipment.

"Whoa. That was amazing." She panned around the room. "To be clear, Simon and I are the only two people in here, and neither of us was touching the K2 meter when it flew off the island. The footage should back me up on that." Her face triumphant, she turned to Simon, and finally put her phone down. "Sorry about the dent in your wall."

He let out a strange laugh. "No sweat. Every wall should have one."

"Are you okay?"

"Not in the slightest." He was shaking. "What was that little performance?"

"Some spirits need to be provoked."

"Do you always go around provoking evil spirits?"

She shrugged. "Pretty much. It's part of my job description."

"I did not like that at all."

"Come on. It was awesome. You have to admit it."

Okay, *she* was awesome. The paranormal activity? Not so much.

"I'll have to review the footage, of course, but it does seem we have a responsive entity. This will go a long way to proving this is an actual haunting, rather than just residual energy."

"Meaning?"

She grinned in apparent excitement. "Meaning this guy might present a challenge, and I do love a challenge."

"Oh."

"Also, he destroyed my favorite K2 meter, and now he must pay."

Simon clapped a hand over his mouth.

He'd never been so incredibly horrified and turned on at the same time.

Chapter Seven

They all regrouped in the front hallway before the vigil ended at six in the morning to share their findings. Adelaide let them know things had been fairly quiet for her and Susannah. She said she'd made contact briefly with Ann Forbes again, but that the spirit woman hadn't relayed anything substantial. Mostly, she had followed them, watching out of curiosity, but she hadn't been willing or able to communicate.

Although she was tired, Edwina told her sisters what had happened in the kitchen with the K2 meter. When she realized Simon still wore a slightly shellshocked expression, she toned down the glee in her voice. "You know I don't like to make premature declarations, but I think it's safe to say this house is haunted."

She ignored the look on Adelaide's face, the one that said *I told you so*.

"Now, I just want to document as much as possible." Edwina turned to Simon. "Do you mind if I shack up with you here?"

His eyes bugged out. "Pardon?"

"Could I stay in one of your empty rooms? Now that we've gotten some good reactions from our spirit friends, I want to be on site as much as possible."

"Oh, right." He rolled his eyes. "Of course. Will you all be staying? You're welcome to. We have plenty of space."

Susannah shook her head. "Not me. I've got all my research notes back at the hotel."

"What about you, Adelaide?" asked Simon. "Want to join the party?"

Adelaide didn't respond. She stared down the hall toward the kitchen, fingering her necklace.

Edwina touched her shoulder. "Addy?"

Adelaide snapped back to attention. "What? Oh, sorry." Her gaze strayed toward the kitchen again. "No, thanks, Simon. It's important for me to get breaks from the negative energy."

Susannah, sharp as a tack, stood in front of Adelaide. "Do you see something in the kitchen?"

Adelaide pasted on a smile. "No, I'm good. I was just lost in thought, that's all."

"Okay," said Susannah. "Let's walk back to the hotel and get some fresh air."

As Adelaide headed out of the door, Edwina pulled Susannah aside. "Talk to her. She definitely saw something."

Susannah nodded and left.

Edwina tried to ignore the hot streak of worry that flashed across her forehead. She turned to Simon. "So, roomie. Where can I stay?"

"You can have your pick of the rooms."

"Most of your guests reported activity in the Merlot room. I'll do that one."

"Sure. Anything but camping out in the kitchen. You'd give me a heart attack if you did that."

"Aw." She stifled a smile. "Worried about me?"

"Absolutely."

The heat spread to her cheeks.

"I'm trying to decide if you're courageous or just reckless."

"Come now, Simon. Every courageous person started out a little reckless." She pointed her thumb toward where her car was parked outside. "I'll just get my bag from the car."

"Wait. You packed a bag? You *planned* on staying in my haunted house?"

"It's what I do. I stay in haunted houses, and I always have a go-bag.'"

* * * *

Edwina woke from a long nap in the Merlot room heavy-headed, as if she'd imbibed too much of the actual beverage. As she sat up, she was startled for a moment by the different surroundings. Her gaze landed on the bookshelf where the ship bookend had fallen a couple of days ago. The bookend was now neatly situated on the shelf, right against a stack of novels.

Had she been "reckless" in choosing to bunk in the Merlot room? Perhaps, but there had been activity in the room, and she hoped to catch the ghosts in the act.

It was a beautiful room, decorated with touches of plum and gold. The draperies, so opulent with their golden stitching, might have been custom made. The wine-colored linens were inviting and were soft to the touch. She'd sunk right into the mattress, it was so cushy. A shimmery throw had been sitting neatly at the edge of the bed, but it was now rumpled from where she'd kicked in her sleep. The various knick-knacks around the room bore the stamps of local artisans. There was also a slight nod to maritime tradition in the shape of a golden sand dollar paperweight on the desk and a bottle full of sand and tiny shells on the bookshelf.

Simon had offered her the honeymoon suite, but the white throw pillows and flowing draperies were a little too precious for her tastes. On the off chance that her Doc Martens had any dirt on them, she hadn't wanted to track it all over the bedroom. She was much more comfortable in the Merlot room with its darker furnishings.

She took a quick shower in the ensuite bathroom, almost crying out in sweet relief as the pressure from the rain shower head hit her back. After dressing and towel-drying her hair, she headed downstairs to find Simon. As she walked toward the kitchen, the most wonderful smell greeted her.

Bacon.

Edwina peered into the kitchen. Simon stood at the stove, his back to her. He had an apron tied around his waist, which brought a huge smile to her face for some reason. Perhaps it was because the tie at his waist cinched nicely over his firm ass. His tongs clinked against the pan as he moved the rashers around.

There was something incredibly sexy about seeing him preparing breakfast for her, especially considering he was probably unhappy about having to do it in a haunted kitchen.

It might explain why he had Britney Spears playing full blast on the kitchen speakers.

"Hi," she called, entering the room.

Simon whipped around. "Oh. Hey, it's you."

"Sorry. Didn't mean to sneak up on you."

"No, it's okay. I was just concentrating on not burning your breakfast."

"It smells amazing. I like your choice of music, by the way."

"Do you? It's from my 'Stressed Out' playlist. Britney helps me shake that shit right off."

Edwina didn't like hearing he was stressed, but his comment still managed to charm her. "We all need a playlist like that, I guess."

He turned back to the stove but glanced over his shoulder. "I hope you were comfortable. How did you sleep?"

For some reason, the question caught her off guard. It was likely because she couldn't remember the last time anyone outside her family had asked her that question. Declan had certainly never bothered to ask, not even after depriving her of sleep so many times. Maybe it was because there was something intimate about the inquiry, and Declan didn't do intimacy. There was a sort of comfort in knowing another human being cared about how you slept, and Edwina spied that in Simon's eyes. He wanted her to be cozy in his house, and it felt nice. "I slept well, thanks. The Merlot room is better than any hotel room I've ever been in."

"I'm glad to hear it. You, uh, definitely don't look like you lost any sleep last night. I mean, this morning."

There was a compliment in there, and it brought a smile to her face. "How about you? Did you sleep well?"

"Not a wink."

Edwina ran a hand up his arm. "Oh, I'm sorry. I know this is a lot to take in." As her hand gravitated toward his biceps, she pulled it away. The need to touch him and soothe him was becoming an urgent one. She couldn't seem to keep her hands to herself.

Not that Simon seemed to mind. In fact, he held his breath when her fingers met with the skin of his upper arm, and his gaze met hers for a hot moment.

But then he released that breath, and they both took a beat.

He passed the tongs from one hand to another. "I have to confess, I feel like there are eyes on me all the time now. Is it wrong that I want to go back to being a clueless unbeliever?"

"No. Ignorance is bliss, right?" The bacon was almost as enticing as his biceps. To appease her hunger, she snuck a cooked rasher from the plate he'd set aside, and devoured it. "Ohmigod, this is so good."

His lips curled up as she chewed, then his gaze lowered to take in her outfit. "You look really nice."

"I do?" She'd thrown on some black jeans and a black Foo Fighters T-shirt. Not exactly her fanciest attire.

He shut the stove off, put his tongs down on the counter and faced her. Leaning against the counter, he crossed his arms over his chest, which highlighted the lean muscles in his forearms. "I don't think you quite understand your own appeal."

Edwina had an urge to dismiss his compliment but tried not to scoff. She wasn't ignorant about her own appearance. She knew she was attractive by most people's standards, but Declan had messed with her head in such a way that she still sometimes forgot she was cute.

Only Simon wasn't looking at her as if she was cute. He was staring at her as if she'd rolled up like Venus on the half shell. His hooded eyes and open lips said he wanted to devour her.

It was tempting. She hadn't been devoured in a while.

"So, um," Edwina said, fighting the urge not to jump his bacon-scented bones right there. "Where's Connie?"

"She's off for the next couple of days."

So there was no one around to stop her from jumping the aforementioned bones. Aside from the ghosts.

Right. The ghosts. "I should probably review the footage from last night."

"At least have some breakfast first. I mean, lunch? I'm not even sure what time it is." Simon opened the oven and pulled out a couple of other hot plates. "I made a few things because I wasn't sure what you liked. There's a cheese omelet with Gruyère. There are also some home fries, bacon and a fruit salad. Oh, and I still have a couple of those croissants you like. Have as much as you want. You can take it to your room, if you want to be on your own."

"Have you eaten yet?"

"Nope."

"Let's eat together, then."

Simon's smile warmed her to her toes. "All right. Could you grab those plates for me? I thought the dining room might be a bit formal, so I set a table in the parlor." He picked up a couple of the items and led her into the parlor, over to the table closest to the window. There was already a silver carafe of coffee waiting on the table, as well as a number of specialty teas in an ornamented box.

"Wow. You went to a lot of trouble."

"Nah. I mean, without any guests, the food's been sitting here, going to waste. This is just what breakfast looks like at the King Street B&B. I hope you like it." The earnestness in his expression told her she might have gotten the VIP version of the breakfast. She certainly never put Gruyère in her own omelets.

She couldn't remember the last time Declan had so much as tossed her a piece of dry toast on his way out of the door.

Stop it.

It wasn't Edwina's intention to make so many comparisons between the two men. They just sort of made themselves.

They sat, and after asking what she'd like to drink, Simon poured them both some coffees. Edwina took a sip of the heady dark roast, relishing the heat at the back of her throat. They chatted a bit about the weather and Simon answered her questions about the renovations they'd done on the building. He was an excellent host, always animated and focused on what she was saying, and he cooked one hell of a meal. Everything was delicious, from the melted cheese in the eggs to the crispy bacon to the perfectly browned home fries.

It made her want to stay a while. It also made her want to let her guard down a little.

"Thank you for letting me invade, Simon. I hope you don't mind me being in your space."

"Not at all. I'm in hospitality. I'm used to people being in my space." He blushed. "Of course, none of them are as fierce as you are."

"Thanks." *Fierce*. She'd never really thought of herself that way. She just did what needed to be done. "I texted my sisters when I got up. They're going to keep to themselves for the rest of the day. Addy usually needs some time to regroup after an intense vigil. She calls it 'restocking the psychic pantry.'"

"Is she okay? She seemed a little distracted at the end."

"Yeah, she did." Edwina had asked Susannah if she'd dug up any dirt on how Addy was feeling, but their younger sister had clammed up. "I'm sure it's nothing. The vigils take a lot out of her. I know Susannah would have loved to have stayed here too, but we talked earlier and decided it might be best if someone sticks close to Addy."

"I see."

"Of all of us, Addy feels it the most. She's basically absorbing the emotions of others, never mind dealing with her own."

"And how are *your* emotions?" Simon reached out his hand. For a moment, Edwina thought he was going to clasp her hand, but he only ran a finger along the edge of her plate, fiddling with a crumb.

Oh, to be that crumb. Her disappointment in that moment was acute. "I'm fine."

No sooner were the words out of her mouth, when an image formed in her head. The specter from all those years ago, hovering over her bed in the middle of the night. It had a familiar face, one she loved dearly. But that face had changed, turning into something surprising and terrible.

"Ed? Are you okay? You spaced out there for a second."

She blinked a few times. "I think I should get out of the house this afternoon. You know, just for a bit, to clear my head."

"Excellent idea. My head could use some clearing too." He leaned in, a sly glint in his eye. "Tell me, what are your thoughts on ice wine slushies?"

She followed his lead and leaned in as well, captivated by his game. "Well, Mr. Teal, I've never had one."

His dramatic sigh would have made a Shakespearean actor envious of his technique. "That's a damn shame. Luckily, my friend owns one of the wineries nearby, and because I feature his fine beverages on my menu, I get ice wine slushies whenever I want."

"Perks of the job, huh?"

"Stick with me, kid." He pretended to buff his fingernails. "This business might be failing, but there are still some ridiculous perks to be had."

"Hmm. You and me, getting a beverage together. That sounds an awful lot like a date."

"It would verge into date territory."

"I don't date my clients, though."

"Then we won't call it a date. We're just clearing our heads, remember?" Simon looked at her from over the tops of his glasses. "Although, I'll just put this out there, and you can tell me to mind my own beeswax. Aside from not wanting to compromise your investigation, why not date your clients?"

She didn't really have an answer for that. It wasn't as if their relationship was taboo, and they didn't tend to get repeat customers anyway. And frankly, Simon was the only client to whom she'd ever been attracted. "I suppose one little slushie wouldn't compromise my investigation."

He sat back and smiled.

Of course, there was a distinct possibility his cocky grin would do what the slushie didn't.

* * * *

It was a good thing Edwina could hold her liquor, because the ice wine slushie was doing its best to knock her down. They'd begun by sampling a tiny amount of the red, then the white variety. Both packed a punch, but the red wine beverage threatened to obliterate Edwina. It was headache-inducing stuff. However, the white wine slushie, while still potent, went down much more easily. Still, it was tempting to suck back the frozen drink. She learned from the first few draws that it went straight to her head.

Simon's friend, the owner of the winery, had set up a pleasant little patio in back. With colorful umbrellas and happy day-trippers and tourists at the other tables, it felt festive and bright. The sun was shining and not a single cloud drifted past in the sky.

No ghosts here, clearly. It was just the breath of fresh air that Edwina had needed.

Their time away from the bed and breakfast gave Edwina another opportunity to see Simon in his element. His pal Martin, the winery owner, stopped by their table and chatted for a few minutes. He was seriously cute too. A tall Asian man with impressive arms, he looked like he hoisted wine barrels as part of his workout routine. Martin had a wide smile and an infectious laugh, as well. Edwina couldn't help but notice the way he and Simon attracted the attention of the others on the patio. On their own, they were both hot, but together, it was almost too much sexiness for mere mortals. People kept looking over at them, clearly drawn to their handsome looks and genuine rapport.

Especially the bridal shower party a couple of tables over. Edwina could tell a couple of the bridesmaids, if not the bride-to-be, were fantasizing about being the meat in a Simon/Martin sandwich.

Just before heading back, Martin clapped a hand on Simon's shoulder. "It's good to see you smile, my friend. I haven't seen that since your early days with Carly."

Carly? Edwina tucked that little detail away.

"Right," said Simon. "Thanks for the drinks, bud."

When Martin left, Edwina twirled her straw around in her glass. "Okay, I'm going to ask because we're both a teeny bit drunk, and it seems like an obvious question. Who's Carly?"

He closed his eyes for a moment. When he opened them, there was a hint of resignation there. "My ex."

"And why didn't you smile when you were with her?"

"It's a long story." A muscle in his jaw twitched. "Short answer? Because, fairly early on in our relationship, she hooked up with my brother, Rupert. The jackass. Although I didn't find out about it until later."

"Oh, Simon. I'm sorry. That sucks donkey ass."

"It really does. The thing is, to hear them talk about it, it ended up being the love of their lives. You know, at least until the next one comes along. They're actually engaged now. I got the wedding invitation a while back. *You are cordially invited to the wedding of Carly and*

117

Rupert. Come on, doesn't that sound like the wedding for a couple of cartoon Golden Retrievers?"

"Yeah, it does."

He lifted his straw out of his drink and sucked on its bottom to empty the contents. "It wasn't really the cheating that got me in the end. The worst part was my family telling me I should just get over it. I should have expected it. Rupert has gotten away with acting like a dick since he was a kid, and he just gets patted on the back every single time. Our father thinks it's a hoot that my brother has tried to steal every girlfriend I've ever had, like it's some sort of test of masculinity. To be honest, things are really strained in the family right now, but they all blame me for holding a grudge."

"Even though you're entitled to it, from the sounds of it. What does your mom say?"

"Oh, my mom? Well, because there's a wedding that she can help plan, she's able to distract herself from the real issue of our crumbling family dynamic." He shook his head. "Sorry. I don't talk about this a lot, because if I allow myself to think about it for more than a few seconds, I realize that I'm still incredibly pissed."

"You have every right to be."

"Yeah." He stuck his straw back in his drink. "I'm not great at sharing things like this. The last couple of years have left me feeling like a failure, in more ways than one."

"You're not a failure, Simon. Carly missed out on something great."

"You think so?"

"I do." She stifled a laugh. "And I'm not the only one who does. As a matter of fact, you are currently being appraised by the bridal party two tables down."

"How do you know it's a bridal party?"

"The pink sashes that say, 'Bridal party' are a dead giveaway. The maid of honor is totally checking you out. Don't look now."

Only he didn't look around at all. If anything, he leaned in closer to Edwina.

Declan would have totally checked out the other woman, and he would have done it right in front of her. He might have even winked at the maid of honor, then told Edwina she was seeing things when she called him on it.

"Really?" Simon said without interest. He focused his gaze on her instead. "Your cheeks are pink."

His low tone caused a thrum in her belly. Another few sips of the slushie, and she just might offer him a peek at her other cheeks. "I hope your story, combined with this slushie, wasn't part of a wicked plan to seduce me."

"Are you always turned on by stories of woe?"

"Let's just say I've always had a thing for the wounded type."

"Oh, baby, have I got wounds for you!" He laughed. "No, I wouldn't do that. I know how powerful these drinks can be. I would never try to seduce you under the influence of a wine slushie." He moved his chair closer to hers. "If I *were* to seduce you, you would be completely alert, capable of making decisions, and on board with the idea."

"Ah. So, if I were on board with the idea, how would you conduct this grand seduction?"

"Come on. I saw how quickly you reached for the bacon. Obviously, the way to your heart is through your stomach."

"True. Go on."

"I might convince you to watch one of those shark movies that frighten you, just so I could put my arm around you and comfort you in your moment of need."

"You do have very nice arms."

"Do I?" asked Simon. "I had no idea you'd noticed."

"I notice lots of things."

"You did see Martin's guns, right?"

"Couldn't miss them, but I happen to like yours. What else would you do?"

"Let's see." He tucked a stray strand of hair behind her ear, then gently wrapped his fingers behind her neck. "You spend a lot of your time helping others feel safe. I think any decent seduction plan would have to include a bit of pampering for you. Maybe a long back rub in a candlelit room."

"I happen to love back rubs."

"I will keep that in mind, Ms. Darke." Simon brought his hand around to cup her jaw, grazing his thumb against her bottom lip.

Damn! The lower lip graze! It was the move that usually brought her to her knees.

Edwina was just about to ask if she could kiss him when her cell phone vibrated on the table. She swore under her breath and sat back. She picked up the call from Susannah. "Hey, Suz. Everything okay?"

"Yeah. Where are you? I hear laughing in the background."

"Simon and I just grabbed a quick...ice wine slushie."

Susannah cackled. "Edwina Frances Darke. Are you planning on fornicating with that man?"

"No!"

"Hmm. That's too bad. You clearly have the hots for each other. Simon would make a great fuck buddy, I bet. The man runs a B&B. He knows how to be discreet. And he lives far enough away from Toronto that you wouldn't have to see him all the time, if you didn't want to."

"Why did you call, sister dear?" She drew loudly on her straw for Susannah's benefit.

"Listen, unlike some people, I've been working on the case. As you know, I've been putting out feelers, and now my precious little research babies are coming home to Mama."

"Stay on track, please." Susannah could get a bit weird when her head was stuck in history books.

"Okay, okay." Susannah paused for effect. "There are still members of the Forbes family living nearby. I have an address on the Niagara Parkway."

"That's just down the road."

"I know. I already spoke to the woman and get this. She's the direct descendant of Ann's cousin. Her name is Martha, and she's been collecting documents related to the family for years. She's willing to talk to us."

"That's amazing." Edwina gave Simon a thumbs-up. "Does she want to see us now?"

"No, she's busy for the next couple of days, but she did give me some info over the phone. It's big."

"Put me out of my misery."

"Martha lives on a piece of property that was owned by Ann's relative. It's been in the family for generations. There's a small burial plot in her backyard. Niagara has several pioneer graveyards, and many were on family properties." Susannah hummed in excitement. "Ann Forbes is buried in Martha's backyard."

"Holy shit. I just assumed her grave might be in the churchyard."

"Me too. I think it would be nice for us all to pay our respects. And maybe Addy will be able to pick up on some info while we're there."

"Great job, Suz," said Edwina.

"Thank you. Anyway, you sound like you're having fun, and Addy's still out of sorts."

"Is she okay?"

"Well, she's holed up in her room, and I'm pretty sure I heard her talking to herself there. You know, normal stuff. Anyway, let's give her the night off and regroup tomorrow night."

"Sounds good."

Susannah chuckled. "Enjoy the rest of your hot date."

"Ohmigod, shut up. Bye."

Edwina hung up and told Simon what Susannah had relayed, leaving out the bit about fornicating with him and suggesting she take him as a long-distance fuck buddy. That was Susannah's tactic for dealing with men. She kept them at arm's length. Even though Edwina admired her sister's ability to maintain boundaries, especially with men, she knew it also came with its own set of problems.

"That's incredible," he said. "What now?"

"Now? I'd really like to review the audio from the vigil. It would be great to have some robust evidence before we meet Martha."

"Can I help you with that?"

Sitting with Simon in close quarters, listening to the same audio? It was probably a bad idea because it would give her plenty of opportunities to sniff him and feel the heat from his body. But she was weak, and she really wanted to see if he'd touch her again. "Sure thing."

As Simon arranged a taxi to come pick them up, Edwina fidgeted in her spot. She wasn't sure why she was feeling so uptight about her attraction to Simon. God only knew her sisters would encourage her to have a fun little fling. They'd been there when Declan left her in his wake. They'd been the ones to pick her up and dust her off, and they'd encouraged to get back in the saddle.

Only, she hadn't. Not really, anyway. There had been a couple of half-hearted dates, but nothing to excite her.

Simon excited her, but she was worried about losing herself in a relationship again. Simon seemed nice, but there was no doubt he was dealing with some heavy family shit, and that kind of stress made people do stupid things sometimes.

Still, when in his presence, it was easy to forget her fears. And when he brushed his thumb against her lower lip, she was ready to forget the rest of the world.

Here, on this patio, she just wanted to lean into his magnetism and soak him up.

Weren't you trying to convince yourself this was a bad idea? Because you're doing a piss-poor job of it.

She had allowed herself to get distracted by the sunshine, some very good wine and Simon's charm. If she allowed herself, she could get carried away.

Only she wasn't even sure she wanted to fight it.

Chapter Eight

"I'm not much of a gadget guy." Simon pulled out a chair for Edwina, and they sat at the parlor table. "You'll have to guide me."

Edwina shuffled closer to him, and he had to resist the urge to reach for her hand or run his fingers through her hair. They'd had a moment back at the winery, a very nice one at that, and he was now suffering from *momentus interruptus*. Her distinctive perfume teased his nose, making him want to throw caution to the wind and kiss her neck. Hell, he just wanted to touch her, in any small way, to see if the electricity was still there. He suspected it hid just under the surface, and that once they allowed themselves to succumb, the reaction would be explosive.

Edwina had six EVP recorders set out on the table. They had previously been set up in various rooms around the house during the vigil. "These things are pretty straightforward. It's the same button to play or pause. Normally, Susannah and I would wear headphones to block out any external noise, but it's pretty quiet here. Let's just listen together for now, and see if we can come up with anything."

"So, I should be listening out for, what, growls and moans?"

"I have heard a couple of those before, but mostly it's just voices or sounds that don't belong. I wasn't able to capture anything on our first walk-through, so cross fingers." She set the nearest recorder between them and pressed Play.

This was the recorder that had been positioned in the upstairs hallway during the vigil. They listened to the familiar conversation as the group entered the bed and breakfast that night. Simon's gaze strayed toward Edwina and he maintained eye contact as the vigil unfolded before them once again.

Her eyes were beautiful, so dark and warm. He'd always loved women with brown eyes, but she made his imagination race. As she blinked, her long lashes moving in a delicate sweep, his stifled emotions raced to the fore.

It wasn't just her looks, though. She was brave and caring, and so fucking intelligent. Every time she opened her mouth, he was awestruck. And they loved the same wine slushies! How cool was that? There was so much about Edwina that made him want to try opening his heart again.

Are you sure about that? Look what happened last time.

His inner voice, the one that was riddled with an anxiety most people never saw, stirred up chaos. He wanted to reach inside himself, tear it out, and throw it away.

Edwina made him want to take chances that terrified him.

They reached the part of the recording in which Adelaide told them she had sensed Ann's spirit again. Moments after she began to talk, a staticky sound erupted over the audio.

Edwina grabbed his hand and froze. "You heard that, right? It's not just me?"

"Not just you." He gave her hand a gentle squeeze. Now that he was touching her, he wasn't about to let her go. When she didn't remove her hand, he almost let out a joyful shout.

With her free hand, she rewound it. "It's possible the recorder went on the fritz for a second, but let's just listen to that again."

They both drew closer to the device, and to each other. Their eyes met as Adelaide's voice filled the room again. Frankly, he loved having an excuse to stare at Edwina.

"There," Simon exclaimed. "When Adelaide mentions the spirit woman, the static starts. Could that be some sort of ghost communication?"

"Hard to say. Let's see if it comes up again."

They continued the recording. When Adelaide mentioned Ann being in mourning, a woman's voice could be heard in the background.

Clear as day, the mystery woman spoke.

"James."

Edwina's eyes grew wide. "Who the hell is James?" She had a notepad next to her, and she finally released his hand so she could scrawl the name.

Simon's adrenaline was pumping, and it wasn't just because he'd got to hold Edwina's hand for a few minutes. They had another name now, and were that much closer to figuring out what the hell was wrong with the property.

As she started up the recording again, his breath came quicker. Edwina's chest was rising and falling too, and her eyes were bright and alert. For a few moments, there were no unusual sounds. But when they got to the part where Edwina said Ann's soul deserved peace, that strange, disembodied voice said something else.

"Perry."

"Perry?" Edwina repeated it, mulling it over. "As in the name? Or could it be 'to parry,' as in to ward something off?"

"I would think the name is more likely, but what do I know?"

"That's two possible names to research. That should help us narrow things down."

They finished off the recording from the vigil. For the most part, the rest of the recording was fairly uneventful, although there was the odd creak on the stairs. Simon tried to rationalize those creaks, but they still left him unsettled.

But then they heard something that took his breath away. Despite his best efforts, he couldn't explain it, and it raised every hair at the back of his neck. It was right at the tail end of the recording.

Susannah had just asked a troubled Adelaide if she'd seen something in the kitchen.

After Addy responded, a man's voice could be heard.

"Come back, Adelaide."

Simon had been the only man in the house that night, and he certainly hadn't uttered those words. Even if he had, there was no way he would have produced the low growl that followed.

When Edwina reached for his hand again, she didn't let go for a good, long time.

* * * *

"Edwiiiiiii-naaaaaa."

The soft, singsong voice teased her out of sleep, as it had so many times before. Grasping her covers, Edwina pulled them up to her forehead. She squeezed her eyes shut and waited in the darkness for the inevitable onslaught.

"Edwina, my love. Why are you hiding?"

"Go away." When she spoke, her voice sounded wrong. It was too high, too scared.

It was the voice of her seven-year-old self.

"I've made cookies for you and your sisters. Snickerdoodles, your favorites. Now, come on out and give your grandma a hug." Her grandmother's sweet tone changed on that last word, becoming something deep and guttural. "Come out and play."

"You're not my grandma!" Little Edwina shivered under the covers. "Go away. I hate you!"

"I'll never go away, Edwina." The monster threatened, not even trying to disguise its voice anymore. "I'll always be with you. You can't get rid of me!"

Then, as it always did, it began to tug on her covers. Although her tiny fingers clutched at the fabric, it slid away from her body.

She knew she had no choice but to look. It never went away unless she confronted it.

So, little Edwina opened her eyes.

The creature had her dead grandmother's face, but in place of her kind eyes, there were terrible white orbs that saw everything. It was dressed in Gran's clothing, cotton pants and a sweater that was embroidered with tiny giraffes. It lunged at her in a cloud of lavender decay.

Edwina threw up her arms and screamed.

"Ed!" Another voice broke into her consciousness. Warm hands held her by the arms. "Ed, what happened?"

She opened her stinging eyes for real this time. Tears still clung to her lashes and she swiped them away.

"Are you okay?"

She struggled in the person's grip. Someone had turned on the lights. Another scream built in her throat.

"Edwina."

Simon. How did he get into her house? Why wasn't he wearing his glasses?

And what happened to his clothes?

She glanced around the space. It looked nothing like her bedroom. Only then did she remember she'd been sleeping in the Merlot room.

Simon had woken her up. He'd scared it away.

Wearing nothing but blue boxer briefs and with a head of tousled hair, he might have been a sexy angel, appearing just in the nick of time to slay her demons. Only he was so wonderfully human. She fell into his embrace and wrapped her arms around his chest.

"Hey." He passed a hand over her hair. "Did you see something, or was it just a bad dream?"

"I'm never quite sure."

A rumble of concern reverberated in his chest. He pulled away, just far enough to be able to tip up her chin. "Is this a regular thing?"

She nodded.

He sat next to her, pulling her tightly against his side. "Tell me about it."

"I've, um, had this recurring nightmare most of my life. When I was seven, my grandmother died. I loved her so much and it hit me hard. She was the first person I knew who had passed away, and I found everything surrounding the funeral and the wake pretty scary."

"I'm sorry. Of course, you'd find it scary. You were a kid."

Tears filled her eyes again. She took a deep breath and exhaled. "A few days after she died, I saw this *thing* in my room. I had been sleeping, but was woken up by a voice calling my name. I remember being confused because it sounded like my grandmother's voice, but something about it wasn't right. I sat up in bed. The closet door opened, and it came out, smelling of her perfume. It was my grandmother, only it wasn't. Her face was all hollowed out, and her eyes were white. It rushed toward me, so I screamed. My parents ran into the room, but it had disappeared. And, of course, they never believed me. They said it was a nightmare caused by stress."

She clamped her hand on his bare knee. "I realize I was little, Simon, but I know what I saw. It wasn't a dream, at least not that first time. It was something evil."

"Shit. Come here." He pulled her into the space between his legs and proceeded to give her a backrub.

She sighed as he worked out the knots in her shoulders. One by one, they relaxed, and her breathing returned to its normal pace. "I've dreamt about it ever since."

"That's awful."

"The dream happened several times over the years, each time a little different, but it always ended the same way. When I was about fourteen, I had it again, but it was really bad. It felt like it dragged on forever. I must have been crying, because Addy and Susannah came into my room. They woke me up and stayed with me in my bed for the rest of the night. I remember huddling with them under the covers. They held my hand and wiped my tears away. I'm the big sister. I should have been comforting them."

"It's because you're an amazing big sister that they wanted to comfort you."

"Even then, Addy said such funny things. She was only ten at the time. And I remember her saying in her high little voice, 'It's okay, Edwina. What you saw years ago wasn't Grandma. It was just a bad spirit pretending to be her. It came to you because it knew you were sad. But it's gone now. Maria scared it away.'"

"Jeez," said Simon. "Can I be real here and admit Maria scares me too?"

"I know." Edwina managed a quiet laugh. "But she and Addy are a package deal, it seems. To be honest, I'm grateful for both of them, even though Maria still freaks me out too. It did help, knowing it wasn't really my grandmother in my room. For years, I'd thought that Grandma was trapped in some sort of terrifying limbo, or that she'd somehow come back changed. When I have the nightmare now, I try to remind myself of that."

"Probably doesn't make it any less scary, does it?"

"No. And despite Addy's assurances, I still worry it'll come back, that it'll find me. It's why I'm such a bulldog when it comes to DPI and what we do. I feel like I'm on this quest for answers, even though I know I'll probably never get them." She swallowed through her scratchy throat. "You asked what scares me. *That* scares me. Never finding the answers."

She shook her head, lost in memories, and turned around to face him. Their legs tangled in her sheets, and she suddenly remembered how little she was wearing. Just her panties and a sleeveless tee.

Simon seemed to realize it at the same moment. He did a slow perusal of her body then his eyes met hers again, full of awareness. "I, uh, should probably head back to my room."

"Simon."

"Yeah?"

"Could you—?"

"I'll do anything you need."

It felt as if all her hopes were pent-up in the sigh that escaped her. "Kiss me?"

"God, yeah. I'd love to."

His tender grin destroyed whatever was left of her resolve. She hauled him toward her by the shoulders. As their lips met, she remembered in horror that she probably had morning breath. Or middle-of-the-night breath, at least.

Only Simon didn't seem to care. He groaned, angling his head so he could deepen the kiss. And somehow, in that kiss, she felt grounded again. She was suddenly hyper-aware of her surroundings and of how much she loved the glide of his tongue against hers. She ran her hands along his strong shoulders and down his chest, where his nipples tightened at her touch.

What else could she make his body do?

She reached for his waistband.

"Hang on." Grinning, his cheeks red, Simon pulled away. "Let's take a breath."

"I'm sorry. Have I messed everything up?"

"No." He cupped her cheek. "Not at all. I'd be lying if I said I didn't want to be in your bed. But Ed, I don't want to take advantage of you. You had a nightmare and it made you sad. And, well, when we do this, I'd rather there weren't any tears in your eyes." He brushed his thumb against her temple, wiping at the tracks of her tears.

Damn.

"But, if you're up for it, I give a mean cuddle."

She couldn't help comparing him to Declan once again. There had been a couple of times when Declan had woken her from her nightmares, only to either suggest she needed serious counseling, or to use it as an opportunity to get into her pants.

And she'd let him every time, grasping onto any crumbs of intimacy he might allow.

Usually, it was the physical sort.

Simon was offering her something more. Being the greedy girl she was, she took it. "I like cuddles."

Simon drew her into his arms as they lay down on the bed. He spooned her, pulling the covers up over both of them, then curled his arm about her middle. Her shirt had ridden up a bit, and his hand came to rest over her waist, a respectable distance from both her boobs and her pussy. His breath was warm and lovely at her neck, and he dropped the odd kiss there, reassuring her of his presence.

Every so often, his stiff cock would nudge her butt, and he'd groan, making them both laugh.

"Let the record state that I was willing to help you with that," she said.

"I know. It's greatly appreciated, and we will revisit the situation another time."

The last tendril of fear slipped from her body. "I hope you realize you scored some points tonight for doing the honorable thing."

"Did I?"

"Yeah. You scored a bunch of points."

"Awesome. Now go to sleep. Next time, you can encourage me to be less honorable."

Edwina drifted off on a happy thought. Next time, she would absolutely encourage him to be a scoundrel.

Chapter Nine

There was no denying it.

Edwina had taken top spot in Simon's mind, and it seemed nothing would shake her from that position.

Even now, as the two of them prepared the bed and breakfast for another night vigil, he couldn't stop looking at her, couldn't stop thinking of her.

Of course, he really wanted to sleep with her. Since waking up that morning with her in his arms, he'd been painfully hard and frustrated.

But there was also something hot about that feeling of anticipation. Edwina had admitted she wanted him too. It would happen, he just knew it, and it was only a matter of time. The knowledge was both overwhelming and exciting. Neither of those feelings had been part of his emotional vocabulary in a while.

As they went about their work today, there were plenty of shy glances and soft touches. In truth, it was a different Edwina he saw this morning, and he suspected she didn't show this side of herself to too many people.

He'd have to find out why. After sharing his dirty laundry with her, the most amazing thing had happened. Something hard and knotted at the base of his spine had unraveled. He'd felt lighter and had stood straighter than he had in a while. It had been nice to have her support and understanding, and he wanted to do the same for her.

In this whirlwind week of remarkable adventures, Simon had become very attached to Edwina, and it wasn't just a physical thing. He enjoyed being with her, loved listening to her, and even though their time together hadn't been full of merriment, her laughter had changed him. He found himself dreaming up ways to make her break into that throaty laugh of hers.

Of course, there had been a few more kisses that morning as well, ones that had obliterated the memory of any kisses he'd ever had with other people. Definitely an interesting development.

In ways that boggled his mind, going on this bizarre ghost hunt with her, being in such close quarters, his emotions seemed heightened. It was as if their relationship was on some sort of fast track, and they'd barely even touched each other.

Of course, sometimes Simon wondered if it was all in his head, and whether or not he was just affected by the situation at the bed and breakfast.

It would be nice to get away from all the ghost stuff and see Edwina in her day-to-day life. Would the fierce attraction still be there?

Just then, she walked by him in the hallway, holding one of her gadgets. Her luscious lips were turned up in a secret smile. As she passed, she bumped her hip against his, and hummed in amusement.

Goosebumps arose on his skin.

Oh yeah, he was fairly certain the fierce attraction would still be there. In fact, he was convinced that even watching her tie her shoes or brush her teeth would fill him with fascination.

"Okay," she said. "Before the others arrive, I want to try to capture some more EVP. We had lots of luck with it last time. I'm just going to walk around the house and poke my head into all the rooms. Want to join me?"

Of course he wanted to join her. He was beginning to think he'd follow her through the gates of hell. "Yeah, sure." He pasted on his best nonchalant grin. It was probably best not to let her know exactly how needy he could be, especially where she was concerned.

Because she was Edwina Darke, and it took nothing short of full-on demonic possession to rattle her, she started in the kitchen. Simon hung back a little, still marveling at her chutzpah.

What would his family think of her?

Fuck, dude. Why do you even care? You haven't sought their approval in a long time.

And yet, his mind still went there.

He could already envision it. His parents would only ask her about her theater work, ignoring her ghost hunting altogether, because they'd consider it a waste of time. They'd tell her they saw *Phantom of the Opera* seventeen times, the height of sophistication in their eyes. Then, they would proceed to talk only about themselves. It was what they did best.

He had no clue what Carly would think of Edwina. He had no clue what Carly thought of anything anymore, even though she was about to become his sister-in-law.

And Rupert? Well, he would try to sleep with her. Simon would have to think long and hard before introducing Edwina to the train wreck that was his brother. Not that she wouldn't hold her own. If Rupert ever tried anything with her, she'd probably lay him out with one kick from her Doc Martens.

Actually, I'd pay to see that.

He just didn't want to expose her to that, or to anything remotely unpleasant. He wanted to surround Edwina with lovely things. Puppies and roses and sunshine. Ice wine slushies and, heck, even haunted houses, if that made her happy.

He was getting ahead of himself. *Just focus and let her do her thing.*

She planted herself near the island and cleared her throat. "Okay. I'm talking to the man who haunts this kitchen. You left a message for my sister, Adelaide. I want to be very clear. If you're planning on messing with her, you'll have to go through me. Got that?" She paused, holding up the EVP recorder. "Talk to *me*. Tell me why you're here, and what it'll take to get rid of you. Is your name James? Or is it Perry? We will find out, you know."

She paused, and Simon held his breath, in case the spirit man decided to finally say something out loud.

As the quiet lengthened, Edwina changed tactics. "Would you rather talk to my friend Simon? He's right here, waiting."

"Thanks for that."

Edwina winked. "Come on. Do something. You sure liked playing with the devices last time. Do it again. Smash another one. I dare you."

Nothing happened, at least, nothing that they could see.

They hung out in the kitchen for a good half hour. Simon even tried talking to the ghost.

If anyone had told him a couple of weeks ago that he'd soon be conversing with wraiths, he would have thought they were off their rocker. But here he was, beckoning to a possibly dangerous entity, all because a hot woman thought it was a cool idea. Unbelievable.

Despite their many entreaties, the kitchen ghost remained silent.

"Fine." Edwina let out a small huff. "I'm not going to beg, even though I get the sense you'd like that." She set the recorder on the island. "I'm going to leave this device behind. Feel free to speak into it. In the meantime, I'm going to see if anyone else is willing to talk to us. Maybe Ann Forbes will be more cooperative."

Just then, Simon's phone vibrated in his pocket, almost giving him cardiac arrest. He motioned silently to Edwina, and pulled it out to check the oncoming text.

For fuck's sake. It was Rupert.

Give me a call.

Honest to God. The guy never asked. He always demanded.

Maybe Simon *would* give that entitled fuck a call and tell him all the things he'd been storing deep inside all these years. Maybe he'd tell him…

He he he he.

The deep chuckle erupted right over Simon's shoulder.

Edwina grabbed his arm. She'd heard it too.

It might have been Simon's imagination, but a soft blast of cold air whispered past his ear. He sucked in a breath and gestured over his shoulder.

She nodded and aimed her cell phone at him. "Ah, so you are here. What brought you out of your hole? Was it because I mentioned Ann? Are you worried about us contacting her? Maybe she'll expose you."

The draft ran down the back of Simon's neck. He held still, fighting the urge to vomit. Was fear-induced vomit a thing?

Something told him this particular visitation wasn't about Ann at all. The sensation was too intimate, too close. He couldn't shake the sensation that the entity was focused on *him*.

Previously, he would have argued that the draft was created by natural, albeit unseen, means. Now, he wasn't so sure. The waft turned colder, its pressure harder, like an icy finger being dragged down his spine.

Terrible thoughts filled his head, although he couldn't even come up with words to describe them. For a moment, his field of vision just went dark. He blinked until it cleared, but those few seconds temporarily robbed him of all hope and serenity.

Edwina caught his eye, radiating calm. "Ann Forbes might reveal your identity," she said to the ghost. "I think you like hiding in the dark, scaring people. You won't be able to do that once we know who you are. We're going to take all your power away."

She and Simon stood like that, eyes locked on each other, until the cold sensation finally dissipated. As Simon's body temperature started to regulate, he confessed the depth of his fear. "It was as if someone had shoved a six-foot block of ice behind me. I could feel a presence, and it almost made me sick. The last time I felt like that was when I was a kid, and Rupert pulled me into this creepy funhouse at a fair, then ran off on me. I was too scared to run to the exit."

Edwina grunted in disapproval at his funhouse story. "This thing understands its own power. I think it gets off on frightening people. Didn't you say that your guests had experienced a lot of cold spots around the building?"

"Yeah, but that was in the bedrooms."

"Addy said this guy likes to move around. Ann's spirit made it cold for us too, but without that sense of foreboding. He uses it to assault people." She paused, nibbling her lip. "Is everything okay? You got a text."

"Oh, that. Just my brother, being a dick as always."

"I see." Another pause, a longer one this time. "Want to talk about it?"

Simon's instinct was to brush it off and bury it deep, as he always had, but he knew that would hurt Edwina. It couldn't be easy for her to extend herself and ask, after he'd dismissed her questions before. So he swallowed his pride, and did the thing that scared him. "I would like to talk about it with you, but let's do it later, when we're not being actively haunted. Is that all right?"

"Absolutely. As long as you're comfortable."

He closed the short distance between them and reached for her hands, bringing them both to his lips. "I'm more comfortable talking to you than I've been with anyone else. Is it wrong to admit that so soon?"

"Not wrong at all." She wrapped her arms around Simon. "I appreciate you being honest with me."

Look at that. He'd begun to talk about his feelings with her, and he hadn't burst into flames. To celebrate, he kissed the corner of her mouth. Dragging himself away from her soft lips, he glanced around the room. "Come on. I feel like we're being watched."

They conducted some EVP sessions in the other main-floor rooms then headed upstairs. Simon's guests had reported activity in each of the bedrooms, but there were a couple that the Darkes hadn't explored fully yet.

Edwina led him toward the Chardonnay room. In truth, this room was Simon's pride and joy. It had a gorgeous view of the ravine behind the house, and even though it had been decorated with a modern touch, it oozed history. He and Connie had furnished it with a gorgeous four-poster bed and a roll top desk that he'd found at an antique show. The draperies and linens were all in soft shades of cream. Eggplant-colored pillows and a rich blanket at the edge of the bed provided pops of color.

"This room is amazing," said Edwina, a note of awe in her voice. "You know, when our investigation is done, you might have some new regular guests on your hands."

Simon pulled her toward him and happily brushed his lips along the column of her neck. "You, madam, are always welcome here."

She relaxed into his arms. "I'm glad."

Christ, she smelled good. It was some kind of spicy scent, and it reminded him of mulled wine and cookies. "Is that cinnamon I smell?"

"Yeah. I use a perfume oil. Is it too strong?"

Hell, no. "You smell delicious." Simon allowed himself a small nibble of her flesh, just a taste of what was to come. Edwina sucked in a breath, one that came out as a sigh.

"Do you like being bitten?" he asked.

"God, yes." She arched her back, pressing her breasts against his chest. "Do it again."

Delirious at hearing those three words, Simon nuzzled her neck again. He let her feel his teeth right in the delicate valley where her neck met with her shoulder. He didn't apply too much pressure, not sure if she'd appreciate marks, but he looked forward to learning everything that drove her wild. "What else do you like?"

She pulled back, but just by a fraction. "You really want to know?"

He didn't trust himself to nod, because he'd end up looking like a crazed bobblehead. He had to use his words. "Of course, I want to know. I want to know everything."

Her quiet laugh of disbelief almost broke his heart.

"Did I say something wrong?" asked Simon.

"Sorry. You haven't said anything wrong. I guess it's just been a while since anyone has asked me what I want. My last boyfriend, well." She grimaced. "Never mind. This isn't the time to talk about him."

Simon swallowed hard, suppressing the streak of white-hot rage that lanced through him. Had her last boyfriend not met her needs? Worse still, had he taken advantage of her in some way? She might not be ready to have that conversation yet, and he'd respect her on that, but they would have it eventually. He passed a hand over her hair and cradled her skull. "You deserve to have your needs met, Edwina."

"So serious." She tried to laugh off his sentiment.

"Yeah, I am being serious." Simon stared at her, hoping he could impress upon her his desire to make her happy. Not only happy, but downright delirious. "You, Edwina Darke, are an incredible person, as well as the sexiest thing I have ever seen. And if your last boyfriend was too much of a dipshit to understand that, I'm glad he's your ex. He doesn't deserve you."

Her lips formed an O.

"Now," said Simon, his body quaking with need, "I would really like you to tell me what you want, because I don't want you to come away with any regrets."

"I want you to touch me."

"I can do that." He ran a hand over her collarbones, then toward her breast. He found her swollen nipple with ease, despite the barrier of her bra and shirt, and pinched it between his fingers. "Is this okay?"

Edwina gasped and nodded. She was so responsive, so attuned to his touch.

How would she sound as he coaxed an orgasm out of her? How would she react? Would she dig her fingernails into his skin? So many delicious scenarios raced through his mind.

"I just—"

"What do you want, beautiful? Tell me."

Her mouth fell open, showing just how adorably flustered she was. "I just want to come. I've wanted to come since last night."

"That's good to know." Simon removed his glasses and set them on the bedside table. "Because I really want to make you come."

He sought her mouth with greed, and she opened to him, clearly just as hungry. Clinging to each other, they stumbled to the bed. With one hand, he whipped the covers back, and urged her onto the mattress. She spread her legs, welcoming him there. He ground against her, desperate to relieve his ache.

"Fuck," he muttered.

"You're as hard as a rock." She reached a hand between them. "Let me help you with that."

"No, no, sweet thing. This is all about you right now." Simon tugged on the hem of her shirt. "Is this okay?"

"Take it off," she said, with the cutest little pout. "Take it all off."

"Yes, ma'am." Barely able to contain his glee, Simon helped her undress, leaving her only in her bra and panties. Her underwear was mismatched, a black bra and dainty pink panties, but somehow that was totally Edwina. She probably didn't give a shit about matching her undies to her bra. Or maybe she had a whole drawer at home, one full of coordinated silky bits and pieces.

He'd have to ask her about that too.

For a moment, he could only look at her. She was fucking exquisite. All hips and lips and tight, beautiful nipples.

Unbelievably edible, and he was famished.

Simon lowered his head, taking one of those adorable nipples into his mouth, right over her bra. She writhed below him.

Only it wasn't good enough to satisfy him. He needed to taste her skin. Her bra, while soft and satiny, was too much of an impediment. He needed it gone, and now.

His movements deft, if a little frenzied, he unclasped that blasted item and tossed it to the side.

Damn.

Those big dusky nipples would be the death of him. In awe, he traced one with his finger, admiring the way it made her skin tighten even further. He latched on to it, sucking until she cried his name. As he teased her breasts, moving leisurely between them, she ground her hips against him.

"Not enough, beautiful?"

She shook her head.

"Use your words, or I stop," he teased.

"Simon, please." She wiggled her hips again. "Please make me come."

He slid a hand between them, giddy at the wetness of her panties. He danced his finger along the elastic, away from where she needed it most. "Do you want me to lick you here?"

"Please."

"Such a good girl." Simon rose, even though the brief lack of skin-to-skin contact almost took a year off his life, and knelt at the side of the bed. He insinuated his finger under the elastic of her panties. "Can I take these off?"

She lifted her head. "Jesus, Simon. Are you always such a tease?"

"It's all in good fun. Just creating a bit of anticipation. Besides, I want you to understand you're in control. I won't do anything you don't want me to do."

"I appreciate it, I do." She threw her head back. "But fuck, you're killing me."

"So dramatic. I like it." To reward her for pleasing him, he lowered his head and nibbled her clit over her panties.

She bucked on the bed, letting out a strangled cry, and dug her nails into his shoulders. "Yes!"

Intoxicated by her scent and her reaction, Simon's head swam.

This.

This was all he wanted to do for the rest of his life. Just eat Edwina's pussy until Judgment Day. It was literally all he needed to sustain him.

And he hadn't even tasted her properly yet.

Undone, feeling feverish, he dragged himself away just long enough to remove her panties. Then, Simon pried her hands off his shoulders and tangled her fingers with his. Closing his eyes, he feasted. He tasted every last inch of skin until she was fluttering against him.

As her legs tightened, he released her hands. Holding her wide open, he returned to her clit, but gently this time. He sucked at that miraculous little button until she came apart.

So fucking beautiful.

He had to see that again.

He kept licking, softening his touch, until she was squirming once more. Before long, the telltale flush covered her skin, her caresses turned into grasping, and her quiet panting transformed into the most glorious sound ever.

"Ohmigod, I'm going to come again."

Simon smiled. *Yes!*

He got up and reached into the bedside table, to pull out a condom from the courtesy kit he left in every bedroom.

"B-but this isn't your bedroom," Edwina stammered.

"We leave these in every room for the guests. Thoughtful, don't you think?"

"So thoughtful." She raked him with her gaze. "Take your clothes off, Simon."

She didn't need to ask him twice.

He dispensed with his clothes, probably at an Olympic sprinter's pace, and rolled on the condom.

Edwina sat up on her elbows. "I'd be happy to return the favor first."

"Oh, you will. Another time. I really need to be inside you." Simon situated himself between her legs. "Would it be all right if I fucked you now, beautiful?"

She locked eyes with him. "Fuck me."

"With pleasure." He thrust deep and stilled. She felt so good all his cares slipped away. All that was left was him and Edwina and the sound of their breath mingling. He buried his face in her neck. "Tell me how you like it."

'Hard. Please."

"Thank Christ." He began to move, and each gorgeous slide into her body only made him hungrier. He'd certainly had sex before, and wasn't in the habit of comparing his lovers, but there was something profound in the way his nerve endings seemed bound to Edwina. Each of her moans spurred him on, filling him with the sort of energy he hadn't had since he was a horny teenager. Lost in a world of wonder as he learned what made her squirm, Simon wanted to shout in triumph.

She was perfect.

They were perfect together. At least, he hoped her noises meant she was on the same page.

"Does this feel good?" he asked, hanging on her answer.

"It feels amazing." She practically purred. "You feel amazing."

Thank God.

"Oh, Simon. I'm close."

Never in his life had he heard four such delicious words. They filled him with giddy hope and light.

He positioned her legs over his shoulders and slid a hand between them. Her labia were swollen and pink, but he found her clit with ease. It was like coming home to a place that he never wanted to leave. He breached her again, and she threw her arms out to the sides. Grasping the sheets, she cried out. Simon had never felt so strong, so special, and he knew immediately that he was addicted to the feeling.

His cock was painfully hard. He'd never been this eager for release, but he needed to take care of her first. Still thrusting, he circled that precious little clit. "Come for me, Edwina."

She seized her next breath and held it. Her body quaked and tightened around him. So fucking beautiful. *Yes!*

Safe in the knowledge that he'd made her come again, Simon ground over her and fucked her until he reached his own shocking orgasm.

Then he just held her.

He didn't want to move, not ever. He wanted to lie like this for all time.

Awed by the wave of emotion that washed over him, Simon kissed her. He wished he could kiss every inch of her skin, leaving an indelible mark.

Even though he was exhausted and overwhelmed, he wanted her again.

She ran her hands down his back toward his ass and clutched him there. "I think you broke me."

He chuckled against her neck. "For real? Did I hurt you?"

"Only in the best way possible. Simon, that was… I have no words."

Would it be in bad taste for him to pound his chest like an alpha beast? *Probably.* "That's good, right?"

"It's excellent."

Yeah, he might pound his chest a little in private later. "Good. Don't move. I'll be right back." With another kiss, he got up and went to dispose of his condom in the bathroom.

He grabbed a clean washcloth and wet it with warm water, in case Edwina might want to wipe herself...or have him do it for her.

But when he returned to the bedroom, the most wonderful sight greeted him.

Edwina lay on her back, running her hands over her breasts. She writhed in the most exquisite of dances. Meeting his gaze, she pinched her nipples. Then, slowly, so as to torture him, she walked one hand down between her legs. She licked her lips and smiled. "Come back to bed, handsome."

Simon usually needed a few minutes' recovery time, but he hardened at once. *Well, fuck me.*

He tossed the washcloth over his shoulder and knelt before her. She was a queen, and he was prepared to worship her.

Chapter Ten

"Hang on," said Susannah, after Edwina had updated her sisters on what had happened in the EVP sessions. "You're telling me we have a possible James, a possible Perry and the creepy guy said 'Come back, Adelaide?'"

Edwina nodded, casting a glance at the silent Adelaide. They sat in the parlor, where it was cozy. Adelaide was in a big plush chair, one that engulfed her, making her look like a little girl again. All of a sudden, Edwina was filled with memories of their kid sister trailing after her and Susannah, wanting to be with the big girls. How many times had she helped her tie her shoes? How long had she sat with her, teaching her how to braid her hair?

There were the other memories, like the ones of standing up to the bullies who had tormented Adelaide in school. Those girls had called her a freak, among other choice epithets, and they'd turned on Edwina and Susannah for defending their sister.

They'd all been freaks from then on. Edwina had begun cultivating her armor around that time, the armor that now failed so spectacularly whenever Simon was around.

She still couldn't believe they'd slept together. Not that she was filled with any sort of regret. Hand on heart, it had been the greatest moment of physical intimacy of her life. Other guys had certainly touched her the same way Simon had, and sometimes to great success, but her growing connection to Simon had underscored each movement with an unfamiliar urgency and desire.

It wasn't just that, though. Her head was still whirring because of the careful way he'd held her afterward, as if she were a thing to be treasured.

Focus.

Susannah gripped the armrest of the chair she was sitting in. "Maybe we should reconsider this investigation."

Edwina glanced over her shoulder to see if Simon was in earshot, but she could hear his voice in the distance, making calls in his office. "We can't do that, Suz. Simon and Connie need us."

"I realize that, but the entity is calling for our sister. I think we all know that's a bad thing." Susannah turned frustrated eyes toward Adelaide. "Addy, back me up, here."

But Adelaide said nothing. She just fingered her necklace, her eyes unfocused.

Adelaide always played with her necklace when things got dicey on the spiritual front. It was a necklace their grandmother had given her, the same grandmother who appeared in Edwina's nightmares. She'd had the same sorts of abilities as Addy, and it was a piece of jewelry that she'd worn to help her stay grounded. The chain itself was simple, even old-fashioned with its heart pendant. Set in the heart were several colored birthstones, representing the births of Gran's children. Addy had been a toddler when Gran died, and so Gran had passed it on to their mom, with strict instructions to give it to Addy.

Even all those years ago, she'd known. Somehow, she'd held her little granddaughter, and had recognized her rare gift.

Edwina appealed to them. "Look, I was shocked when I heard that EVP too. I don't want anyone to be uncomfortable, but if our presence here has unleashed something, then we have an obligation to clean up the mess."

Susannah wasn't buying it. "Not if it puts us at risk. We have one rule at DPI. *One.* If things get dangerous, we get out. It's that simple."

"I know," said Edwina. "But this thing hasn't touched anyone. It hasn't hurt anyone. And we have dealt with worse. Remember Yorkville?"

When they'd first started out, they'd helped a gallery owner in Toronto's posh Yorkville neighborhood. The activity there had been terrible, with gallery patrons being scratched. Even the Darke sisters had had their hair pulled. Edwina had found some bruises on her body too. By the end of the investigation, they'd had to bring in an exorcist to clear the place. She walked over to where Adelaide was sitting and crouched before her. Edwina grabbed her hand. "I'm not trying to make light of this situation, Addy. I'll defer to you here. You know best in these matters."

For the first time since they listened to the EVP together, Adelaide met her sister's gaze. She arched an amused eyebrow. "Can I get that in writing?"

"You know I would never compromise your safety, neither of you. You understand that, right?"

"Yeah," said Adelaide.

"I just want to finish what we started," said Edwina.

A slow grin unfurled on Adelaide's face. "Like Simon, you do?" she asked, in her Yoda voice.

Okay. It can't be that bad if she's doing her Yoda impression.

"Yes." Edwina stood and took turns glaring at both her sisters, while holding in a bemused laugh. She plopped back into her chair. "I like him, okay? More than I've liked anyone in a while, and I want to help him. He's kind and funny, and he makes me smile. He's had such a shitty time lately, and he gets no support from his family, and well, he's got a really good... tongue."

"I knew it!" Susannah shouted, then clapped her hands. She lowered her voice. "I *knew* you were fornicating with him."

"Suz, that word is so old-fashioned. You know you can just say 'fuck,' right?"

"But 'fornicating' is a great word. It sounds so dirty," said Susannah, filled with glee. "And I bet Simon is a dirty boy, isn't he?"

Edwina hung her head. Saints preserve her from her sisters.

Adelaide joined in the fun. "You'll have to show him your sex swing."

"It's not a sex swing, you weirdos," Edwina said in defense. "It's my hammock."

Adelaide snorted out a laugh. "Which you keep in your bedroom."

"I use it as a reading nook!"

"And have you read any good books in your nook lately?" asked Susannah.

"I don't know," mused Adelaide. "I've never seen a hammock with stirrups before."

Edwina narrowed her eyes. "Back to the matter at hand. Are we good to finish the investigation?"

"It's your call, Addy," said Susannah. "That thing called your name, not ours."

Adelaide closed her eyes for a few moments, engaged in a silent conversation with Maria. They'd seen her do the same thing many times over the years, only to get spooked whenever Maria made herself known. Edwina listened for the telltale whooping cough, but it didn't manifest.

Adelaide finally opened her eyes. "There is a malevolent spirit here, and he'll do his best to scare us. But Ann is trapped here too, and she's innocent. Maria and I discussed it. We want to help her. I wouldn't feel right leaving her alone. She's been on her own so long already."

"Okay," said Edwina. "We're decided, then. But Addy, if you sense real danger, will you let us know? Because we'll hightail it out of here."

Adelaide's gaze wandered toward the hallway.

"Addy?"

She turned back to them. "Don't worry. I won't let him near you."

Edwina frowned. That wasn't what she'd asked.

* * * *

Simon sat at his office desk, putting off the call to Rupert.

Fucking Rupert.

What the hell did he want?

The sound of the Darke sisters laughing in the other room distracted him. They sounded so happy, like siblings who actually liked each other. They might have been unicorns, they seemed so fantastical to him.

He had no idea what it was like to admire his brother. He couldn't even remember the last time that he'd liked him in some small way.

Simon glared at the text again. When was the last time he'd spoken to Rupert? It must have been that awkward Thanksgiving, when Rupert had brought Carly along to a family event for the first time. Carly had tried to give Simon a hug, but he'd stood still, unable to return the embrace. And Rupert...he'd just given Simon that perverse little grin that said, 'No hard feelings, champ. The better man won.'

And now he expected a callback? Fuck him.

He massaged his temples. If he didn't call back, there was a chance Rupert would keep at it.

Maybe he was calling to say he and Carly had broken up, not that it would impact Simon's life in any way. He and Carly were through.

Or maybe, for the first time in his life, he was hoping to make things better. Simon wasn't sure he'd ever heard his brother apologize for anything, but could he have finally seen the light?

The sooner you find out, the sooner you can get back to Edwina.

Edwina.

Damn. She had him in knots, but he relished the burn of each sweet twist of his gut.

Since meeting her, he'd been trying so hard to keep it cool, but he failed miserably every time she turned those gorgeous brown eyes on him.

He'd accused her of being a little reckless in her dealings with ghosts, but he wanted to throw all caution to the wind whenever she was around. Hell, he'd never been big on tattoos, but he was ready to get Edwina's name written all over his body in ink.

He really resented Rupert for distracting him from the incredible woman in the next room.

The conversation in the parlor had quieted. They were waiting for him to join them before they began the vigil.

Just do this.

Taking a deep breath, Simon picked up his cell phone and clicked on his brother's number.

After five or six rings, Rupert answered. "Hey, little brother. I thought you'd dropped off the face of the earth. How are you?"

"Do you actually want to know?"

"Listen, I don't have long. Carly and I are just checking out reception halls, and we're going into a cake tasting. I have a question for you. When would you be available for a tux fitting?"

"Sorry, what?"

"You know, tu-xe-dos." He pronounced each syllable slowly, as if Simon needed help understanding. "For the wedding, champ. The best man needs a tux."

"Best man?" Simon made a face at his cell phone.

"You do know what a best man is, right?"

"Yeah, I know what a best man is. I just don't understand why you're asking me. And why you're doing it over the phone." *Tacky piece of shit.* "Actually, scratch that. You didn't ask me at all. You just assumed I'd be up for it."

"Come on, bro. We're family."

"In other words, Mom made you do it?" Given the way Rupert mumbled his response, Simon took it as an affirmative. "I don't believe this. You want me to stand there, in the wedding party of the people who betrayed me."

Rupert's sigh grated on Simon's last nerve. "You know what? The wedding's not for a few months yet. Maybe, by then, you can sign up for some nice anger management courses, and offload the chip on your shoulder? Are you still seriously pissed about all this? It's time to move on, Si."

Simon's free hand curled into a fist. He dug his fingernails into his palm. "Let me be clear, *bro*. I'm not actually pissed about the cheating anymore. I've come to expect that from you. What *does* bother me is the fact that none of my family members seem to care about my feelings at all, in any situation. You never fucking apologized for cheating with Carly. Not once."

"I'm not going to apologize for falling in love, Simon."

"Fair enough. What you *should* apologize for is for even thinking my girlfriend was available to you. You didn't just fall for Carly. You targeted her. While you're at it, you can apologize for being a shitty brother my entire life. You've never cared about anything I'm doing. You've never been around to lend a hand or to give advice, or even just to shoot the breeze. You've made it painfully clear that you couldn't care less about me. Not once have I ever looked to you as a role model. In fact, I basically live my life doing the exact opposite of what you would do in any scenario, because then I know I'm in pretty good shape. You suck as a human being." He grabbed a breath. "Oh, and in case it's not already clear, I will *not* be your best man, because I won't be at the wedding. You, Rupert, can go take a flying fuck."

"Hey—"

But Simon didn't stick around to hear what he had to say. He ended the call.

His heart hammered. He'd told off his brother before, but never quite like that.

It felt...good?

No, good wasn't the right word. He was too angry for this to be good.

Even though his blood was racing, he suddenly became cold. He shivered, and his breath appeared in front of his face. He grabbed his phone, tempted to whip it at the wall.

From deep inside his being, a voice spoke. *Do it. You'll feel better. Smash it. Destroy it. Burn it all down.*

What the hell? He refrained, confused by the adamant tone.

He rested his head in his hands for a moment, and tried to gather his swirling, muddled thoughts. As the cold enveloped him, he forgot about Rupert.

But he didn't forget the fury he'd inspired.

His vision darkening, Simon got up and stumbled into the parlor.

Chapter Eleven

When Simon joined them in the parlor, Edwina did a double take. Of course, she'd been doing lots of double takes around him lately. She seemed unable to avert her gaze from him for long.

But this was different. His fists were clenched, showing white at the knuckles, and there was a darkness in his eyes that she hadn't seen before. In fact, if she didn't know any better, she would almost swear their color had changed from their usual periwinkle to a cold slate blue.

It must be the muted lighting in the room. It was late summer, and the shadows were starting to lengthen.

"Hey," she said. "Were you able to make all the calls you needed to make?"

Simon looked up at her as if noticing her for the first time. His mouth opened and closed, then he nodded. An aura of chilly detachment surrounded him.

"Great." Edwina continued the conversation but kept an eye on him. She didn't like the look on his face. "So, I've brought Suz and Addy up to speed."

"Did you now?" He almost spat the words. Turning to Susannah and Adelaide, his expression was that of someone who'd just encountered strangers in his home. Indignant surprise.

"Simon, are you okay?" asked Edwina.

He walked over to behind the pool table and paced, muttering to himself.

"No, he's not," said Adelaide. "The spirit man just slunk in behind him. He's hovering all around Simon." She squeezed her eyes shut for a few seconds and shook her head. "Yes, Maria, I see him."

"What?" Edwina's hands shook. How *dare* that ghost fucker try something with her —

Her what? Her boyfriend? Her favorite new hookup? She wasn't sure yet, but either way, she was pissed.

Susannah turned on one of the EVP recorders. "Has he been possessed?"

"No," said Adelaide. "Simon's still in control, but the other guy is messing with his thoughts."

"Stop talking about me like I'm not here!" shouted Simon. He continued pacing. "I'm sick and tired of people not taking my feelings into consideration. I'm not a doormat."

Edwina stood and slowly drew nearer. "We don't think you're a doormat, Simon. Why don't you come have a seat? You seem upset."

"I don't want to take a seat." He mimicked her tone. "And I have every right to be upset!"

Adelaide's face was pinched. "Don't get too close, Ed." Her gaze was focused on the empty space next to

Simon. "Leave Simon alone. You and I both know he's not the one you want."

What the hell did Addy mean by that? Edwina was growing concerned by her sister's cryptic comments. They would need to have a serious talk, and soon.

A man's laugh echoed throughout the parlor, and it wasn't Simon's.

That laugh…it was the exactly the same as the one they'd caught on the previous EVP.

"What the hell?" Chilled to the bone, it took everything Edwina had to pull out her cellphone in order to film what was happening. It wasn't that she looked forward to showing Simon, but they might need the evidence later.

"Addy, what do you see?" Susannah's face, normally of a peaches and cream complexion, was now white. "Who *was* he in life?"

"He says it doesn't matter who he was. What's important is who he is now. He likes what he's become. It makes him feel strong. He's been working on his powers, day by day, year by year. Right now, he's showing himself to me as a dark cloud, one that will engulf anyone who comes near." Adelaide looked up from under her lashes. "But he says he'll tell me his name if I allow him to get a little closer."

"Well, fuck that, mister," shouted Edwina. "We don't need your name to figure out what's happening here. Now, let go of Simon."

Simon was shaking his head over and over. "No one listens to me. No one cares. They think I'm insignificant. A dog they can kick for their amusement. I won't stand for it anymore. I'll make them listen to me. I'll shut their mouths so I don't have to hear their laughter. I will silence those who have wounded me.

The pretty Ann was not the first to feel my wrath, and she will not be the last. I will not be disregarded any longer, and not by an ungrateful bitch in heat!" Simon let out a garbled cry then punched the wall behind him.

"Simon!" Edwina flew to him. "Oh my God."

As Simon removed his bloodied hand from the broken drywall, he turned to them. His mouth was open, and horror made his eyes bright. At least they were the right color again.

Had the spirit man left?

"What happened?" asked Simon.

"You hit the wall," said Edwina.

"I don't remember." When she reached for his hand to check out his injury, he flinched. "No. Stay back. I don't want to hurt you."

"It's okay. I know you wouldn't hurt me."

Tears filled his eyes and he blinked them away. "I'm sorry."

In the silence that followed, a child's cough filled the room. Its pained sounds grew louder and louder.

Maria.

They all turned to Adelaide.

Adelaide sat in her chair, gripping the armrests. "You're not welcome here. Get off me. Get *off* me, you bastard!" She shivered for a minute, then calmed. "He's gone. Maria took him away." As if in confirmation, the whooping cough noises faded to nothing.

Simon gawked at the broken drywall. "I don't know what happened back there. Was that thing *inside* me?"

"Not literally," said Adelaide. "But sometimes they can feed off our emotions, and it gives them strength."

Edwina rubbed his shoulder. "Out of curiosity, how were you feeling when you came in here?"

"At first, I was thinking of you, and I was happy." Simon adjusted his glasses. "But then I talked to my brother. It didn't go well."

"I'm sorry," said Edwina. "Can you move your hand?"

"Yeah." He wiggled it around. Apart from some nasty cuts, it didn't appear to be broken. "I'll keep an eye on it for swelling and bruising, but I think it's okay." He glared at the wall. "Which makes me question whether or not my builder used a good quality drywall. What a way to find out your contractor cut corners, huh?"

Edwina gave him a sympathetic smile. "So, you don't punch a lot of walls?"

"Ed, please believe me. I would never do that. I'm not a violent person."

"It's okay. I get it."

Susannah wandered over to check out the hole in the wall as well. She peered into the space behind the sheetrock. Frowning, she aimed her cell phone at it and turned on the flashlight. "Uh, guys? There's something in there."

"Let me guess." Simon's shoulders slumped in defeat. "Cigarette butts and empty pop cans?"

"No," said Susannah. "It's right on the floor. Do you have something I could scoop it up with?"

"Yeah. In the front hall closet, I have one of those grabby sticks. You know, the type with the claw at the tip?" He made a face. "I've had guests who leave nasty crap under the beds."

Susannah, eyes wide, was already sprinting out of the room. "I'll get it."

Edwina had seen that look on her sister's face before. The first time she'd seen it was when they were kids, and their parents had taken them on a trip to England. They'd gone to Hampton Court, and the costumed interpreter who worked the massive roasting spit rotisserie in the Tudor kitchen had let Susannah take a turn cranking it. Somewhere in their parents' house was a photo album that contained a picture of a beaming Susannah, poised at that massive fireplace. Ever since then, Susannah had assumed that orgasmic expression any time she was about to touch a piece of history.

Of course, she also had a similar expression when she watched her favorite sexy historical drama, the one about the Victorian doctor who was having an affair with the neglected wife of a cranky old baronet.

Susannah reappeared with the grabber, her cheeks pink and her smile wide. She reached carefully into the wall hole with the stick and poked around. "I'm not one hundred percent sure, but I think I've seen one of these before. Oh, dammit. I keep dropping it."

"Want me to try?" said Edwina.

"Nope." With her tongue peeking out at the corner of her mouth, Susannah made another attempt. "I've just about got it. There!" Moving gingerly, she extricated the item from the hole and placed it in the palm of her hand.

They all gathered around.

"It's a button," said Adelaide. "An old one."

"Yes, it is." Susannah's voice trembled. "In fact, I believe this is a button from a soldier's uniform. I know it's corroded in places, but look in the middle. There's the number forty-nine. The 49th Foot Regiment took part in the War of 1812, although if I recall my military history, they'd been stationed in this area for almost ten years by that point. Guys, this was Isaac Brock's regiment, *General* Isaac Brock. It's entirely possible that whoever wore this button fought alongside the man who would later be known as the Hero of Upper Canada."

They were all silent, caught up in the magnitude of the moment.

"Can I hold it?" asked Edwina.

Susannah handed it to her. "I know, right? It's one thing to talk about history, but it's another thing to hold it in your hand."

Edwina smoothed her finger over the rusty forty-nine. All of a sudden, her ears began to ring again. It had been a while since she'd experienced the cloying sensation, and she'd forgotten about it. Now, her ear practically throbbed with the layers of sound. It wasn't enough to deafen her, but it demanded all her attention and filled her with urgency, like the sound of a child crying in the night.

She thrust the button toward Susannah. "Take it. I don't want it."

Addy gave her a look, but Edwina ignored it.

"Wow," said Susannah. "Maybe we could use this as a trigger item."

"What does that mean?" asked Simon.

"Sometimes in investigations," said Susannah, "we use historical artifacts to trigger a response from the spirits. In cases where we've had the alleged ghosts of children, we've used old teddy bears or antique dolls. They're items that the spirits will recognize, items that might provoke an emotional response."

"I'm not sure our spirits need any additional provoking," grumbled Simon.

Edwina turned to Adelaide. "Addy, do you think you can get something from the button?"

"Did you?" asked Adelaide.

Edwina's face streaked with heat. "Of course not. What's that supposed to mean?"

But Adelaide held her tongue.

"I'd like to have it authenticated first," said Susannah. "There's an antique dealer in town. I noticed the sign in his window. He seems to specialize in military artifacts. As long as that's okay with you, Simon. It's your button."

"Of course. Find out all you can." Simon's lips quirked up in a half-smile. "So, it's not such a bad thing that I almost got possessed and punched the wall?"

Edwina ran her hand up his arm, massaging his tense muscles. She had a suspicion about why the angry spirit latched onto Simon, and she wasn't sure he'd want to hear it.

She still owed it to him to tell him, even if he ended up hating her for it.

* * * *

They didn't stay at the King Street B&B that night. After Simon's unfortunate encounter with the wall, then finding the button, they were all too agitated to continue the vigil and decided to call it a night.

Susannah and Adelaide headed back to the hotel, but not before Susannah wrapped the antique button in one of the soft washcloths from the B&B. She carried it out of the house with it cradled in her hands. A contestant in an egg-and-spoon race couldn't have moved with more care.

Edwina convinced Simon to get his hand checked out at a local emergency clinic. He fussed and moaned a bit, insisting he was fine, but relented when she pointed out the fact that his knuckles were turning a garish color.

It took three hours to see a doctor, at which point both Edwina and Simon were ready to punch another wall. However, at least they got the good news that Simon's hand wasn't broken.

Of course, she hadn't really minded sitting with him in that dingy medical office. Even though the magazines were all about ten years old and their conversation was constantly interrupted by a sweet old man who wanted to chat with everyone while he waited for his wife, Edwina enjoyed being with Simon.

For those few hours, it felt like they were just a regular couple, doing run-of-the-mill things. Taking care of each other, instead of trying to prove the existence of paranormal beings.

Because they were in mixed company, they didn't talk about what had happened at the house, but the memory of the spirit man's cruel laughter stayed with Edwina. To say nothing of the issue with her ears.

Maybe she needed to book an appointment with her own doctor. Although she suspected a doctor couldn't cure her of this ill.

Eager for a distraction, she obliged when Simon asked about her work in theater. She was happy to tell him some of her colorful stories from her time with the Canadian Opera Company and the National Ballet of Canada. Between those experiences, and her other stints backstage, she'd collected a few unusual tales.

While at the medical office, they didn't discuss his conversation with Rupert. After they saw the doctor and filled Simon's prescription for some pain pills, she convinced him to stay the night in her hotel room. She'd retained her reservation at the hotel, knowing she might need to retreat there at some point.

It was close to midnight when they rolled up to her hotel. After picking up a courtesy toothbrush for Simon at the front desk, they made their way to her room.

"Of course," he whispered over her shoulder as she unlocked her door, "the only reason I'm staying here with you is so that I can check out the competition. You know, sample their toiletries, examine the thread count on the sheets and stuff."

"Right."

"It's not because I'm terrified to sleep in my own bed or anything."

"Of course not." She turned on the lights and led the way in, dropping her key card on the TV table. "Make yourself at home."

Simon kicked his shoes off inside the door and dropped into the cushy chair by the window. Edwina had left the blinds open when she was last in the room, and the dark streetscape lured her to the window. Her room was on the third floor, and the view encompassed everything between Queen Street and the waterfront. There were some scattered lights, but because they were in Niagara-on-the-Lake, and not the twenty-four-hour hubbub of downtown Toronto, it was mostly swathes of darkness where residents had retired for the night.

The twinkling lights, lonely pinpricks in the darkness, reminded her of the spirits with whom DPI had been in contact over time. They hurled their energy into the abyss in a final attempt at connection, trying desperately not to be muffled forever by the velvety expanse.

Edwina opened the window and breathed in the night air. "Do you ever wonder where we go, you know, after we die?"

"Whoa. That's a deep question for this time of night." Simon removed his glasses and set them on the side table. Although deep shadows underscored his eyes, he didn't avert them in disinterest. He was completely focused on her.

"I guess so."

"Honestly, I don't know. Before meeting you and your sisters, I figured death was the end. A long sleep. Now, I'm not so sure."

"I'm not sure either. Sometimes, I worry about ending up in some sort of hellish nightmare, but Addy says it's not like that. I guess I won't really believe it until I see it, but I've been questioning my beliefs a lot lately." She walked over to where he was sitting and knelt between his legs. She dropped a kiss on his arm, just above where his hand was bandaged. "How are you feeling?"

"Shattered."

"Don't take this the wrong way, but you look shattered."

"I guess family drama, a near possession and a violent outburst will do that." He ran a finger along her eyebrow, tracing the arch. "You, on the other hand, are still luminous somehow."

Ripples of delight coursed through Edwina's chest. "Oh yeah? You should see me first thing in the morning."

"I have seen you first thing in the morning, remember? You're a fucking goddess."

Overcome by emotion, Edwina was at a loss for words.

"Thank you for coming with me to the hospital. I really hated the idea that I might have scared you away with what happened tonight."

"I'm not scared of you, Simon, but I was scared *for* you." She grasped his good hand and stroked it. "I think we need to talk about Rupert."

He groaned. "Do we really have to? I'm not trying to be closed off. I just… Is it wrong to say I'd like to trade my family in for a different model?"

She rested her head on his strong thigh and gave him the space he needed to unburden himself.

"Rupert asked me to be his best man tonight."

"What? You've got to be kidding me."

"I wish I were." Simon's breath escaped in a huff. "I mean, he didn't do it because he wants me there, although I'm sure he would appreciate the opportunity to gloat. There are only two reasons he would bestow that *honor* on me. Either our mom made him do it, or he's already alienated all his friends by sleeping with their wives."

"Yikes. Did he really?"

"I've heard a few stories, so yeah, I have no trouble believing that. He'll cheat on Carly one day too. I know he will. He can't help himself."

Ah. The C-word. Edwina asked the question that had been simmering in her gut. "Do you still care for her?"

"No," he said without hesitation or artifice. "I feel sorry for her, but she was an active participant. She knew what she was doing. Cheating is a hard stop for me. I could never trust her again."

Edwina thought back to a couple of her conversations with Declan. Before him, she'd always believed cheating was a hard stop for her too. And yet, she was ninety-nine percent sure he'd cheated on her, and she'd allowed him to sweet talk her until she took him back.

Like a fool.

Don't look back. Don't ever look back.

"In hindsight, I know I made mistakes with Carly," he said. "I probably wasn't as attentive as I should have been. I was trying to get the business off the ground, and it was stressful. By the time I realized I'd alienated her, I'd also realized we weren't meant for each other. But I always encouraged her to talk to me, and I was always honest with her. I just regret that she didn't feel comfortable coming to me."

"I get it. Shit happens in relationships. People need to be able to talk it through." Edwina sighed. "I'm guessing you won't be best man, then?"

"I more or less told him to shove his tuxedo up his ass." He shook his head. "Actually, I said a lot worse than that, and now I'm feeling guilty. I told him he was a shitty brother, and that he always had been."

"Is that the truth?"

He seemed to be choosing his words, but settled on a sad, "Yeah."

"Then maybe he needed to hear it. I'm sorry, Simon."

"I think I need to step back from my family for a while. I know I'm not perfect, but their patterns are toxic as shit. They're not good for me, at least, not right now. I'm not sure they know how to be."

"Have you ever thought of getting some counseling?"

"Me? They're the ones who need it."

"Probably so, but do you honestly think they'd ask for help?"

His laugh held no amusement. "Are you kidding? I've seen both my parents sneer when their friends have mentioned their therapists. And Rupert, well, he's never wrong. It's always the other person's fault."

"Okay, then. So maybe it wouldn't be such a bad idea for you to work out your feelings with a professional."

He searched her eyes. "Do you really think so?"

"It's helped me."

"You see a therapist?"

"Yeah. My last relationship fucked me up, but I'm better now."

He cupped her cheek. "One day, you're going to tell me the full story of this last relationship...including the details on where this person lives, so I can fuck them up."

"It's okay. I'm not actively seeking vengeance anymore. But if I change my mind, I'll give you a call."

He laughed as he raised his bandaged hand then dropped it back onto his lap. "Please do. I didn't actually break any bones this fine evening, so I can go another round."

"All kidding aside," she said, rubbing his thigh, "I think the reason that spirit latched on to you tonight was because of the anger you keep inside. Like Addy said, they can feed off our emotions, they gravitate to us. We're like lanterns on a foggy night."

"You really think I should release my pent-up anger, huh?"

"I don't think it would hurt. Better to discuss it in a calm environment than to have it sneak up on you."

He quietly played with her hair, twirling his fingers in it. Edwina hadn't lost sight of the fact that she was wedged between his legs, and that her face was level with his crotch, but she became even more aware as he touched her.

It would be so easy to ease his zipper down and take him into her mouth.

Would Simon want that right now, after what they'd discussed?

"You've convinced me." He tipped her chin up. "I'll call someone tomorrow."

At his words, her heart expanded, filling her chest. She smiled, happier than she would have expected to be.

"God," he murmured, "you're beautiful."

Edwina glanced at the bulge in his jeans and licked her lips. "There's something I really want to do for you."

"I have a feeling I really want you to do it too."

They undressed, and she helped him because of his tender hand. Simon cursed a couple of times, but every time he did, she stopped him with a kiss.

"I just won't be able to touch you the way I want to," he said.

"Let me be in charge, then." She grabbed a towel from the bathroom and set it on the chair. Then she gestured for him to sit there, and she positioned herself between his knees again. "Let me take care of you."

"I wouldn't dream of saying no."

Edwina began by dropping a couple of soft kisses on his cock and watched in fascination as it bobbed. She was going to love making him lose control, but she would take her time bringing him to that point. Angling her head, she placed open-mouthed kisses along his length, letting him see every time her tongue darted out. Even though her intention was to softly tease him to the point of delirium, she couldn't keep it up for long. She wanted him too much. Greedy, ravenous, Edwina took him into her mouth.

Simon fisted his good hand in her hair. "You are very good at this."

"You make me want to be bad." She teased him with barely there licks, lulling him into a false sense of security, only to take him right to the back of her throat.

"Fuck." Simon strained on the chair, sliding toward its edge. "Bed."

She got up and walked to the bed, swinging her hips for his benefit. When he rewarded her for her impertinence with a sweet slap on her ass, she almost came right there. She wanted to do anything and everything with this man. She wanted to take him to the highest heights, and plummet with him through the air.

But most of all, Edwina wanted to help him forget his horrible evening, and anything that had ever made him sad.

Simon deserved to be happy.

With me. I want him to be happy with me.

The wish took shape in her mind, becoming something tangible and necessary.

Could she have a future with him?

She crawled onto the bed, intending to finish off the blowjob, but it seemed Simon had other ideas. He pulled her toward him, ass first, and palmed her derriere. "So fucking sexy." His good hand slipped between her legs and found her clit.

Edwina cried out at the beautiful invasion, and her knees buckled.

Simon supported her against his hip. "I've got you, sweet thing. Trust me."

She did. She absolutely trusted him, knowing full well she had never offered her trust to anyone else so quickly.

Maybe she could even trust him with the pain of her past.

It was hard to even think of that pain when he touched her. Over and over, his fingers circled her clit. Every so often, he dipped a couple of fingers inside her, drawing out her anticipation. Whenever she moaned, he chuckled, obviously pleased with his handiwork.

She ground against him, hoping he'd take the hint.

He only slapped her ass again. "I'm going to need you to be patient, Edwina."

God, she loved it when he said her full name in that serious voice.

Simon knelt behind her at the edge of the bed. "Spread your legs for me."

On all fours, she widened the distance between her knees.

On a hungry moan, Simon buried his face in her pussy. "You taste so fucking good."

Her entire body shook. "More licking, less talking, dude."

"Not ladylike at all." He continued his leisurely exploration of her body, dipping his tongue into the most wonderful places. At this point, Simon probably knew her better than she knew herself.

It was a scary thought, caring enough to show someone everything.

As the tremors began in her core, they were followed by a frightening crest of emotion. It might very well knock her over and under, but right now, she was only too willing to explore its depths.

Biting her ass, Simon returned his hand to her pussy and massaged it. Three slow circles of her clit was all it took before she fell apart in his hands. Why was it that each orgasm this man gave her felt like such a momentous discovery?

As she caught her breath, he rummaged in his jeans pocket. She rested her head on the bed, more than delighted by the sound of a crackling condom wrapper.

"Are you ready for me?"

"God, yes."

He entered her as if they had all the time in the world, making her crave each inch of his length. But as he began to move, Edwina got the sense Simon was losing his last shred of control. He began to pump, and before long, each smooth thrust was accompanied by a frenzied curse.

"I'm close." He ground out the words.

"Do it." She just wanted to feel him unravel. "Fuck me hard."

"Jesus." Simon entered her again, gasping with each thrust. His fingernails met with her skin, and would no doubt leave marks.

She didn't mind. She was happy to wear them all over her hips.

Balls slapping against her skin, he took his pleasure. After two more fierce thrusts, his body tightened with his own orgasm. He let out a string of obscenities and a protracted groan. As his body stilled, he lowered his head to her neck. "You're incredible. Holy fuck. That was intense." They remained in that position as they caught their breaths, caressing each other's skin. Simon brushed his lips all over her throat, pausing only to tell her how beautiful she was in a whisper. He then slid away from her and went to tidy up in the bathroom.

Edwina rolled into the bed. She felt so full, so satisfied.

She'd been laid bare, and yet she still wanted to give him more. She wanted to share all her hopes and dreams with this man, and the knowledge frightened the hell out of her.

She could get really hurt here, if things didn't go well.

And yet, for the first time in a long time, she didn't care about getting hurt, and was willing to take a risk.

Simon joined her in bed and spooned her, pulling her close. "You okay?"

"Yeah. You?"

"I'm bloody marvelous, thanks for asking."

They both collapsed into giggles. She turned to him, still nervous to show him everything in her heart, but needing to make some sort of statement. "Simon, I like you."

God, it sounded so inadequate.

However, he didn't scoff or laugh. He smiled and kissed her nose. "I really like you too."

As she drifted off to sleep in his arms, a lump formed in her throat, but she swallowed past it.

Simon's embrace was becoming her sanctuary, a place where she could always find passion and caring.

She dared to hope that it might always be that way.

* * * *

Edwina was hearing voices again.

As she lay in bed, her eyes still squeezed shut, she lingered in a semi-dream state. When the hushed conversation continued, she realized it wasn't a product of whatever was happening with her ears.

It was Simon, and he was talking on his cellphone.

She glanced at the display on the bedside table clock. It was nine thirty, and she hadn't meant to slumber this long. He must have let her sleep in.

He stood outside on her hotel room balcony, wearing one of the hotel bathrobes. He'd left the door partially open, and she couldn't help overhearing his conversation.

"Yes," he said to the person on the other end of the line. "As soon as you can squeeze me in, please. I'd like to get this taken care of soon. The seventeenth with Dr. Warner? That sounds perfect. Yeah, an email confirmation would be great. Thank you. Have a great day."

Had he taken her advice about seeing a therapist? She hoped so.

She sat up and brushed her hair out of her face, bunching the covers up around her bare breasts.

Simon disconnected the call and stepped back inside the room. He stopped short upon seeing her awake in bed. "Hey. You're up."

"Hi."

He stood still, his lips parted.

"Are you all right?"

"Yeah. Sorry." He chuckled quietly. "Every time I wake up next to you, I'm caught off guard."

"Oh."

"No, it's a good thing. Trust me." He sat next to her and brushed his lips against hers. "I just can't believe my luck."

"Simon."

"I mean it. Wrinkled sheets look good on you. And the way the sun is hitting your hair... Amazing."

Edwina's skin erupted in goosepimples. She was going to get a big head around this guy. Every time he looked at her, it was with a mixture of fascination and awe, and she wasn't sure she deserved it.

"Would you mind if I took your picture?"

"My eyelashes are crusty and I forgot to take off my makeup last night."

"You're perfect." He waved his phone. "May I? It won't go any further than this. It's just for me."

If it had been anyone else, she would have doubted his sincerity. But this was Simon, and she believed him. "Okay." Suddenly bashful, she clutched the sheets and offered him a tease of a smile.

Simon took the picture. Upon reviewing it, his eyebrows rose. "Yeah, I am never deleting this. I won't be able to stop looking at it." He showed her the phone.

Edwina was surprised by the photo, but not for the same reasons. There was such hope and vulnerability in her eyes. It was an expression she hadn't seen on her own face in some time.

And it was because of Simon.

Something pinged inside her chest, suspiciously close to her heart.

"So," he said, after taking a deep breath. "I just made an appointment with a therapist."

"I'm proud of you."

"Thanks. I'm proud of me too. But to be honest, I'm not sure I would have done it without your encouragement."

"You think so?"

"I know so. Actually, the whole time I was making the call, I heard my father's voice in my head, telling me to man up and rise above my problems. Telling me I was weak for sharing my business with a quack."

"Well, I happen to think you're strong. Asking for help is not a sign of weakness, and I'm sorry you got those messages from your dad." A flare of anger shot through Edwina's core as she contemplated the kind of pressure Simon must have been under all his life. If she ever met Simon's folks, she'd have to be very careful she didn't blast them for it.

She knew not everyone was comfortable with the idea of seeking therapy, but it wasn't right of them to criticize someone else for choosing that path. If Simon chose to discuss his concerns with a professional, that was his prerogative. Personally, she appreciated him being proactive. It meant he prioritized his mental health. After knowing people who actively sought to tear down the mental health of others, it gave Edwina hope.

She wanted to drag Simon into the bed and into her arms and keep him there for a very long time.

However, they had plans for the day, ones that didn't involve naked snuggling. At least, not immediately.

He tucked a stray lock of her hair behind her ear. "Anyway, thank you for listening, and for being there, especially during the last wacky twenty-four hours."

Edwina wanted to be there for him a lot longer than that. The realization arrived with gravity and excitement and an almost-painful desire to not screw things up.

"Hey." He set his cellphone on the bedside table. "What time do we meet your sisters?"

"In an hour."

"An hour, huh?" Eyes hooded, Simon tugged at the sheets covering her breasts. "You know, if we shower together and grab breakfast on the go, that still gives us plenty of time."

"Showering together does seem ecologically sound. I guess we have a few minutes to spare. What do you want to do?"

Simon grinned and lowered himself onto her body.

Edwina closed her eyes, most appreciative of how he managed his time.

Chapter Twelve

"Make sure you try the raspberry scones. The bakery in town makes them fresh every morning, and they're absolutely decadent." Martha Cook turned the platter of sweets around so they were all visible. She sat back and folded her manicured hands on her lap. "Well, this is exciting. It's not every day that I get to entertain a lovely bunch of young people with my family history."

Martha, the descendant of Ann Forbes' cousin, was one of those older women who simply sparkled with positive energy. When they introduced themselves, she looked them straight in the eye and held each of their hands for a moment, as if to say, "I see you." She was a tall white woman with flowing gray waves, a prominent nose and more grace in her pinky finger than Edwina had in her whole body. She wore a bright red tunic over her wide-legged trousers, and her outfit was complemented by scarlet lipstick and a beaded necklace.

Edwina grabbed one of the scones and munched. Although she had nothing more than first impressions to go on, she had the sense Martha didn't take any bullshit. She immediately recognized her as a kindred soul.

"Thank you so much for meeting with us," said Susannah.

"You have a beautiful home," Edwina chimed in.

"Thank you." Martha beamed. "My husband and I have worked very hard on restoring it and keeping it faithful to the period. Because our home isn't located in the heart of town, in the designated heritage district, we had a bit more freedom with what we could do. If you live within certain streets, you can't even paint your house without using one of the approved colors. Still, we had to apply for special permits any time we wanted to do a bit of renovation."

"I remember that process," said Simon. "My bed and breakfast is just outside the heritage district, but getting a permit to do anything was still a headache."

"Right?" Martha nodded enthusiastically. "I understand why they're so rigid. You don't want someone coming in and destroying a heritage property. Even still, the folks at the council office can be unnecessarily strict. They've heard from me a lot over the years, but sometimes you just have to shake up those old bureaucrats. I'm certain they have a dart board with my picture on it somewhere in their coffee break room. I bet they take turns trying to land one right between my eyes." She grinned, obviously thrilled with her reputation as a troublemaker.

Yep. Edwina adored Martha.

Nestled along the picturesque Niagara Parkway, the winding road that led from the center of Niagara-on-the-Lake toward the more touristy area of the Falls, Martha's house was one of the original homes. It too had been burned down in 1813, but her branch of the Forbes family had built it back up again. The red brick structure was ornamented with black shutters, a white picket fence and a rose garden in front. Very different from Simon's place, but no less charming.

They all sat in her gorgeous front room that overlooked the Parkway. Martha had decorated it with an eclectic mix of antique and modern furniture. Newly upholstered Louis XV chairs nestled next to a streamlined leather settee.

"So," Susannah said. "Your ancestor Sophia Forbes was Ann's cousin?"

"Yes." Martha's brown eyes shone. "And the girls spent a lot of time in each other's company. They were just about the same age, and by all accounts they were quite fond of each other. Of course, they would have run in the same circles, and would have learned skills from the same tightknit community of women. In those early years in Upper Canada, a woman's work was literally never done, even for young women like Ann and Sophia, who came from families with a bit of money. They would still have been responsible for most chores, the family meals, and first aid. They would have learned to plant vegetables and herbs for their food, and they would have taken care of the cooking and the harvesting. They would have been expected to care for the ill and the elderly in their households and that care would have extended to neighbors as well. Sophia and Ann would have relied on each other in many of these situations. They were confidantes as well as cousins, and Sophia was crushed when Ann died."

"Your branch of the family survived when the town was burned down?" Simon reached for a cookie covered in chocolate ganache.

"They did," replied Martha. "Ann was the only one from my family who died that horrible winter, but she wasn't the only townsperson to perish. December tenth has been recorded as a cold, blustery day, and there were snow drifts several feet high. Sophia later wrote about the invasion. Apparently, they blew up the powder magazine at the fort first. She said the vibrations from the explosion could be felt all across Newark."

"Wow." Edwina snuck a chocolate biscuit from the sweets plate.

Martha smiled at Edwina. "Oh, good. You're eating. When people visit my house, I like to know they're being fed. Anyway, back to the story. The Americans then set fire to the barracks. Sophia wrote that she heard cheering as the flames shot into the sky. Of course, the enemy wanted to make sure the British could no longer use the fort." Martha glanced out of the front window. "Sophia said that when she looked out of her window, she saw a multitude of American soldiers advancing, regulars and militia men."

"She must have been terrified," said Simon.

Martha nodded. "Her mother apparently begged the commanding officer to spare their property, but he said his orders were to burn everything they saw. Sophia described it as total chaos. There were people screaming for mercy as they fled from their burning homes. A lot of townsfolk had waited until the last moment, you see, in the hopes it wouldn't happen. Many escaped with just the clothes on their backs. And, in the meantime, the gang of soldiers went from house to house, destroying every building they came across. Someone tried to start a bucket brigade, but it wouldn't have helped much. All they could do was try to salvage bits and pieces. It was a windy day and the fires spread. The town literally went up in smoke."

Edwina sighed. Even now, so many years later, it was hard not to think about the horrific scenario without feeling sorrow.

"Years later, Sophia recorded all these memories," Martha said. "I'm sure she must have had what we now know as PTSD. She said later that for much of her life, she dreamed of the plumes of smoke and of buildings falling down around her."

"I don't believe we have an accurate number of the casualties from that winter," said Susannah.

Martha shook her head. "We know there were about four hundred people who became homeless that day, but most historians agree we can't know for sure how many died. It would have been a terrible death. I know that much. There were babies and elderly people in that group. Although some of the townsfolk were able to construct crude shelters, others died while trying to find a place to huddle. We believe that's how Ann died. She wasn't with the rest of her family, you see."

"That's right." Adelaide sat at the edge of her seat. "Ann showed me the place. It was an old barn. She refused to go inside. She said there were others who needed the warmth more than she did."

"Did she?" Martha gazed at Adelaide in awe. "You're the one who sees things, aren't you, dear?"

Adelaide nodded.

"Amazing." Martha's eyes watered. "They found Ann on the road about a mile away. She died all alone, out in the elements." She wiped her eyes with a tissue.

"Please excuse me. I get emotional talking about that poor thing. She was unable to marry the man she loved, was harassed by a man she despised, then she had to suffer in death."

"Hang on." Edwina seized on the new information. "What was that part about the man she loved...and about her being harassed?"

"This is where the story gets even more interesting," said Martha, clenching the fabric of her chair. "Ann Forbes had a stalker."

"Whoa." Edwina turned to Adelaide.

Addy nodded, as if to say *It's him*.

"Before you go any further," said Susannah, her face lit up with the joy of a hundred history geeks, "do the names James and Perry mean anything to you?"

"Oh my goodness! They certainly do, and they wouldn't be common knowledge to someone unfamiliar with the family." Martha leaned in with conspiratorial flair. "According to Sophia, Ann was secretly engaged."

"What?" they all exclaimed.

"Aside from her cousin, who only shared the info years later in her memoirs, no one else in the family knew," said Martha. "Ann had begged her to keep it a secret until she could convince her father to approve the match."

"Who was the guy?" asked Simon.

Martha angled her head toward Adelaide. "Care to take a guess?"

A small smile crept across Adelaide's face. "When Ann's spirit communicated with me at Simon's place, she was agitated. I wasn't able to get much from her. But being here now, hearing you speak, I am getting an image. I see a soldier. He's wearing a red coat, one with a medal. This is a man who was thoughtful and considerate, more interested in maintaining peace than warmongering. He was young, and I think he believed he could make a difference. He has dark hair, and he's very handsome. When he smiles at Ann, his eyes crinkle. He clearly adores her. I see them at town functions, but they're not there together."

Adelaide gasped. "Oh my gosh, the way they're gazing at each other from across the room. You can just feel the longing radiating from them. He's desperate to make a life with her." She took a moment. "He's the one named James, isn't he?"

Martha clapped her hands, squealing. "Yes! Sophia recorded his name as Captain James Kingston of the 49th Foot Regiment. He was an aide to General Brock, and from what I've read, he had the ear of his commanding officer. Unfortunately, aside from Sophia's writings, there is no proof of the engagement. I've actually discussed it with a couple of local historians, and they just pooh-poohed me. But I believe her. There was no reason for her to lie about it."

"Incredible," Susannah whispered. "At the B&B, we found a button from a 49th Regiment uniform."

"You did?" asked Martha. "I would love to see it."

"We'll make sure you do," said Simon. "It's just being authenticated."

"There's just one thing about James Kingston that I've never understood." Martha played with the beads on her necklace. "He was a damn fine soldier, by all accounts, and he was devoted to Brock. The two men seem to have complemented each other too. Brock was a popular, respected man, but he was hungry for action, and could be impatient. History records Kingston as having had a more measured temperament. While

Brock could sometimes get antsy about their Indigenous allies, Kingston was quick to recognize their considerable contributions. When Brock's company first received news of the invasion at Queenston Heights, the general and the other officers scoffed. It was Captain Kingston who urged him to listen to the messenger, and that's been verified by contemporary accounts. Although many historians feel Brock's charge at Queenston Heights was a reckless one, I can't help but feel that Kingston would have been there with his commanding officer. He may have differed in opinion from Brock on several matters, but he had a real sense of duty. And yet, he doesn't appear to have taken part in the Battle of Queenston Heights at all. In fact, he's listed in the military records as a deserter."

"What?" Susannah eyes crinkled in confusion. "But that makes no sense. Desertion did happen, but this is an officer we're talking about."

"Exactly," said Martha. "Why would he have deserted, especially if he was secretly engaged to Ann? And yet, Captain Kingston seems to have fallen off the face of the earth immediately *before* the Battle of Queenston Heights."

Edwina was no military historian, but even to her, the story sounded wrong. She glanced at Adelaide. "Any idea?"

"I'm not sure yet," said Adelaide, "but I don't think James Kingston ran away. I see an image of him holding Ann. They're in some kind of forest. Then...nothing. Just darkness. I think he died before Ann did."

They were all silent.

"There has to be a way to prove it," said Susannah.

"You won't find him mentioned in any death records," cautioned Martha. "Believe me, I've checked."

The tiny hairs at the back of Edwina's neck tingled. From deep inside her ears, there was a crackle, like when her ears popped on flights.

Not again.

It bored through her head, but rather than drilling into her brain, it seemed as if something was trying to get out. She shook her head a few times. When that didn't work, she opened her mouth and moved her jaw around, trying to dislodge the popping sensation.

The mysterious rumbling intensified. Like a howl being carried on the wind, it shrieked out of her, but no one else seemed able to hear it.

It was all in her head.

And it was calling to her in a man's voice, one she'd heard before.

Can you see me?

No four syllables had ever worked on her the same way, and she knew she would never forget that plaintive tone.

Out of nowhere, an image occurred. It was of a British soldier from another time, walking alone near a patch of woods. He was distracted, maybe even worried. A dark shadow rushed up behind him, and he never saw it coming. There was a terrible crack as something hard met with his skull. The shadow engulfed him, and the image went black.

Edwina choked on her breath.

They all turned to her, but it was Adelaide's gaze she sought.

Adelaide's eyes were wide with horror and curiosity. "You saw it too."

"Saw what?" Simon touched Edwina's knee.

Edwina couldn't form an answer, not while that dreadful image lingered in her brain. She knew she'd seen James Kingston in that darkness. It was his muffled shout, his pain, and his blood.

But why would that image occur to Edwina?

Maybe, when this case was resolved, she needed to take a good, long vacation from paranormal investigations. The subject matter was clearly getting to her. Not only was her hearing suffering, she was having visions now.

There was no reason for her to envision Captain Kingston's murder. She'd only heard about him today.

Something else was happening here, and it made her want to break into a sprint. Anything, as long as she could escape the ominous attack on her senses.

Even as she pondered the question, the tumult in her ear canal faded. Tempted to stick her finger in her ear and give it a good shake, Edwina sat still and stared at her lap instead.

"Martha," asked Susannah, "could I look at Sophia's memoirs?"

"Absolutely," said Martha. "Although she wrote her memories down as an old woman, she's never struck me as an unreliable narrator. Her sense of detail is too great. To be honest, I've already given you all the info she provided about those incidents. The rest of it is just little stories of how they ran the household through the years, but it provides a lovely snapshot of the era, and there are several references to Ann. Would you like to join me in the library?"

The woman had a library. If Edwina wasn't so consumed with having seen James Kingston's death in Technicolor, she'd be excited.

As they followed her down the hallway, Addy tugged on Edwina's sleeve. "You saw him."

"I don't know what you're talking about."

"Ed, come on. You *saw* him."

"I saw...something. I don't know. It was just a flash. A weird blip." She shook her head. "My imagination got carried away, I guess."

"That wasn't your imagination. I saw the same thing just now. The man near the woods. Someone rushed up behind him. Whatever that thing was, it killed James Kingston, and you saw it, just like I did."

"Not now, Addy. I can't deal with this right now."

"Okay, as long as you understand you will have to deal with it at some point."

Clenching her fists and biting the inside of her lip to suppress the need to cry, Edwina followed the others. She had a feeling she knew what was happening to her, and she didn't like it. If her odd ear noises and the wild sense of urgency in her belly had anything to do with what Adelaide experienced, Edwina wanted none of it.

She hadn't signed up for this.

Neither did Addy.

No, but her sister had grown accustomed to it. She'd lived with it her whole life. The last thing Edwina wanted was to be at some dead person's beck and call.

She wasn't sure how, but she would fight this, and with all her might.

Like storm clouds gathering in the distance, her head began to slowly pound.

Martha's library was a sumptuous wood-paneled room with built-in bookshelves on three of the walls. The leather furniture would have been at home in the most exclusive of gentleman's clubs. Jewel-toned lamps provided a soft glow. Books of every type and genre, many of them antiques, lined the shelves. Family photos from different generations graced each desktop and windowsill.

"Um." Susannah touched a finger to one of the weathered book spines. "I'm having major library fantasies right now."

"I know, right?" Martha laughed. "My daughters always tell me my little library is a bit 'extra.' But I've worked hard my whole life. I deserve it." She went to the large desk and unlocked one of the drawers. After putting on a pair of gloves, she pulled out a yellowed booklet and set it on the desk. "It's fragile, so I hope you don't mind if I handle it."

"Of course not." Her voice hushed, Susannah peered over Martha's shoulder.

"I've read it cover to cover anyway," said Martha. "I'm sure I could recite it, upon pain of death."

As the dire image of Captain Kingston's death began to fade in Edwina's mind, a new thought took root there. "I wonder if the reason Ann is haunting the B&B is because of the confusion surrounding James Kingston's disappearance! I mean, the circumstances around her death are documented. There's no mystery that we know of. But what if she's trying to tell us something about James? What if there's more to the story?" She faced Adelaide. "You said Ann's spirit was looking out of the windows for someone she *mourned*. Ann had to believe James was dead."

"So how did he die?" asked Simon. "Or did someone kill him?"

Oh, someone killed him, all right. Edwina didn't say the words out loud because she had no proof, but she knew it in her heart.

194

As if to confirm, her heart beat in time with the pressure in her head.

"Martha, you mentioned Ann had a stalker?" asked Susannah. "Was that in Sophia's memoirs?"

"It was, although not in those words," admitted Martha. "I'm putting my modern spin on it, of course. Sophia mentions that Ann's father tried very hard to marry her off to his assistant, and that Ann would have nothing to do with the man. Apparently, she despised him, although that didn't stop him from pestering her. His name was Reginald Perry."

"Perry!" Edwina grabbed Simon's arm. "That was the other name we heard on the EVP."

Martha sniffed in disgust. "From the way Sophia describes him, the man was vile. Real creeper material."

"Addy, could the spirit man be Reginald Perry?" asked Edwina.

"I don't know." Adelaide frowned. "He didn't reveal much."

"Well, I'll let you draw your own conclusions." Martha turned carefully to one of the pages in the booklet. "I'll just read this part out loud. In referring to the days after the Battle of Queenston Heights, Sophia writes, 'After the fall of General Brock, there was much sadness in our community. Uncle George believed that was the cause of Ann's tears, and it vexed him to see her brought so low. Indeed, the general was greatly respected and admired, but Ann's tears were for another. I was the only one who knew of her turmoil, and I would not break her confidence, no matter how often my uncle implored me to reason with her. As his sickness advanced, he became impatient with her changing moods. No matter how often he demanded she accept Mr. Perry's proposal, Ann remained steadfast. Until the day she died, she kept faith that Captain Kingston would return, that they could make their engagement known to all. Alas, her dreams were never realized. I never found the strength to tell Ann all the vile gossip, but I fear it reached her ears through other means. To this day, Captain Kingston is regarded as a deserter, and he was much maligned for not being at General Brock's side when he fell. I, for one, do not believe it. Captain Kingston was a better man than most, and he was loyal to his commanding officer. There is one thing that has troubled me all these years, although I made light of it at the time. I am certain that the first time I heard the contemptible rumors about the captain's desertion, they were from Reginald Perry's lips. I recall seeing him spreading his venomous words in town, telling anyone who would listen.'"

"Perry was a civilian," said Susannah. "How would he know that Kingston deserted?"

Martha nodded. "Exactly."

"I'd like to go back and see if I can make contact with Ann again," said Adelaide.

"Of course," said Martha. "Would you like to see where she's buried first?"

They followed Martha into her kitchen. It opened onto a modern addition with a sunroom and patio door. Her backyard was huge and filled with mature trees, and the garden boasted the pristine touch of a professional landscaper.

At the very back of the yard, there were several old headstones. Some lay flat in the earth, but others remained upright. There were a few that had previously broken, and these were now reinforced with steel beams. Edwina marveled at the sight. "I can't believe these are in your yard."

"Old family cemeteries aren't uncommon in this area," said Martha. "This house has been in our family since Ann and Sophia's time, and my husband and I see ourselves as caretakers. I suspect the house will always stay in the family because of the graves. I'd want to make sure they're preserved. We owe a debt to the people who came before us. Without them, we wouldn't be here. Niagara-on-the-Lake might be a comfortable community with some interesting sites and pretty houses, but it's so much more than that. Countless people lived and loved on this land. Indigenous, Black, white people, they all put down roots here. Some went into battle and died here. I still feel them all around me."

"What happened to Sophia?" asked Susannah.

Martha smiled. "Oh, Sophia had a long, happy life, happier than most. She married young, as many did at the time, and had several children. She became involved in several charities and spent a lot of time giving back to a community that had been so scarred and traumatized. I'm proud of her, and I've tried to keep her spirit alive in my own charity work."

"I'm glad she had a good life," said Edwina.

Martha leaned over and brushed some dirt off a couple of the stones. "Sophia's right there, with her family. And here's Ann, bless her."

The stood in a circle, silent. In one of the nearby trees, a cardinal chirped to its mate. Seconds later, the answering chirp sounded.

Edwina had once read that cardinals mated for life, and that, when troubled, they would call to their mates with their lyrical chirps. Her mom had once told her that cardinals were visitors from beyond the grave.

Cardinals appear when angels are near.

Edwina couldn't possibly know if the colorful birds in Martha's yard had anything to do with Ann and James, but the symbolism still gave her pause.

Had Ann Forbes somehow known that her beloved James was dead? Had she cried out for him?

Overwhelmed by emotion, Edwina swiped at her tears. But it wasn't sadness that filled her heart. It was rage, and it burned a path into her stomach.

Someone *did* this to Ann and James, and she would make it right.

Edwina tried to make out the inscription on the headstone, but between her swollen eyes and the weathered stone, it was too hard. She could see Ann's name, but that was about it. She reached for Martha's hand. "I'm sorry she hasn't been at rest."

"It breaks my heart to think she's still suffering in some way," said Martha.

"You have our word, Martha." Simon caught Edwina's gaze and nodded. "We'll do our best to fix it."

Adelaide took a step back from the grave. When she spoke, her voice rang out through the quiet space. "Yes, and I know how to do it." Her cheeks were pale but there was resolve in the faint lines around her mouth. "Ann was silenced in death. We need to give her a voice."

Chapter Thirteen

"What on earth?" Connie brought her face closer to the hole in the parlor wall. "Do we have raccoons?"

Simon still couldn't look at the damn hole in the wall without wanting to bring up his lunch. "Yeah, about that, I wish I could blame it on a raccoon infestation. Unfortunately, it was me. I wasn't exactly myself."

"Did you dip into the good Scotch? I warned you about that."

Simon told Connie about his near possession. Her eyes grew wider with each sentence out of his mouth.

Yup. There was his lunch again. Ham and cheese on rye, with a side of shame. He swallowed. "Sorry about the mess. Once the investigation is over, I'll start calling around for some quotes."

"Leave it to me. Remember my nephew Jason? He just finished his apprenticeship. He could use the business."

"Yeah, Jason's great. Let him know the job's his. I appreciate it."

Just then, Edwina walked into the parlor. "Have you guys seen my... Ah, there it is. I knew I left my phone in here. I want to upload some of the new footage to our YouTube channel." She grabbed the cell phone from the pool table and started to walk out. However, she quickly changed course and walked back over to Simon. Smiling, she mussed his hair, then dropped a kiss onto his cheek before heading out of the room.

Once Edwina was out of earshot, Connie crossed her arms over her chest and stared at him.

"Yes, Connie?" drawled Simon. "Is there something of a personal nature that you'd like to ask me?"

"Oh, you think we have secrets? That's cute. That ship sailed a long time ago. Now, will you please explain to me why Edwina Darke looked like she was ready to mount you like a freshly saddled horse?"

"There may, or may not, have been some mounting recently."

Connie's jaw hit the floor.

"Look—"

"Don't get defensive. No judgment here! I'm just going to say one thing." Connie grabbed him by the arms and drew him in for a hug. "I'm happy for you. You deserve a bit of fun."

"Aw, thanks." Simon patted her back. "It's early days, though. Don't get too excited. I don't want to get ahead of myself."

"I saw the way she looked at you."

A ripple of excitement made Simon's chest expand. "She did give me the look, didn't she?"

"Mm-hmm, and I saw you give it right back. You care for her."

He nodded, his throat tight all of a sudden. "I'm nervous, though. I haven't been sleeping well, and I can't just blame the ghost problem. I can't stop thinking about her. I'm totally under her spell, but I'm worried I'm going to screw things up."

"Simon."

"I did with Carly, and my feelings for her didn't heat up this quickly at all. I feel like my head is constantly spinning. What if I say or do something to piss Edwina off?"

"You will. Absolutely."

It was his turn to glare.

Connie just laughed it off. "Because everyone does, silly. Just make sure you talk it through. Look, Simon. Carly betrayed you, and that's on her. She made a choice. But you pretty much admitted that the lines of communication had already closed. I know it stung because of how you broke up, and because your brother was involved, but that relationship wasn't going anywhere. I think there's potential with Edwina, so just keep talking. I know that's scary for you sometimes."

"Talking, huh? Is that how you and Margie have lasted all these years?"

"Yup. That, a whole lot of hot sex."

"Aaaand I think it's time for this pep talk to come to a close." He laughed. "But I appreciate what you're saying."

Thankfully, Edwina chose that moment to walk back into the room, sparing Simon from any further discussions of Connie and Margie's vigorous love life. Not that he didn't aspire to what they had. God only knew he'd been treated to many ear-bending stories over the years. Connie was extremely comfortable talking about sex. He could learn a thing or two from her.

As Edwina entered the parlor, she stopped short, rolled her eyes and went back out into the hallway. She seemed distracted, which was unusual for someone who was always so focused and prepared.

He'd noticed that she'd had words with Adelaide back at Martha's house, and both of them had seemed bothered by the conversation. He hoped everything was okay between the sisters.

Later, he'd try to talk to her about it. The last thing he wanted was for the Darkes to end up like him and Rupert, full of resentment and unspoken feelings.

Edwina returned with a laptop, and she set it up on one of the parlor tables. Connie took that opportunity to slip out of the room, wearing a look on her face that said, 'I'll give you two some privacy.'

"Check it out, Simon." Edwina dropped into a chair in front of the laptop. "Once we're done with the investigation, I'll put together a full-length episode for our YouTube channel. In the meantime, I've been uploading some teaser bits of footage for our subscribers. We've been getting lots of views and comments."

"Great."

"Some of them are about the B&B. See? 'That place is amazing. I want to stay there the next time I visit Niagara.'"

Simon sat next to her and read a few more of the comments. "Nice. If we ever open up again, maybe we'll get some new customers out of this."

"You'll open up again. I promise."

Edwina leaned in for a kiss, and Simon happily obliged. Tasting her lips, he closed his eyes and allowed himself to get lost in the banquet of delicious sensations. Simon had kissed a few people in his time, but something about Edwina made everything seem brand-new. Maybe it was the way she dug her fingertips into his back, holding him as if she never wanted to let him go. Or maybe it was the small moans of delight that accompanied all her kisses.

Whatever that magic quality was, he was captivated by it, and he hoped he made her feel the same sort of passion.

When they ended the kiss, both of them practically panting, she touched her lips. "Hmm. Tingles. I forgot what they felt like."

"You shouldn't go a day without feeling tingles." If he were lucky enough to have Edwina at his side, he'd make sure she was tingly right down to her toes, and as often as possible. He searched her gaze for any hesitance, and the answering warmth made him bold. "Of course, you realize it's now my mission to deliver as many as I can."

"I'll take you up on that." When her laptop pinged with a notification, she glanced at the screen. Her face fell. "For fuck's sake."

"What is it?" Simon checked out the comments on the screen. The most recent one was a doozie, a crude message that made several references to Edwina's anatomy. "What the hell? Who the fuck is Gary69lover?"

"Just one of our regular trolls."

"This happens a lot?"

"Yup. I should have blocked him long ago, but I thought he was a fellow paranormal investigator. Turns out I was wrong. He's just some asshole." She clicked a few buttons, removing the comment, then blocked him. "There. Done. No need to scowl."

"That guy's a turd, and there's every need to scowl. How many of those comments has he posted? Are you sure it's not someone you know?"

The Darke sisters were easily searchable online. What if this dipshit decided to try out some in-person trolling? Once again, Simon marveled at the white-hot fury that coursed through him any time he thought of someone hurting Edwina. He knew that guy was just some internet douchebag, and that most of them never ventured out from behind their keyboards, but it didn't mean he didn't want to throttle him.

"I'm sure. I know it's gross, but it's just words. I'm okay." Edwina snuggled up against him. "But I appreciate your willingness to drag that guy into a dark alley so you can commit some sort of atrocity on my behalf."

In that moment, he was more than willing. He was ready to hire a hacker to discover the identity of Gary69lover, so he could do horrible, painful things to him. Preferably with a crowbar. No, a pair of tweezers. Then, he could draw the torture out longer.

Whoa. Back up, buddy.

Connie was right.

He cared for Edwina, and the feeling was growing deeper every day.

There were moments when he thought it might very well knock his feet out from under him.

It was scary, but good, and he definitely wanted to see where it would go.

"So," he said, changing the subject to steady his nerves. "Is Addy still determined to do a séance tonight?"

"She doesn't like calling them séances. She calls it channeling. She thinks the only way we'll get some concrete answers from Ann Forbes is by inviting her to speak through her."

He glanced at the hole in the wall. "Like what happened to me?"

"Not exactly. Addy will be in control. Still, it's a big deal. Addy doesn't usually open herself up that way. She says one needs to be careful when opening a door. You just don't know who might step through."

"Are you worried?"

She took her time replying. "Yeah, actually. This case...something feels different about it. From the very beginning, even as I read your email, I felt this sense of urgency. I can't explain it."

"You and Addy had a quiet conversation earlier. Is everything okay?"

"Sort of." She rested her elbows on her knees, taking a few deep breaths. "Simon, back at Martha's house, I think I *saw* James Kingston die. It was clear as day. He was murdered. I don't know how I was able to see it, but I'm convinced I did."

"Okay."

"I've been having these bizarre feelings, and sometimes I think I even hear voices. Something's happening to me, and it's really creeping me out." She tipped her head up to gaze at him. "Do you think I'm a freak?"

He let out a sigh and drew her back into his embrace. "Ed, I think you're amazing. Nothing short of amazing."

"I know Addy wants to make something of this, but I'm sure it's just some weird sort of one-off. I mean, it's not like I always go around envisioning people's gory deaths. Look at me. I'm not a medium! It's just this investigation. All my synapses have been firing, and I don't know why."

She trembled in his arms so he kissed her forehead. "Hey. Don't get ahead of yourself. One mystery at a time, okay? Whatever's happening, you'll handle it." He smoothed his fingers along her soft cheek. "And I'd like to help you."

"I'd like that."

"Good."

"I just wish I could get rid of the sinking feeling in my gut. I'm nervous, but I don't think we have any option but to push forward. I'm not going to leave you and Connie in the lurch."

"Your safety's more important," said Simon. "If you decide not to go any further, we still have options. Maybe we could find a buyer."

"No." Edwina shook her head. "You guys have put your hearts and souls into this bed and breakfast. And even if you were to sell, what would happen to Ann?"

Simon understood. It was one thing when he and Connie were musing about the possibility of a haunting, but now, they had names and places. Ann Forbes was a real person who had led a tragic life.

Where was she now? In some hellish purgatory, unable to move on, a victim to circumstances beyond her control?

No. This felt too personal. They had to help her.

"I remember when I first saw the real estate listing for this place," said Simon. "It just grabbed me. I'd been working long hours, and everything had just fallen apart with Carly. There were plenty of listings, and I could have reasonably set up my business in any of those properties. But when I spotted this house, I had to tell Connie about it right away. Something called to me. Maybe, somehow, that was Ann. Maybe she found a way to summon us all."

Edwina smiled. "Maybe she did."

"We don't sound like a pair of skeptics, you know."

"I'm not so sure I can call myself a skeptic anymore. I still like having proof, but I want to believe."

Simon wanted to believe too. More importantly, he wanted to believe in *them*. He wanted to believe he wouldn't screw up his relationship with Edwina. He wanted to have faith that she would never hurt him. He wanted to believe they could last.

He wanted her, period.

"So, we're agreed then?" she said. "We see this through, no matter what?"

He'd already admitted he would follow her to hell and back. "As long as no one gets hurt." He wrapped his fingers around the back of her neck, luxuriating in the fall of her hair over his hand. "I don't ever want to see you hurt, Ed."

"Likewise."

Her sisters entered the parlor, stopping short when they spotted them on the couch.

"Ooh, they're canoodling," Susannah said in a dramatic stage whisper. "Please don't let us disturb you. Just be aware that Addy and I will award points based on technique and enthusiasm. Isn't that right, Addy?"

"Sure." Adelaide picked at her shirt hem, where a thread had come loose.

Susannah shrugged and pretended to hold up a sign. "That's a five from this Canadian judge. I want to see some acrobatics."

"Harsh." Edwina walked over to Adelaide and put her arm around her. "I'll have to see if I can bribe this judge. Can we talk later, Addy?"

Adelaide's mischievous grin could only indicate one thing. She'd forgiven Edwina for being a stubborn ass...and her Yoda impersonation was about to make another appearance. "Talk later we will, youngling."

"Ugh," said Edwina. "Simon, you do realize that if you continue to hang out with me, you'll be exposed to even more of my sisters' oddities."

Odd or not, Simon was becoming fond of the Darke sisters' banter. It was so unlike anything he had with his own brother. They had their disagreements, but at their core, they were tight. They talked things out.

Hmm. Connie was right. Talking didn't have to be a painful experience.

Adelaide gave Edwina a noogie, for which Edwina retaliated by tickling her.

Yeah. Being a part of the Darke family didn't strike him as much of a hardship at all.

Frankly, he was so smitten with Edwina, he would have put up with her sisters even if they'd been actual ogres.

Had they encountered actual ogres in their line of work?

Nope, never mind. He really didn't want to know.

* * * *

As they gathered that night, Edwina's skin tingled. Already in a state of hyper-awareness, she couldn't shake the sensation that she was being watched. That they were all being watched.

But by whom?

For someone who'd always insisted on finding reasonable explanations for spooky phenomena, expecting spirit activity was now becoming her go-to reaction. She went throughout the house, checking on their various pieces of equipment, and kept expecting to bump into some wandering shade. It was off-putting, to say the least, but there was also something cloying about the vibes in the King Street house. It seemed to beckon, a spider luring her into an inescapable web.

Adelaide had expressed a desire to remain upstairs, where Ann's spirit seemed most comfortable, so they met in the Merlot room. While Addy prepared herself, taking some time alone outside in the garden, Edwina and the others set up. She and Susannah positioned cameras and recorders throughout the room, making sure every angle was covered.

Simon brought up a spare table out of storage, one that was large enough for all of them to sit around. Edwina dimmed the lights in the room using the dimmer switches. With the sort of activity they'd seen, she didn't want to have to resort to candles. Edwina sat opposite Adelaide. On her right sat Simon. On her left, Connie and Susannah.

In the middle of the table, Susannah had set the uniform button. She'd heard back from the antiques appraiser, and he'd confirmed it was indeed a 49th Foot Regiment button from the 1812-1814 period. They would use it as a trigger item in Adelaide's session.

Edwina touched it now, and the image of Captain James Kingston in his last moments flashed before her eyes once again. The blood coming from his head seeped into his scarlet coatee.

She didn't need an appraiser to tell her this button had been part of Captain Kingston's uniform. She knew it as well as she knew her own name.

When Adelaide entered the room, she did so quietly, but with purpose. "Is everyone ready?"

"No Ouija board, huh?" A nervous laugh erupted from Simon.

"No." Adelaide sat in her chair, making it creak. "I don't like working with them. It's been my experience that they can act like a magnet for the wrong spirits. It's important to stay focused when channeling. Our intention here is to speak with Ann, and Ann alone. I don't want to attract anyone else."

"That all sounds incredibly ominous," said Simon.

"We'll be okay," Adelaide replied, "but I'll be honest with you. What you see tonight might be disconcerting and even a little scary. If there's anyone here who'd rather leave, it would be good if you said so now." She turned her gaze upon Edwina. "Whatever happens tonight, whatever any of you may see or hear, just be open-minded. The dead can't hurt us if we don't allow them in."

Edwina wasn't so sure about that.

As if understanding her fears, Adelaide said, "We're only looking to talk to Ann tonight. If anything else tries to come through, Maria and I will shut it down. Let's join hands."

Edwina clasped hands with Connie and with Simon. He gave her hand a squeeze.

His warm skin against hers grounded Edwina. *We can do this.*

Together.

Adelaide began with a prayer of protection, similar to the one she used before vigils. "I would like to reach out to the spirit of Ann Forbes. Ann, you have been kind enough to communicate with us since we've been here, and I'm asking you to make your presence known tonight as well. You may use the devices that we've set up around the room, if you wish, but I would like to invite you to use my body so that we can speak with you directly. You have been restless for so long, and our hearts go out to you. I don't want you to be in pain anymore, Ann. I would like for you to finally be joined to Captain James Kingston of the 49th Foot Regiment. He's waiting for you. Would you like to see James again?"

At the mention of Captain Kingston's name, the K2 meter on the table lit up in brilliant color and continued to flash.

"Yes," said Adelaide. "Thank you, Ann. You're doing so well, and you've had to be so brave, braver than I ever would have been in your shoes. We met one of your cousin Sophia's descendants today. Her name is Martha and you would be proud of her. She's taken such good care of your resting place, but she's worried about you. We all are. We would like for you to find peace."

He wouldn't let her have peace, not in life, and not now.

The thought sprang unbidden from Edwina's core. Her blood went cold thinking of Reginald Perry. After dealing with so many toxic personalities in her own life, she sympathized with Ann.

Without even knowing much about the mysterious Reginald Perry, Edwina hated him.

A wisp of cold air drifted over her right shoulder, chilling her to the bone. The draft felt almost like a touch from cold fingers, far too intimate a caress for her liking. Somehow, those invisible fingers trailed down her neck and into her shirt, between her breasts.

She was about to cry out, but Addy had already noticed.

So had Maria.

Her pained coughs filled the room, causing everyone to hold their breath.

Adelaide's jaw tightened. "No," she almost shouted. "You are not welcome here! Get out."

A deep voice rumbled over Edwina's shoulder. The knowing laughter was the most sinister thing she'd ever heard.

But Maria's coughs were louder and stronger, and they drowned the laughter out.

Just like that, the chilly grip on Edwina faded. Footsteps creaked on the stairs, descending. There was some shuffling downstairs that seemed to be coming from the kitchen. Then everything went quiet, including Maria.

"He's gone, but he'll try again." Adelaide shut her eyes. "Ann, come into me now, and tell us your story. With truth, comes peace and light. We need to hear what happened to you. I know it's hard, but I'm begging you to communicate with us."

She tightened her grip on Simon and Susannah's hands. "Yes! Use me as a vessel. Take my voice and make it your own. Use my eyes and tell us what you see. It's safe for you here. I will give you shelter from the cold, Ann. You've been wandering in winter for too long. Be warm now. All you need to do is step across the threshold."

There was a low humming noise. It was coming from Adelaide, but it wasn't a sound she could have produced. It was almost as a cat had fallen asleep in the next room, and its soft, satisfied purrs were reverberating through the walls. The lights on the K2 meter wouldn't stop moving. The entire unit was lit up.

Then the lights in the room went out, but it was only for a second.

When they came back on, Adelaide opened her eyes.

Right away, Edwina knew it wasn't her sister looking back at them. Not entirely, anyway.

Adelaide's eyes, normally a warm brown, had lightened. They now shone hazel, made bright by curiosity and fear. Without even having seen a picture of Ann Forbes, Edwina knew the woman now sat before them.

"Goodness," whispered Susannah.

They'd seen Adelaide channel spirits before, but they'd never seen such a stark change in her. Maybe it was just the light playing tricks, but there was no denying the myriad tiny differences. The shadows altered Addy's round face, giving the impression of high cheekbones. There was also something about her lips that signaled another woman was present. Addy's bowlike mouth was suddenly wider, more generous. Even the curve of her shoulders seemed different, the angles more pronounced. Addy had clearly taken a step back so that Ann could shine. Now, Ann gazed at each of them with those unblinking hazel eyes, perhaps seeking answers as much as they were. Although she still held on to Susannah and Simon's hands, she seemed ready to bolt.

"Ann Forbes of Newark?" asked Edwina. "Is that you?"

"It is I. What is this place?"

Edwina glanced at Susannah, who shook her head in amazement. That voice…it wasn't Adelaide's at all.

The timbre was all wrong, and certainly not something their sister could fabricate. Ann had a high, clear soprano, so different from her sister's deeper tones.

"This is your home, Ann," said Susannah. "It just looks a little different now."

"Everything is different now." Ann's sigh was heavy, mournful. "I cannot find him."

"You mean, James Kingston?" said Edwina.

Ann pinned her with a glare, but her expression softened. "That's Captain James Kingston, and an aide to Major-General Brock, himself."

"Of course. I'm sorry. I meant no disrespect." Even though the spirit woman had gently called her out, Edwina wasn't offended. Ann was protective of her lover, and Edwina respected her for that.

"He said he would come back for me, but he never did." Her eyes filled with tears, and they spilled over her cheeks. "Something went wrong. I can feel it in my marrow. Will you help me find him?"

"We will." Edwina knew it was probably wrong of her to make promises to a ghost, but it seemed like a kind thing to say.

"Ann, when was the last time you saw Captain Kingston?" Susannah asked.

"It was the night before the invasion at Queenston Heights. James met me under cover of darkness, in our usual place. We always met under the large willow tree, in the wilderness beyond the garden. He said nothing would keep him from coming back, but something did. Someone took him from me. I know it to be true. The shadows never lie."

"What shadows?" asked Simon.

"The shadow people." Ann tilted her head. "They always come when someone is about to die. They came for me as well, on that day in December, when the cold bit into my flesh and my breath froze inside my chest. They come for all of us, in the end."

Next to Edwina, Connie sucked in a breath. Edwina squeezed her hand.

"Who would take James from you?" demanded Edwina.

"The one who took everything from me. Reginald Perry." Ann sneered.

"Because he wanted to marry you?" asked Susannah.

"Because he wanted *everything*," she answered. "My body, my soul, even this house. He wanted it all. Not a day went by that he didn't try to coerce my father into forcing me to marry him. He followed me everywhere I went and sent me numerous tokens of his vile *love*. No matter how many times I rebuked him, he returned. Sometimes with words that were sickly sweet, sometimes with threats. I finally had to tell him —" She broke off with a cry.

"What?" asked Edwina. "What did you tell him?"

"That I was betrothed to James! The only person I'd told was my cousin Sophia, and I had begun to broach the subject with my father. But Father wouldn't hear of it. He didn't trust James because he didn't trust anyone in the military. He was unwell, you see, and his illness made him confused and suspicious.

"Perry scoffed upon hearing of the engagement," Ann continued. "He said my bond with James was nothing compared to the bond he would forge with me. Everywhere I went, he appeared, watching. He watches me still. Even here, in my sanctuary, he torments me."

Ann paused, her gaze unfocused. "Shortly afterward, James disappeared. Perry took great delight in delivering the news to my father. He called my James a deserter, as if it were possible." Her gaze hardened. *'Give yourself to me,'* he said, *'or wither away, with only your memories of a coward to warm your bed.'* But he was wrong. James was no coward, and he would not have forsaken his duty."

"How can we prove it?" asked Susannah. "We'd like to clear his name, but we need proof."

Ann let out a noise of exasperation. As she moaned, her eyes flashed, flickering between her bright hazel and Adelaide's brown tones.

They were losing her.

"Ann, please," implored Edwina. "Stay with us. We need more details on Perry."

"Reginald Perry was a monster, but he was also a traitor. He threw in his lot with the Canadian Volunteers. It was he who brought the enemy militia to our door. It was bad enough once Newark was in enemy hands. Our lives had become a nightmare. We couldn't walk the roads, especially at night, because they would taunt us and threaten us for not supporting their cause. Every night, I went to sleep, wondering if Perry would finally grow tired of being civil. I had to sleep with a rifle under my bed.

"When that day came, I saw them coming. I had been reading by the window when they appeared through the trees. Perry led them right to us. He hurled insults at my father, who had quickly grown infirm. As they turned my family out into the cold, he grabbed me by the arm and said, *'There is still time. You and I are more alike than you know, and we could be formidable together. Come with me, and you will be spared.'* I did not understand his strange words. I was nothing like him. So I spat in his face. He threw me to the ground, and said to the other Volunteers, *'This one's a harlot and a witch. Use her however you wish.'* But they were too occupied with the task of setting the town ablaze. They had mercy on me that day, if one can call it mercy."

Edwina choked back a sob.

"I will never forget the flames." For a few seconds, Ann's eyes flashed, as if the fires of Newark were reflected in them. "At first, there was just shock, as frightened townsfolk gathered in the streets. Some cried. Others tried to bargain with our enemy. It was no use. After a time, the roar of the fires drowned out the shouts of alarm and the weeping. The Volunteers left us in the rubble and snow, our only light the eerie glow of the sky."

"What happened to Perry?" asked Susannah.

Ann's shoulders drooped. "He is bound to this place by his evil, as I am bound by my loss. He killed my James. I know it in my heart. And until he is punished for his crimes, I will not rest." She closed her eyes and hung her head. Another low hum signaled a change in the room's energy.

When Adelaide lifted her head, her eyes had turned back to brown. She blinked a few times. There were bags under her eyes, as if she hadn't slept in days, and her head was heavy.

"Addy?" said Edwina.

"I'm okay. Ann's gone." She still held hands with those next to her. "I'm not sure if it will work, but I'd like to do a prayer of progression, to help her move on."

They all bowed their heads.

"Ann Forbes, dear spirit of light," Adelaide began, her voice cracking. "We thank you for your time, energy and wisdom. May the Creator watch over this place and the people in it, cleansing it with holy light. We ask that no harm befalls or follows the protected circle here. May all lost souls be permanently healed and reunited and taken into the light. Go, Ann, to the place of peace."

Although it terrified Edwina to open herself up to the unnatural energy that had allowed her to see James' death, she searched her heart for some sort of sign that Ann had moved on. But there were no images of Ann, no fleeting glimpses of her ascending to paradise, or whatever it was that happened after death. Nothing had changed, and the rooms of the King Street house still vibrated with weariness and sorrow.

"Is she gone?" asked Simon. "She said she couldn't be free until Perry was punished. How are we supposed to punish a dead man?"

"She's still stuck here. I can feel her all around me. Something's keeping her here." Adelaide shook her head, then stood and headed for the door. "I couldn't help her."

"Addy." Edwina got up. "Where are you going?"

"Just outside," called Adelaide from the hallway. "I'll be in the garden."

Edwina was about to follow her, but Susannah touched her arm.

"Give her some space," said Susannah. "Ann mentioned the Canadian Volunteers. They defected to the American side and acted as scouts, taking part in skirmishes. Because of their active participation in the burning of Newark, they were reviled in Upper Canada."

"So, they were real bad guys?" asked Connie.

"I guess it depends on who you ask," said Susannah. "I mean, there were those on the American side who considered the Canadian Volunteers to be brave rebels. Others said the Volunteers used the war as an excuse to seek revenge on Loyalist neighbors who'd angered them. I've read accounts of them destroying property and tormenting people."

She shrugged. "We have to remember each side had an agenda in this war. The British were protecting their assets, while the Americans thought we would be an easy conquest. Meanwhile, the Indigenous people wanted to retain their land, and the townspeople just wanted to be left alone. It was a tinderbox. Nevertheless, many historians agree that the Canadian Volunteers did a horrible thing by participating in the burning of Newark. They targeted helpless civilians in the dead of winter."

Simon cocked an eyebrow. "Charming."

Susannah nodded. "They were led by a man named Joseph Willcocks, a politician and former resident of Newark. Willcocks had originally been allied with Brock, but he became disenchanted. Once he offered his services to the Americans, he was guilty of treason. In burning Newark, he took revenge on those who he believed had wronged him. He had begun his career as a promising young man, but his legacy is one of terror. He sounds like just the sort of guy Reginald Perry would have liked."

Susannah brought out her cell phone and began to scroll. "Several of his buddies were executed for treason as a result of the Bloody Assize of Ancaster in 1814. I know Willcocks escaped to the States, and died in battle there. I wonder if something similar might have happened to Perry?"

"Which would mean he was never punished," added Connie.

"If I were Ann Forbes, I think that would be enough to make me want to come back as a ghost," said Susannah. "I need to find out what happened to Perry after the burning of Newark."

"I'm going to check on Addy." Edwina stood.

Simon went to her side. "Want me to join you?"

"No, it's okay. She's just out back." She grabbed onto him and nuzzled the bare skin at his throat. Things were coming to a head, and her body was sending out all sorts of warning signals that she didn't understand. The voices in her ear were clamoring and her head throbbed as she tried to tune them out. But when Simon held her, it kept the voices at bay a little. "Wait for me?"

"Of course." He dusted her lips with the gentlest of kisses.

Edwina hurried downstairs and out of the door. She walked around to the other side of the porch and scanned the back garden. At the far end, where the property met with the wooded ravine, Addy disappeared into the trees, the soft glow from her cell phone as her only light.

The voices demanded she follow her sister.

Edwina swatted the air around her ear. "I know, I know. I don't need ghosts telling me what to do. I'm quite capable of making my own decisions, thank you very much."

Addy might be accustomed to shooting the breeze with dead folks, but Edwina hadn't gotten the hang of it yet.

Holding her breath, touching the flashlight button on her own cell phone, she walked into the dark garden.

Chapter Fourteen

Edwina found Adelaide about fifty feet from the edge of Simon's yard, where the woods dipped into the ravine. A trail of tall sycamores lined the edge of a small creek, one that wound into the distance, behind other houses and into another section of woods. Edwina couldn't help admiring the patchy trunks of the sycamores, with their camouflage-like bark.

It was exactly the sort of place where one could hide from the world. She was tempted to do so herself.

Adelaide stood under a massive willow tree, framed by its drooping branches, facing its trunk.

Edwina approached quietly, so as not to startle her. "Addy?"

"Come here. I want to show you something."

Sweeping aside the canopy of willow branches, Edwina closed the distance between them.

"Grab my hand."

Edwina hesitated. The voices weren't letting up. They hunkered down, insistent, squatting inside the channel of her ear. She wouldn't be able to swat them away for much longer.

"It's okay," said Adelaide.

"I don't know. Why do I feel like I'm about to pass the point of no return?"

"I promise you it's not the end of the world. Take my hand."

Just do it. Simon called you a badass, so act like one. Without stalling a moment longer, Edwina reached for her sister's hand.

The noises in her head began to peel apart, and distinct voices could now be heard. However, it was all garbled, with each voice trying to drown out the others. A chunk of bile slid up Edwina's throat, as she realized the implications, but she swallowed it down. There was so much turbulence in her head, all of it distracting.

Was this what Addy felt like every time she did a vigil or a reading? How could she even hear her own thoughts?

"I know it's a lot," said Adelaide. "You'll reach a point where you can tune out the chatter. I can teach you some exercises, even some good meditations."

"No!" Edwina dropped her sister's hand. "I don't want to learn your exercises and meditations. I don't want to see what you see, Addy, and I don't want this!"

"You don't have a choice, Ed. It's time you confronted the fact that you have the gift too."

"Gift," she scoffed. "Not much of a gift, if you ask me. It's more like a curse."

"I won't lie to you, it has its moments. There have been times when I've wanted to take it back to the shop for a full refund, but it doesn't work that way."

"It'll change everything." Tears sprang to Edwina's eyes. "I saw what it did to you. I've heard what people have said about you. I've seen their reactions. God, Addy, have you forgotten all the times you were bullied in school by that awful Cheryl Ladmore and her mean-girl pals?"

"Considering I was the one being bullied, no, I haven't forgotten."

"You're right. I'm sorry."

"It's fine. We're not kids anymore, and I'm not worried about bullies calling me names. I don't even think about those people nowadays, not much anyway."

"I do. I think about them a lot."

"Oh, come here." Adelaide gave her a hug. "That's because you're my big sister, and you and Susannah have always bent over backward to help me. So, let me help you now."

"What does that even mean? Am I a medium all of a sudden?"

"You've always been able to see and hear those who've crossed over. You just haven't been ready to face it. The lines of communication were…buried, so to speak." She laughed softly. "You're pretty stubborn when you want to be."

"Thanks, I guess?"

"It's not necessarily bad. It has shielded you somewhat, but over time, something had to give. I think, if you look back, you've had experiences you couldn't explain. Remember how that thing in your closet appeared to you as Grandma?"

"Don't remind me. I've been dreaming about it again."

"I'm not surprised. Your abilities will need an outlet. If you suppress them while you're awake, they'll come out when you're asleep. Not even Edwina the Great Debunker can hold it off forever."

It made sense. Edwina had always suffered from bad dreams, and not just the one about their grandmother. Even the good dreams had always been so vivid — too vivid — and each one had left her in a state of numbness. Many of them had been peopled with dead family members and acquaintances. In her teens, there had been a troubling period during which she'd experienced a frightening sort of déjà vu. She would frequently see random images or scenarios in her mind, only to have them occur in real life a while later. But with the onset of adulthood, she'd managed to quash a lot of those curious sensations, until she forgot all about them.

At least, she mostly forgot about them. Truth be told, she always knew a day of reckoning might arrive.

With a touch of her sister's hand, they all came back to her, and in luminous color.

"Why now?" asked Edwina. "And why me?"

"It runs in our family. As for your first question, I'm not sure." She turned to the willow tree and rested her hand against its trunk. "But I think it might have something to do with Ann and James. I think this is their willow tree."

"That makes sense. It's huge. It's probably been here a long time."

"I suspect Ann has tried to communicate with the living before. Thus, some of the activity we've heard about. She probably needed people like us to show up."

People like us. That was going to take some getting used to.

"Want to try something with me?" asked Adelaide. "Put your hand on the tree next to mine and close your eyes. Just concentrate on Ann and James and ask them to come to you. Maybe together, we can see more than I was able to see by myself."

"Okay." Edwina had certainly dealt with worse than talking to these particular dead people. At least Ann and James weren't malevolent. She closed her eyes and touched the tree trunk. *Ann, James, I know I'm a little freaked out here, but it's okay if you want to talk to me. I'm ready to listen.*

Edwina's inner ear buzzed to life, as several voices fought for dominance. As she continued to reach out to Ann and James, two voices separated themselves from the fray. One was deep and warm. The other was one she'd already heard, the same high tone that had bubbled out of Adelaide earlier.

They were here, and she wasn't afraid to look at what they were willing to show her.

The darkness behind her closed eyes began to shift, fading into a fog. Ann rushed forward, like a ray of sunshine cutting through a cloud, and shot right through Edwina. Suddenly, she was seeing things through Ann's eyes.

As Ann, she appeared at a social function in Newark, and her heart was light, untroubled by war and strife. A lovely table was set out, one laden with cakes, pies and punch. The ladies were dressed in their finery, and there was much happy gossip. There was a small orchestra in the next room, and the dancing had just begun. The 49th Regiment had been invited as well, and a handsome young captain had just asked her to dance. His smile was kind, and his warm hands clasped her trembling fingers.

The scene changed. She was in a church now, one filled with congregants. Throughout the service, Ann glanced toward where James was sitting. His expression of secret yearning matched the gaping hole in her heart. Her father cleared his throat, and she turned around, saddened.

Once more, the setting shifted. In this scene, Ann picked her way over the undergrowth in these same woods, hurrying toward the willow tree. She spotted the telltale scarlet of James' coat and ran to him.

He embraced her hard, like a man who never knew when it might be the last time. Her heart beat rapidly against his chest, and she could barely catch her breath.

My love, he said, as his lips found hers.

Ann moaned with pleasure, and Edwina's pulse sped up. As James moved his strong hands lower on her body, Edwina's sex began to throb with desire, the same longing Ann must have felt in life.

James glanced about, to make sure they weren't seen, then lowered Ann to the ground. She spread her shawl out beneath them. She lay back, and he adjusted his trousers, freeing himself.

My darling, hurry, Ann urged. *I need you.*

Then you shall have me, again and again.

Overcome by conflicting emotions, Edwina shut out the vision. Even though Ann had clearly allowed her to see them that way, it didn't seem right to be a voyeur.

The moment Edwina closed herself off to the image, another took its place. This time, James manifested in that same rush of light. He filled Edwina's core with his spirit, and she now viewed everything through his eyes.

Once again, they were under the willow tree, but this meeting was filled with trepidation.

Did you hear that? Ann asked, her voice wobbling with fear.

But James wasn't worried about the rustling in the bushes. Other concerns had clouded his mind that night. General Brock had granted him some time to come see his sweetheart, but he would need to return to the fort swiftly. *It's nothing. Just an animal in the undergrowth. I don't have much time. The general believes an attack from the Americans is imminent.*

James, no!

We've received word from Major Evans this evening. He was sent to reconnoiter with the enemy about releasing prisoners and caught wind of their plans. I was in the officers' dining room when he told the general, and heard it all myself. He's been ordered to make all the necessary preparations for an assault.

Major Thomas Evans had been exhausted and drenched upon arriving back to Fort George. He'd had to paddle back from the American side of the river to warn them. At first, General Brock and the other officers had met his claims with disbelief. It was only after James convinced his commander to speak privately with Evans that General Brock had given the necessary orders.

We'll be ready for them. General Brock has positioned over a thousand men at Fort George. We are allied with the Mohawk chiefs John Norton and John Brant. Our numbers are strong. Mark my words. I shall return to you in no time and we'll make our engagement public. I'll speak to your father. Surely, he'll see sense.

Ann began to cry. Oh, how her tears destroyed him! James begged her to be strong. She twitched in his arms, and her eyes grew wide with fear. Then his beloved bunched her hands up in the fabric of his coatee, so much so that one of its buttons fell off in her hand.

Although he kept his uniform pristine, he couldn't bear to pry it from her hand. Besides, there was no time to mend it.

Come back to me, James. I will not rest until you come back to me. I swear it.

I will always come for you, my darling Ann, whether in this life or the next. I am yours, and you are mine, and no one shall ever part us.

Another kiss, and he sent her back to her house, where she would be safe.

He would fight to the death to keep her safe.

He'd left his horse tied up just over the ridge, by the sycamore trees. As he walked away from Ann, lost in her rosy scent and the memory of her soft hands on his skin, he never noticed the man who approached him from behind. He didn't hear the *whoosh* of the club until it was too late to react.

All James knew was an exploding pain and a crushing, unending darkness.

But now, he saw everything, and he showed it to the Darke sisters.

He allowed them to see the smirk on the man's face as he hit him once he was down. He showed them how the scoundrel ran back to the willow tree, to make sure Ann had disappeared. And he made them watch as the villain dragged his body to the place where he and Ann had made love so many times.

Before the sun ever arose on the morning of October thirteenth, 1812, the fateful day of the Battle of Queenston Heights, Captain James Kingston lay dead and buried under the old willow, just a few yards away from Ann's family home.

The last thing he showed them was the cruel snarl on the man's face as he walked away. He opened their ears to the sound of his laughter.

There's nothing stopping me from finding a home between the pretty legs of Ann Forbes now. You'll be Mrs. Perry soon enough, my dear Ann, and your father's business will be mine. Just you wait and see.

James appeared to Edwina and Adelaide as he'd been when he took his last breath, battered and bloodied and defeated.

I'm still here, under the willow. Find me.

A swirling haze surrounded his figure, and he disappeared from Edwina's sight.

With a gasp, she opened her eyes and turned to her sister.

"You saw it too?" asked Adelaide.

"I saw everything. James wasn't a deserter at all." Edwina bent down and scratched her fingers through the dirt. "He's here, Addy. I can feel him."

"Yeah." Adelaide nodded. "And we have to bring him home."

Chapter Fifteen

When Edwina returned with Adelaide, her face was pale and drawn. She flew to Simon as soon as she saw him.

"Hey," he murmured into her hair, "What's up?"

"He's here. James. In the ravine, behind the house."

Simon didn't respond. He wasn't sure what to say, so he just held her.

She turned her face toward him, her eyes filled with a vulnerability he'd never seen in them before. "Can I stay with you tonight?"

"Of course."

Connie and her sisters left shortly afterward. Edwina was shaking, and he wasn't sure how to calm her. He was just about to ask her what she needed from him, when she made it abundantly clear.

She grabbed his hand, pulled him into his room, and began to tug at her clothing. "I need you."

"Are you sure? I know you saw some terrible things tonight."

"That's why I need you." She let her shirt drop to the floor and dispensed with her bra just as easily.

Simon didn't hesitate after that. An unusual energy crackled between them, a new understanding of the frailty of life. He met her kiss for kiss, and touch for touch. Somehow, even though she was the one who'd borne witness to Kingston's murder, he felt changed too and he was desperate for a physical connection as well.

Only it wasn't just physical. It never was with Edwina.

Their bodies came together in a hot crush. He tried to slow things down, to leisurely worship her body, but that wasn't what she wanted.

"Please," she whispered. "I want to feel you inside me."

He couldn't deny her that, or anything else for that matter. He fished a condom out of his drawer and rolled it on in record time. As he filled her, thrusting deep and slow, he realized it was exactly what he needed too.

Simon had left the window open, and a summer breeze drifted through it, cooling them. Cuddling in his bed later, their chests and foreheads still touched with perspiration, they lay still and watched the curtain move. He stroked her hair until they both fell asleep.

Thankfully, the spirits stayed away. Although Simon knew he would have fought any demon that tried to disturb Edwina now.

* * * *

The others returned early the next morning. Although the weather had been bright and beautiful the last couple of weeks, clouds now gathered in the sky. The weather report threatened rain, but not enough to set them off their task. No one wanted to wait another day. It was time to act.

It was time to recover the ill-fated captain.

Simon wasn't sure at first. "Shouldn't we be calling the police?"

"There's no use in doing that yet." Adelaide's jaw was set. "They'll want evidence, not a psychic medium's word. I've worked with a couple of police departments before, and if I've learned anything about it, it's that they're not quick to believe someone like me. They'd laugh us out of the station if we showed up with nothing more than a ghost story."

"You and Connie are the business owners, Simon," said Susannah. "Fortunately for us, the area around the willow tree, while part of the ravine, still falls within your property line." One corner of her mouth quirked up in a sly smile. "And there's no reason you can't do a little digging on your own property."

Connie's dark eyes were lit with an inner fire. "Let's do it, Simon. If anyone asks, we were gardening."

"Right." Simon glanced out of the window at the darkening sky. "Gardening in the rain."

"It's not raining yet." Edwina touched his shoulder. "Look, if all goes well and we find something, of course we'll call the cops, and it won't stop there. If we find remains, the medical examiner will have to investigate for foul play. The Registrar of Cemeteries will need to determine if this area was part of an old burial ground, possibly an Indigenous one. And, of course, they'll need an archaeologist."

"Because of who James was," Adelaide added, "we might even need to involve someone at Fort George eventually. Oh, and we should keep Martha posted too. It's only right."

"I want you both to be prepared," said Edwina. "It's entirely possible that when the media gets a whiff of this, we might end up with a circus on our hands. If you prefer, we don't have to do anything more. As far as I'm concerned, *we* know what happened to James Kingston. I just don't know if it will be enough for Ann." Her voice broke on the last couple of words.

Simon pulled her in for a quick embrace. He knew a hug wouldn't change the fact that this was an outlandish situation, but if he could help Edwina feel even a bit better, he would. "Like Connie said, let's do this. We can't leave him there."

They gathered up the shovels they kept in the garage. They only had a couple, but they brought out some smaller gardening implements as well. They brought flashlights, in case the weather worsened and it got too dark to see in the ravine. At least, with the weather being what it was, they wouldn't have any nosy neighbors prying into their business. Thankfully, no other homes in the vicinity overlooked that part of the ravine.

Adelaide and Edwina conferred and mapped out where they believed Kingston's body lay. Using large rocks, they marked out a rough boundary.

His arms wobbly with nerves, Simon began to dig. It was hard getting through the first layer of soil, thanks to a sprawling patchwork of willow roots. Luckily, the root system was shallower than he expected. Working up a sweat, he dug past it.

When his breath started to come heavily, the others took turns with the shovels. Before long, a trench had been dug. They went slowly, so as not to damage any remains.

Once they were a few feet down, Adelaide got into the trench. Touching her pendant, she turned slowly around in the hole. "Help me, Maria. Show me where James is." She stared at the earth, as if she were trying to see through it. She then brushed her hand along one side of the trench. "Here. We should dig here."

"Let me." Simon helped Adelaide out and got back in the hole. Using one of the smaller implements, he scratched at the soil. He used smaller motions, not wanting to disturb anything. Bit by bit, he peeled away the layers of earth and time.

Until his tool met with something hard. "I've hit something."

"Can you dig around it?" asked Edwina.

The women drew closer, getting on their knees around the hole.

Simon continued gently digging until he'd removed all the soil around the hard item.

It was a skull. It was facing downward and still seemed to be connected to what he assumed were neck bones.

Even with his rudimentary knowledge of anatomy, Simon could see the fracture in the back of the skull would have been enough to kill the person.

"Oh, my stars," Connie exclaimed.

We've got him. Simon's head spun, as if someone had just tried to clobber him. He touched the skull. "Hello, Captain Kingston."

The others started discussing next steps, but Simon barely heard them. He just ran his finger over the bones, unable to process what was happening. He watched from his vantage point, in a daze. In a way, he felt a lot like the ghost of Ann Forbes, lingering in the hallways, observing the action but not capable of participating.

The most horrible feeling insinuated itself into his core. Fleeting images from his own life passed before his eyes, all of them disjointed and startling.

If it hadn't been for the Darkes, no one might ever know about Captain Kingston's demise. He would have remained in the ground, possibly forever, and Ann would have continued to suffer in her realm.

Was she watching now? Could she see that they'd found him?

Was she free?

Out of nowhere, it occurred to Simon that he hadn't heard from his brother, or his parents, since giving Rupert the old heave-ho. Not one of them had called to say, "Hey, Simon. Are you okay? Want to talk about what just happened?"

He'd been cast aside. Forgotten, like poor James Kingston in his hole.

If he walked outside right now and got hit by a bus, would any of his family members even bat an eye?

A few minutes later, he managed to rouse himself from his stupor. He climbed out of the trench, not wanting to be there anymore. As the Darkes continued their discussion, he stood back.

He must have looked like a sad sack, because Connie brought him a coffee.

Funny. He hadn't even noticed her going back into the house.

She patted his arm after handing it to him. "Here. Drink. You were looking extra pasty so I put a little something in it."

He took a sip. *Ah, sweet alcohol.* "You're a good friend."

"Just good? I think I'm in the top tier."

He choked on a laugh. His throat began to sting, and it had nothing to do with the strong beverage. "You're definitely tops, Connie. You're my best friend."

"Oh." She got misty too. She waved her hands in front of her eyes. "You too, Simon. Now, drink your spiked coffee."

As she went off to see if anyone else wanted a coffee, Edwina joined him. "Susannah's calling the police. Are you okay?"

"Yeah. Have a sip of this. Connie put the good stuff in it."

She took a sip and sighed. "That hits the spot." She set the mug down on a dead tree trunk, wrapped her arms around his middle and rested her head in the crook of his neck.

Although Simon had been taught to hide his feelings, he knew that was no longer an option. Recent events made him want to share everything about himself with Edwina, even the gnarly, nasty parts and the scared, confused parts. "Can I ask you something? It's going to sound weird."

"I bet it won't."

"If I got murdered and ended up like our friend over there, would you haunt the place until they found my body?"

She pulled away so she could look at him. Her gaze softened with understanding. "Simon, I would be your fucking avenging angel. I would haunt the place so hard the rafters would shake and every doorknob would rattle."

And just like that, the scratchy ball in Simon's throat began to disintegrate. He'd probably always bear the scars of his upbringing and a shitty sibling relationship. But, as he looked around this yard, and as he held the woman he was growing to love, he knew he had family. There were people here who loved him, people who cared about what might happen to him. People who would miss him one day.

Maybe he wasn't alone after all.

Chapter Sixteen

It all came home for Edwina when the yellow emergency tape went up around the yard. It was around that time that a pit of anxiety formed under her ribs. As the day progressed, it hardened, digging into her sides.

They'd really found a dead man on Connie and Simon's property.

Of course, they were in Niagara-on-the-Lake. There was a good chance someone had died on every square foot of the town. Still, they had confirmation now. Despite having seen James's murder herself, a part of Edwina had been hoping they'd been mistaken.

The police had responded quickly to their call. Apparently, it wasn't unusual for Niagara residents to stumble upon old bones. In fact, there had been a recent construction project that had unearthed the remains of several American soldiers from the 1812 era. Once their remains had been examined, they'd been given a military funeral and had since been repatriated.

Edwina had read about the event and recalled several Canadians had been in attendance, wanting to pay respects to the fallen men.

People tended to feel strongly about bringing their heroes home.

So, despite their peculiar story, the local police department hadn't actually treated them like pariahs.

That didn't mean the detective in charge was above shooting them the odd suspicious glance as his team continued with uncovering the remains.

"Quite the coincidence," mused Detective Emery, "that you folks had been conducting a ghost hunt on the property. You suspect there might be a body on the premises, and voila! You find one, and a possible military figure from the War of 1812, no less."

"Yup," said Simon. "That's how it happened."

"Look, Detective." Susannah sighed. "We called as soon as we found the first bone. I mean, I suppose we could have kept going, but it's my understanding that improper interference with human remains is an indictable offense under section 182 of the Criminal Code."

The detective peered at her. "What are you, a lawyer?"

"We're just trying to do the right thing," said Susannah.

"You should have called as soon as you suspected there might be remains," Detective Emery countered.

"Oh, really?" said Adelaide. "And you're telling us you would have been happy to come, on the *off chance* there might be a body?"

He remained silent.

"I think," said Adelaide, "we can call it a happy accident. And once those bones are examined, and our theories are proven, there's going to be a bit of a fuss. I'll share something with you, Detective. Major-General Isaac Brock and his other aide, Lieutenant Colonel John Macdonell, both perished at the Battle of Queenston Heights. They got a flashy dual funeral that was attended by thousands of Upper Canadians. Their caskets were carried through lines of militia and Indigenous soldiers. Cannon boomed every minute during the procession. Even the Americans fired a salute, out of respect."

She paused for effect. "Captain James Kingston would have fought with them at Queenston Heights. If he had fallen there, he might be buried at the Brock Monument alongside them now. But he didn't get that. A villain ambushed him from behind, smashing open his skull, then dumped him under a tree. Captain Kingston was a man who offered his services to our country, a man who fought side by side with figures of national importance, figures who are revered today because of the way they bolstered a young country's sense of nationhood. We wanted to be respectful of his legacy and of his family, and that's why we called you."

Although a new respect warmed his eyes, he bristled. "It'll take some time to prove his identity. We might never make a positive ID."

"We understand," said Adelaide. "But it's better than having him rot away under that tree. He deserves dignity, the dignity he wasn't afforded at the time of his death."

Grumbling, Detective Emery went to check on the work.

"That was a pretty speech, Addy," said Susannah. "Nice touch, by the way, with the details on Brock and Macdonell's funeral. That funeral was a huge event in

Upper Canada and it rallied the people as nothing else ever had. Only, I don't remember sharing it with you."

"You didn't. I just know."

For the first time, Edwina regarded her sister's talents, and her own, with something other than fear. Maybe it wouldn't be so horrible to have a special sort of sight.

Maybe one day, she'd be able to help people like Addy did. She might be able to put people's minds at ease about the ones they'd lost.

She still wasn't sure it was "a gift," but whatever it was, it had been given to her to use wisely.

She prayed she'd know how to do so when the moment arose.

Edwina watched as the officers arranged a tarp around the grave. It was all still so surreal. An actual body, and she'd seen it first. The image of a bloodied Captain Kingston still lingered at the back of her mind. He'd been so young, so earnest. So in love, and ready to do his duty.

Now, he was nothing more than bones.

All of a sudden, it became hard to catch a breath. She bent over at the waist and grabbed her knees. *Hang in there.*

Simon was behind her in a flash. "Hey, you."

She was spiraling. She felt her control slipping away, sliding into nothingness.

Simon rubbed her back. "Ed? You okay?"

"A body. We found a body."

"I know, sweetheart. Breathe. It's going to be okay."

"Is it? We don't know that. What if nothing changes? What if Ann is still stuck here? What if I have to see all these terrifying murders the rest of my life, and it doesn't accomplish anything?" Her breakfast twisted in her belly, churning into acid. When she opened her mouth, a noise of distress emerged. She darted away from Simon and hurried over to one of the bushes. All at once, she began to vomit.

He raced over to her and held her hair back. "I've got you."

Once the final spasm died down, she reached into her pants pocket for a tissue, and wiped her mouth. She then fell into Simon's embrace. "I'm glad we found him, I am."

"I am too."

"But I wanted to be wrong."

* * * *

The rain never did fall, and the activity at the King Street Bed and Breakfast proved to be a source of excitement and speculation for Simon's nearest neighbors as they ventured out of their houses.

At one point, after talking to officers for a good hour or so, Simon went outside for some fresh air. It wasn't long before he heard the familiar click of men's dress shoes half a block away.

Bernard Granger approached.

Bernard was a fixture in the neighborhood. An old theater man who'd spent much of his career at Niagara-on-the-Lake's Shaw Festival, he was beloved in the area. He walked up and down King Street every day, like a modern-day dandy. A tall Black man, he always wore a bright red beret, one that complemented his dark complexion. He clutched a polished walking stick and sported shimmery eyeglasses that Elton John would have coveted. At his side was his dog, Maggie, a black terrier who, in Bernard's own words, "loves people who give her treats but hates other dogs." She could often be seen snapping at other people's canines from across the street. Although Bernard would admonish her, Simon had always gotten the sense he was secretly proud.

As Bernard sidled up to Simon, Maggie strained on the leash. Simon had snuck her some kibble in the past, so he was on her list of cool people.

He bent down to pat the dog. "Sorry, Mags. I wasn't ready for you this time."

"Simon, what on earth is going on?" asked Bernard. "Hazel Patterson called and asked me if I'd seen the police cars, so I thought I ought to hurry over and offer my support."

"Thanks, Bernard."

"Did you kill someone, dear boy? If it was Mabel Cummings from down the road, I'll back you up and provide you with an alibi. Anyone in the neighborhood would swear she had it coming. She never picks up after that beastly thing she calls a pet. Poor Maggie trod in that creature's excrement just the other day. I had a few words for Mabel, let me tell you."

Maggie growled, clearly just as offended as Bernard.

Bernard stroked Maggie's back. "I know, my precious. That yappy little thing isn't nearly as well-behaved and beautiful as you are." He looked back up at Simon, intent on receiving an explanation.

"No, I didn't kill anyone, but we may have found some 1812 bones on the site."

"Ah. Is that it? We probably all have a few of those in our backyards. Well, at least it's good to know we don't have a serial killer in our midst. Ha! Not that I would have believed it of you, my dear boy."

"I appreciate that."

Edwina chose that moment to join Simon on the sidewalk, but she stopped short a few feet away from them. "Oh my goodness. Bernard Granger?"

Bernard beamed and bent at the waist in a courtly bow. He loved being recognized. "I'm afraid so, and in all my glory. Have we met, my lovely?"

"No, I'm just a huge fan," Edwina gushed. "I saw your *Lear* a few years back. It was the best performance I've ever seen. Like, life changing."

"Aren't you a dear? Thank you, kindly. I would never compare myself to a McKellen or a Gielgud, of course, but the *Toronto Star* did call the performance 'a dazzling swan song.' Alas, my days of treading the boards are over, but I still manage to make a nuisance of myself on the Shaw Festival Board of Governors. It keeps me young and active." Bernard sighed and tugged Maggie's leash. The terrier had begun to growl because someone had dared to walk a German Shepherd across the street. "Simon, where on earth have you been hiding this delightful creature?"

Simon did the introductions and hung back as Edwina and Bernard talked theater for a few minutes. It was a blessed distraction from the gruesome business in his yard.

Although Bernard loved recounting his own exploits, he was gracious and asked Edwina about her experiences as a theater tech. She gave him a quick rundown of some of the shows she'd done.

Bernard arched an eyebrow. "Well, young lady, if you ever decide you'd like to work at the Shaw, give me a call." He reached into his pocket and handed her a business card. "You strike me as a go-getter, just the sort of person we like. If you're interested, I could get you in there like that." He snapped his manicured fingers.

"Thank you." She glanced at Simon. "I'll keep that in mind."

"Come now, Maggie," said Bernard, as he proceeded down the street. He called out to them in the booming voice of a classically trained actor, "Good luck with the dead body, Simon! Call me if things go pear-shaped, and you need a character reference. Ha ha ha!" Within seconds, Maggie was pulling him toward the German Shepherd.

"Bernard freaking Granger. Incredible." Edwina shook her head. "Did you know that Derek Jacobi called him the greatest Shakespearean actor of his generation?"

"I didn't know that. It was very nice of him to give you his card. He's a good egg, and I will always appreciate him trying to lure you to Niagara-on-the-Lake."

Grinning, she grabbed his arm and they headed back to the house.

The medical examiner arrived and, after conducting an *in situ* examination, was able to attest that the remains were not recent ones. However, more work needed to be done, and it would take some time.

That night, Simon went back with Edwina to her hotel room. It had been a long day and he was weary. By the way she slowly dragged her ponytail elastic out of her hair, looking past herself in the mirror, he could tell she was still feeling the effects too.

Simon dropped onto the bed. "I hope she knows. Ann, I mean."

"I hope so too. I didn't feel her presence anywhere today."

"Look at you," he teased. "Talking like your sister now."

She didn't crack a smile. He knew Edwina was still grappling with her newfound mediumship, but she seemed more resolved now, if not quite at peace with it.

"It must have been rough to see James die."

She gave him the side-eye. "You really believe me, huh?"

"Yeah." Implicitly. Old skeptical Simon was gone. New Simon had seen things. He didn't understand any of them, but he trusted in Edwina.

"Thank you. It's hard for me to accept that anyone will believe what I say going forward."

He grabbed her hand. "Ed, you don't need to tell the world, not if you don't want to. This is *your* journey. No one's saying you need to drop everything and start taking clients, like Addy does. You'll figure out how this fits into your life, and until you do, the only one you need to listen to is yourself. You'll come up with a plan soon enough."

"A plan, huh? We'll see." Finally, the corners of her lips turned up. "It was cool talking to your pal Bernard today. I still can't believe he basically offered me a job at the Shaw Festival."

Simon asked the question that had been plaguing him ever since they spoke to Bernard. "Is that something you might consider one day?"

"I've always wanted to work for the Shaw. The opportunity's just never come up."

It would mean she'd have to stay in Niagara-on-the-Lake, at least for the theater season. That ran for about half the year.

They could be together.

"Of course," she said, her voice quiet, "I'd need a place to stay."

"You always have a place with me. I hope you know that." This relationship was still so new, and he didn't want to overwhelm her. "I mean, if that's something you want."

"Would it be something you want?"

"Hell, yeah."

"Good to know."

He grinned. "So, you're thinking of keeping me around, after this investigation is done?"

"I'd...like that." Her dark eyes shone with warmth, but the stiffness of her posture betrayed her fear.

Admissions like this were obviously hard for her. He needed to lay it all out there. "I want to be clear with you. I like you, Edwina. I like you a lot. Actually, I like you so much it's a little scary. It wakes me up at night, because I don't want to miss a moment when I could be thinking about you. But it's a good fear. It tells me this is important, that what we have is important. It tells me that...I'm falling for you."

Her lips parted.

"So, yeah. I would really love it if you kept me around."

"I don't know what to say."

"You don't have to say anything right now. The details will tumble into place when we need them to." Simon took the plunge, hoping she would open up. "I know you've been hurt before. I'd understand if you want to move slowly. I won't pressure you."

She got up and began to pace in front of him. She brought her hand to her chest and rubbed it, as if it were sore.

It broke his heart to see her so close to shattering.

"Ed," Simon said softly. "What did he do to you?"

She stopped pacing and looked at him, gnawing on her bottom lip.

"You can tell me."

She sat back down and took his hand. "Declan never hit me, in case you're worried about that. That sort of abuse was never his style. But he did abuse me emotionally. I understand that now."

She paused, and Simon waited for her to share her feelings in her own time. Even though he felt like punching another wall as he considered all the ways this Declan character might have hurt her, he resisted.

"I met him through work. He's a tenor and we were working on the same musical theater production. He was the leading man, and I was doing the effects. It started out with some flirting, but I didn't take it too seriously because he flirted with everyone. Still, on some level, I was flattered and I allowed it to continue." She laughed quietly. "Looking back now, I realize I let him get away with so much more than any other person I'd ever dated. I'm still not really sure why."

Simon understood. In hindsight, he'd suspected something might be happening between Carly and Rupert, but had talked himself out of it a few times. He wasn't sure why he didn't call it out as soon as he noticed it. Maybe it was just easier to let it all fall to pieces.

"I never dated the performers I'd meet through work," continued Edwina. "I mean, I have a lot of friends in the acting community, and they'd be the first ones to warn me away from some of their buddies and their egos. But somehow, I found myself breaking a lot of rules for Declan."

"What happened?"

"I had just lost a friend, someone who'd been sick for a while, and I guess I was hurting. I think he saw that in me. He was really enthusiastic and attentive at the start. Flowers, messages, romantic dinners, all that jazz. But, little by little, he withdrew, and I found myself getting needier and needier for his attention. Then it hit me. He was doing it on purpose. He went from one hundred percent to only feeding me bits of himself. I think it was always his plan to keep me on my toes, to keep me hanging on an invitation or a scrap of genuine emotion. Every time I mentioned taking things to the next level, any time I asked him to open up, he withdrew. Suddenly, he'd forget to call back. He'd become very busy and unable to see me, but couldn't tell me why. I'd see him at work, having hushed conversations with women in the cast. You know, huddling in dark corners. When I questioned him, he'd say something like, 'Oh, her? We were just going over our blocking. Don't you trust me, babe?'"

"So, he was a gaslighter," said Simon.

"Yeah. I started doubting myself. Every so often, he'd throw me a bone and a lot of pretty words, we'd have sex and he'd become distant again. I ended up in this horrible cycle of feeling treasured for all of five minutes then lonely for weeks. He didn't want to tell anyone at work that we were dating, and now I understand why. I'm sure he was cheating on me. It went on for months, and I didn't even recognize myself at the end. I'd always been so strong, and I ended up being this miserable creature who was desperate for approval."

"I don't think your feelings were unusual. Anyone in your place would have felt the same way."

"I don't know. I've always been able to recognize a player, and when I met Declan, I knew I was looking at a professional level player. But something about him kept me coming back. I *let* him treat me like a used rag. I'm still not sure why all my defenses failed, but whatever it was, it messed me up. And the worst part was I allowed him to see how he devastated me. I let him see my weakness in all its blubbering, snotty glory. Of course, being an asshole, he loved that."

"I'm sorry that's how he made you feel."

"Thanks."

"No, really. Ed, you can't blame yourself for reacting to a situation that Declan created. He obviously saw you were vulnerable and he used that. Just because you reacted a certain way, doesn't make him any less of an asshole. And for the record, I would consider it an honor to see you in all your blubbering, snotty glory, because it would mean you trust me."

"I do trust you."

"And I would never betray your trust."

She smiled.

"By the way," said Simon, "the Edwina I know is a bold, brilliant person."

"Thanks. It took me a while to find her again. Declan almost destroyed that in me."

"The guy's a jerk."

"When I broke it off, he showed no emotion at all. He was completely indifferent. That's when I knew I'd dodged a bullet. But it took me at least a year to get back in the game. To be honest, I've only had a couple of casual dates since then. I haven't let myself get too close to anyone else. Well, until you."

"You were protecting yourself." Simon lay back on the bed and pulled her down with him. He drew her into his arms. "I'm sorry for what he did to you. I don't expect you to just take me at my word when I say I would never hurt you, but I hope you'll give me the chance to prove it to you."

Her hushed tone gave him hope. "That's the weird thing about you and me. I expect others to lie and cheat. I know I put up walls, but with you, I want to tear them all down. I realize we haven't known each other long, but I already know you would never hurt me."

He ran his hand over her hip. "I wouldn't dream of it. For the first time in a long time, I just want to look forward, and I want to do it with you."

"Oh, Simon." His name sounded so soft and special on her lips. "I'm falling for you too."

He drew in a deep breath. "That's amazing. I'm really glad to hear it."

"Yeah?" She spread her legs and urged him to settle between them. "How glad exactly?"

Simon brushed his lips against her neck, drinking in the scent of her cinnamon perfume. "On a one-to-ten scale of gladness, it's at least a nine."

"Only a nine?" Edwina ran her hands toward his ass, pressing him close to her body. "What can I possibly do to inspire a ten?"

"I have a couple of ideas, but frankly, to achieve them, we'd need to take all your clothes off. Is that doable?"

"I think that's doable."

God, she was awesome. He was losing control around this woman, and it was the best thing he'd ever experienced. Her honesty made him want to dare. Her smile made him want to sing. She inspired a rollercoaster of emotion in him, but it was the best ride he'd ever been on, and he didn't want to get off.

At the same time, Simon felt a new certainty, a sense of peace. He was envisioning an amazing future for the two of them. Knowing she felt it too made him downright giddy.

Simon gazed at her, rapt, and traced the arch of her eyebrow. He was going to do his best to make Edwina very happy, and to make every moment with her a memorable one. With that in mind, he lowered his head and claimed her lips.

Chapter Seventeen

Three weeks later

A wonderful nostalgia blossomed inside Edwina as they entered the King Street house again. The Darkes had left Niagara-on-the-Lake shortly after finding Kingston's body to wrap up the investigation and allow Simon and Connie to get back to normal. Although Edwina had been in contact with Simon on a near-constant basis, it hadn't been the same as being in the same room as him.

Coming back here felt a lot like coming home.

There were a few hugs between her sisters and Simon, and when Edwina hugged him, it was decidedly less chaste. He smelled so good, and she loved being enfolded in his arms.

After a quick catchup, they went to the parlor. "How's Connie?" asked Edwina, as they all took their seats. "Hopefully enjoying her vacation with Margie." Because of all the activity in the house, Connie had put off going on a short trip with her wife, but she and Margie had decided to finally take a long weekend away in Montreal.

"I haven't heard from her," said Simon, "so they must be having fun."

Edwina handed him a folder of all the relevant documents they'd collected since they started investigating the house, items of interest surrounding it and its history. "Well, as you know, we're here to give you a debrief. I know you've been involved every step of the way, but we do them for all our clients."

"Think of it as a bit of closure," said Susannah.

"I like closure, especially if it means no more ghosts." He glanced over his shoulder. "Isn't Addy going to join us?"

The same Addy who'd slipped away and was currently wandering around the bed and breakfast on her own? Edwina wasn't sure what more her sister needed to see, but it was annoying her. She should be here with them. "I'm sure she'll be back shortly."

Susannah clicked the laptop keyboard and proceeded to play the video they'd prepared for Simon. "Of course, much of this footage will appear in our YouTube episode, but we wanted you to have a copy of all the anomalies, including the stuff that might get cut."

Together, they skimmed the footage as Susannah went over the highlights, but Edwina watched Simon.

God, she missed him.

Of course, they hadn't ended their relationship. They were simply doing the long-distance thing for now. It wasn't horrible. Most of the time, they talked late into the night. If anything, it had been nice not having to spend their time chasing ghosts.

That didn't mean she didn't want to see his face and run her fingers through his hair. She wanted to sit down with him at the end of the day and ask him how things were. She wanted to talk about goals and dreams and see whether theirs aligned. She just wanted to be with him, period.

Over the course of those few weeks, Toronto had started to feel somewhat foreign. Her nerves had gotten the best of her a few times, and she'd had to remind herself that plenty of people did long-distance relationships.

She never had, though.

A part of her worried that, now that they no longer had a haunted house to bind them, she and Simon would drift apart. Even though Niagara-on-the-Lake was only about an hour and a half's drive from her place, it was still a distance. They were making the best of it, but would they grow weary of it after a time?

Still, it wasn't as if she could have hung out at his place forever. With all the hype from the investigation, Simon and Connie were now fielding calls from interested tourists. Since Edwina had posted their teasers on YouTube, people from all over North America had been wanting to reserve a stay at the King Street Bed and Breakfast. It definitely attracted the ghost enthusiasts, but they were also getting messages from history lovers, true crime buffs and regular tourists who'd happened upon the footage.

Either way, they needed to recoup their losses, and it wouldn't be fair for her to hang around and get in the way. Besides, she had her own work to do. In fact, she'd already started working with a small theater company on their lighting. It was nothing challenging, but it was a bit of extra cash.

More than once, she'd considered calling Bernard Granger, to see if he could wrangle her an interview with the Shaw Festival.

But that would mean upending her entire life. Did she want that?

She still wasn't sure.

But she did want Simon.

Take it one day at a time. You'll figure it out.

In the days after Captain Kingston's body was discovered, the authorities had launched a full-scale investigation of their own. Some bigwig archaeologist from the Royal Ontario Museum had swooped in and taken over. Edwina, fighting a surprising streak of possessiveness, had been hesitant to hand over the remains to a total stranger. She regarded Ann and James as her babies, in a weird way. She knew James was in good hands, however.

There had been an exciting development. In the grave, the archaeology team had found a series of buttons, ones that matched the 49th Regiment coatee button that DPI had discovered at the bed and breakfast. They were currently being examined and compared with Simon's button.

If the numbers added up, and they could prove they came from the same garment, it would be another step closer to confirming James's identity.

It also was a nice piece of validation, in a field that often provided little of the sort. Not that Edwina needed any additional proof. She'd already seen everything she needed to see.

"Watching this footage," said Simon, "I almost can't believe it's the same property. It's been so quiet."

From the moment Captain Kingston's remains were recovered, the atmosphere around the bed and breakfast had apparently lightened. Simon and Connie were thrilled.

There was only one problem. Edwina didn't trust the quiet.

Perhaps her skeptical side wasn't dead, after all. Something told her the spirits at the King Street house weren't done with them yet.

Shortly after finding the remains, Edwina had tried reaching out to Ann Forbes several times to make sure the spirit woman knew her beloved James had been found. She had also tried to contact Reginald Perry.

Neither had responded.

For a house that had absolutely rumbled with activity since they'd arrived, the relative peacefulness struck Edwina as suspicious. For all intents and purposes, it seemed their ghosts had nothing more to communicate. Edwina wanted to be hopeful, to believe they had allowed the spirits to move on, but it just didn't ring true.

Instinctively, she knew they hadn't heard the last from either one of them, and it kept her up at night. She hated the thought that Ann might still somehow be tied to the house. If finding James wasn't enough to move her onto the next plane, what would do the job? As for Reginald Perry, she worried that he might still be lurking in the shadows too.

Simon, on the other hand, appreciated the newfound tranquility and was happy with the results. He said he and Connie had both noticed a change in the vibe, and they felt more at ease doing their work.

"Maybe the ghosts had no other reason to stick around," he said.

"Maybe. Let's hope so." Susannah hummed. "There's just one thing bothering me. We found

Kingston, we've learned about his engagement to Ann, and we can safely assume he was murdered here. Aside from what Ed and Addy saw, we have no proof that Reginald Perry was the killer. There are no records of his death, not in Canada, nor in the States. I can't find anything that tells me what happened to him."

"Ann wanted him punished," said Edwina. "How on earth are we supposed to do that?"

Simon crossed his arms. "In other words, you don't believe this place is actually in the clear?"

"I'm cautiously optimistic," said Edwina. "Maybe, in time, we'll know for sure."

In truth, she didn't buy it at all, but she didn't want to upset Simon. He had enough on his mind, trying to get the place up and running again.

Even though the activity had died down, for her, the house still pulsated with a peculiar energy. It might not be something that Simon or Connie could perceive, but it was there all the same. As tangible to Edwina as the billiards table in the parlor, or the linens on the beds.

It shimmered in her peripheral vision, like a stray sunbeam reflected in a mirror. It moved like a shadow, there one moment, then gone as the clouds appeared.

It waited.

Adelaide was still acting weird and detached. Any time Edwina caught her talking to herself, she tried to use her new talents to see what Adelaide was seeing. It didn't work. Her sister's abilities were much stronger, and it appeared there were things Adelaide just didn't want them to know.

The phone rang at the reception desk, and Simon excused himself to answer it.

Susannah frowned. "I'm going to go find Addy. We've done all we can here. She really shouldn't still be wandering around the place at this stage of the game."

"What's up with her anyway?" Edwina asked.

"You mean, the way she scurries off at odd moments and avoids certain questions?"

"Yeah, that. Do you think we should be concerned?"

"I hope not," said Susannah. "Addy's never been one to take foolish chances. Still, we should be on our guard. What about you?" She waggled her fingertips in a fake spell, like some cheesy fortune teller in the movies. "Can you see anything with your new superpowers?"

"Superpowers, please," Edwina scoffed. "No, something still feels off here. I'll have to find a way to break it to Simon. He deserves to know." As much as Edwina tried to brush off her concerns, they itched like a bad rash.

Edwina had been working on honing her talents. Adelaide had taught her some meditations and Edwina was finding them helpful. It was in those peaceful moments that she learned to trust, that she opened herself up to the other voices whispering in her ear. She was learning that she could still be in charge of the process, and that just because she had the ability to hear and see those who'd passed, it didn't have to overwhelm her.

It wasn't as if someone had thrown her into a pit of vipers. She could control the noise.

It was a little like one of the lessons she'd learned in therapy, actually. If she carved out some time and invited the spirits to calmly speak to her when she was ready, they didn't tend to inundate her when she wasn't prepared. Just like how if she made time to discuss her emotions at set times in her therapist's office, those feelings didn't swarm her at other times.

Susannah went off to collect their sister. In the meantime, Simon returned, a mystified smile on his face. "Another reservation. Talk about feast or famine."

"I'm glad it's picking up, I really am."

"I hear a 'but' in there. Be honest with me."

"I don't know what it is I'm feeling right now," admitted Edwina. "A part of me thinks maybe this whole psychic medium thing is still too new. It's not as if I've ever sent anyone into the light before. That's Addy's department. I don't know enough about how it works. That being said, I wouldn't be surprised if some activity starts up again."

"Let's worry about that if it happens." He pulled her into his arms. "It's a good thing I happen to be in a relationship with a very sexy and talented ghost hunter, then."

"I want you to be careful, Simon. Keep your wits about you until I can visit again."

"I can visit you too."

"You'll be busy."

He touched her chin. "Hey. I'm not too busy for you. If all goes well, I might be able to hire someone to help out. Either way, we'll make it work. If our only issue is logistics, then we're doing fine." He frowned. "Unless this isn't about logistics at all."

"No, I want this. I want you. And you're right. We'll find a way to make it work. It's just all so new."

"I know. Tell you what, I'll come see you in Toronto soon, and we'll make a day of it. Breakfast, lunch, dinner." He nibbled her neck. "And dessert. Lots of dessert."

Edwina laughed. "Sounds like a plan. I'm already looking forward to it."

When Susannah arrived with Adelaide in tow, they pulled apart. "Now, now, love birds," said Susannah. "No need to act coy on our behalf."

"Ready to head out, Addy?" asked Edwina.

But Adelaide wasn't listening. Her gaze was trained on the floor. She gave her necklace a distracted tug.

"Addy." Edwina regretted the sharpness in her tone, but enough was enough. "Is there anything you want to add to the debrief?"

Adelaide approached Simon and grabbed his hand. "I've saged the house and done some prayers of protection. If anything feels wrong, call us right away." She gave him a hug.

Startled, Simon hesitated then patted her back. "Thanks, Addy. I'm sure we'll be fine."

They headed into the foyer. With a final glance down the hall, Adelaide walked outside. Susannah followed.

Edwina embraced Simon. She snuck her hands under his shirt, running them over the smooth muscles on his back. She took note of all the little details that made him feel so good, the stubble at his jaw, the soft press of his lips and his wonderful citrusy scent. She wished there was a way to keep that scent fresh in her mind, but she knew it would fade the moment she walked out of the door. For that reason, she buried her face in the crook of his neck and inhaled deeply. "Until the next time."

He kissed her forehead. "Until the next time." He angled his head and took her mouth in a passionate kiss that shot heat into her toes. "Thank you for everything. Call me when you get home, okay?"

"I will."

"Have a safe drive." He began to follow her outside, but the phone rang. He hesitated, but she didn't want to keep him from his work.

"Go," said Edwina. "I'm fine. Make lots of reservations."

He brushed his lips across her knuckles and raced off toward the office.

Edwina lingered for just a moment, relishing the deep timbre of his voice as he greeted the person on the phone. Then she headed out to her Jeep.

Adelaide sat in the back, while Susannah sat in the front passenger seat. Both of them were absorbed in their phones.

Edwina started up her Jeep and proceeded to make a three-point turn. As she backed up, she glanced over her shoulder to make sure no one was nearby. Her gaze landed on Simon's front porch.

A man stood there. He had pale skin and brown hair that was cut in a nondescript fashion. Both his woolen trousers and shirt bore dark, blotchy stains. Bloodstains.

He smirked.

A voice sounded in her head. *You can't run from me, Edwina.*

She slammed on the breaks.

"Whoa!" Susannah gripped the dashboard. "What's wrong?"

Edwina did a double take, but the man was gone. So was her ability to breathe. Her lungs had emptied out.

Susannah grabbed her arm. "Ed, are you okay? You're white."

Only then did Edwina manage a frazzled breath. "Yeah. I thought I saw something, but there's nothing there. Just my imagination, I guess." As her nerves settled back down, she let go of the brake.

She drove away from the bed and breakfast, rattled. After a few moments, she made eye contact with Adelaide in the rear-view mirror.

Her sister's haunted expression told her everything she needed to know.

Addy had seen it too.

Chapter Eighteen

"I'm sorry, but this is hard to accept. The things you have shown me today have shaken me to my core, and frankly, I think you're enjoying the fact that you've destroyed my entire world view. I'm not sure I can forgive you for this." Simon shoved his hands into his jacket pockets and marched down the park walkway.

"Ha!" Laughing, Edwina caught up to him, "I told you Scoops is the best ice-cream parlor in Toronto! We went to your favorite, albeit inferior, ice-cream place yesterday, and now we've gone to mine. After trying Scoops' Cherry Chocolate Explosion, you have to admit there's no contest." She waved the remnants of her cone under his nose.

Having already devoured his cone, Simon grabbed her hand and took a cheeky bite from hers.

"Hey!"

"That's what you get for shaking that thing in my face."

"Funny." She grinned. "You said the same thing last night."

Simon pulled her under the nearest tree for a Cherry Chocolate Explosion flavored smooch. "You were even more delicious. For the record, you can shake your ass in my face any time you want. In fact, I encourage it." He squeezed her butt cheeks to emphasize his point.

They made their way over to a park bench and sat. As Edwina took her time licking her ice-cream cone, Simon entertained some very dirty thoughts. Most of them involved her licking along the length of his naked body.

All in good time. They still had another evening before he had to get back to the bed and breakfast, and he planned to make her pay for winning their ice-cream contest. He was a sore loser when it came to sex and frozen dairy treats.

He put his arm around her and they sat quietly as she got to work, licking and nibbling the remainder of her Cherry Chocolate Explosion. Every so often, she'd dip that naughty tongue of hers into the cone to make him groan.

The leaves were just starting to change color, and the maples and oaks in the park were tinged in gold and orange. Between enjoying nature's display and Edwina's pornographic ice-cream display, he was having a great time. There was literally nothing better than having Edwina tucked up against him.

Things had been going well since she and her sisters had departed Niagara-on-the-Lake. Of course, he and Edwina had been back and forth a few times. Although she'd resumed her theater tech work, they'd found ways to see each other. Because weekends were tricky for both of them, they had to think outside the box, even if it meant he drove to Toronto on a Monday morning for a breakfast date. All in all, they'd been able to carve out chunks of time to be together.

Although, it was never enough. The moment she left, he missed her, and he spent a fair amount of his time planning out fun dates and adventures for the next time they could be together.

She was a quiet for a time and had stopped eating her ice cream.

"You're pensive," he said.

"Yeah. I'm just trying to find a way to tell you something. You won't like it."

A thousand scenarios charged through his brain, none of them good. Was she leaving him? Had he annoyed her to the point where she just couldn't take it anymore? Was she, God forbid, sick?

Settle down, you dork. "Whatever it is, you can tell me."

"I got this weird message on social media the other day."

His heart fell into his sneakers all over again. "Please tell me it wasn't from Gary69lover." Had the internet troll found another way to harass her?

"No." She grimaced. "It was from your brother."

"Fucking Rupert." Simon stood and stretched out his suddenly tense arms. It took all his fortitude not to punch the tree. It wasn't worth breaking his hand for Rupert. Besides, Edwina had already seen him lash out like that once, even if it was under the influence of a ghost. She never needed to see that again.

But how had Rupert learned Simon and Edwina were dating?

Wait.

There had been one text exchange that Simon had had with his mother, in which she'd admonished him for not being more supportive of his brother's impending nuptials. When she'd asked if he still carried a torch for Carly, Simon had let it slip that he was seeing someone. She'd peppered him with questions, so to get her off his back, he'd told her about Edwina.

Knowing what Rupert was like, Simon had asked his mom not to share that info. Once again, she'd disregarded his feelings altogether.

"Let me guess," said Simon. "He heard we were together, and wanted to reach out and say hello. You know, seeing as we're practically family."

"Yeah, actually. Those were pretty much his words."

"And if you respond, he'll continue the conversation. Then, after shooting you a few lighthearted messages, he'll suggest you meet for coffee, you know, to get better acquainted. No need to involve Simon and Carly, of course. A couple more messages, and he'll be sending you his very best dick pics, and encouraging you to send nudes." He plunked himself back on the bench. "So…did you respond?"

"Yeah," she admitted in a sheepish voice. "I mean, he's your brother. I could hardly ignore it."

Simon's temples began to throb. "Can I ask how it went?"

"Oh, sure." She proceeded to lick her ice cream again. "I told Rupert that I knew what a cheating scumbag he was, that I would be blocking him, and that he could go fuck himself. And I may have told him he could never tempt me because I already have the more desirable Teal brother in my bed." She looked into the final piece of her sugar cone. "Hey, look! One last cherry, right at the bottom." She popped the whole piece into her mouth, chewed and swallowed, then grinned from ear to ear.

Just like that, the pain in Simon's head eased. He wrapped his hand around the back of her neck and brought her face close to his. "Edwina Darke, you are the most amazing person I've ever known. I love you."

Her eyes misted but the gorgeous smile never left her face. "I love you too."

Simon had already come close to expressing it a couple of times, but had held back, not wanting to overwhelm her. Any time he got close to uttering the words, he'd reminded himself it was best to just take things slowly. For a while though, he had seen the same feelings reflected in her eyes, and it had become harder to wait.

No more waiting. Screw taking things slowly. He wanted to conquer the world with this woman, and he wanted it now.

"I know your family has been a source of incredible stress for you," she said, "and I hope you understand I will always have your back."

"And I'll have yours. Always and forever."

"You've made so much progress with your therapist. I would never dream of messing that up."

"Thanks, Ed. I feel guilty sometimes for cutting my family out, but I've come to realize I deserve better than a group of people who have no consideration for my feelings. You've shown me more empathy and caring in the time I've known you than they have my entire life."

She kissed him softly on the nose. "I'll be your family. And, if things change one day, and you decide you want to reconnect with them, I'll support you however you need it. But I thought it was important to establish right away with Rupert that I have his number. Oh, and that I'm capable of breaking his nose."

"You are capable of destroying him body and soul, but I'm still sorry you had to deal with that."

"I've dealt with far worse." Edwina hesitated. "Speaking of which, is everything still fine at the B&B?"

"Still no activity. Connie's happy. The guests are happy. If anything, some of them are disappointed they haven't seen any wee ghosties, but they'll get over it. It's been over a month now. I think DPI has truly done the job."

"That's…good. A nice surprise."

"I know that apparition on my front porch gave you a scare." Simon was careful in choosing his words. He didn't want to come off as patronizing. After all, he hadn't seen the dude. "Maybe, whatever it was, it's gone away too."

"Yeah. I'm sure that's the case."

Simon knew Edwina well enough now to know she wasn't convinced, but there really was no reason for her to worry. If Ann Forbes wasn't haunting the halls, surely that meant she'd passed on, right? To say nothing of the nasty sonofabitch who used to linger in the kitchen.

He sought out Edwina's sweet lips again. God, she was absolutely edible after eating that ice cream. They'd have to return to Scoops soon and try all the other flavors.

For the first time in a long time, hope bloomed in Simon's chest. He was looking forward these days, not looking over his shoulder.

And he planned to enjoy it as long as he had breath in his lungs.

Chapter Nineteen

"Ghost hunt leads to discovery of 1812 remains."
Niagara-on-the-Lake Gazette

It all began with a haunted bed and breakfast in Niagara-on-the-Lake, and an email request for help.

When the owners of the King Street Bed and Breakfast started to hear unusual tales from their customers, they scoffed at the idea that they might have paranormal origins. However, it didn't take long for co-owners Connie Willard and Simon Teal to realize their guests weren't just getting swept away in Niagara's colorful history. Even Teal, a self-confessed skeptic, had trouble disregarding the stories of shadow figures, disembodied voices and phantom hands pulling the covers off at night.

They reached out to Darke Paranormal Investigations. Run by investigators and YouTubers Edwina, Susannah and Adelaide Darke, DPI has an impressive record of capturing unusual anomalies on film. They had a theory about the King Street Bed and Breakfast. Not only was the property haunted by the daughter of its original owner, it was also the possible burial ground of an early Canadian war hero.

In the course of their ghost hunt, they happened upon human remains directly behind the property. Psychic medium Adelaide Darke believes them to be the remains of Captain James Kingston, one of Major-General Isaac Brock's aides.

Adelaide Darke claims to have communicated with the dead since she was a child. Some might doubt her methods, but others have taken a keen interest. DPI's findings also shed some light on what happened to Captain Kingston during the War of 1812. Despite being one of Brock's right-hand men, he disappears from contemporary accounts before the fateful Battle of Queenston Heights.

The claims were enough to incite the interest of local experts in history and forensics. Footage from DPI's YouTube channel was shared thousands of times on social media. Historians clamored for a look at the man who might very well have been an aide-de-camp to an early Canadian hero.

Frank Chambers, head of Archaeology at the Royal Ontario Museum, personally examined the remains. "After conducting an exhaustive array of testing," said Dr. Chambers, "I feel confident saying the remains in the grave are consistent with those of a man who would have lived a similar lifestyle to Captain Kingston's. It is also clear that the wound at the back of the skull is a result of blunt force trauma. Such a wound would most definitely have proven fatal."

Although no clothing survived with the bones, something else had. In the grave, a series of buttons were uncovered, ones that bore the distinctive 49 of the 49th Foot Regiment. These were Brock's men during the War of 1812, and it was Captain Kingston's regiment.

Bob Goodwin, an expert on military uniforms and a War of 1812 reenactor, was eager to examine the buttons. "These are absolutely the sort of buttons that would have appeared on a captain's coatee. One button, however, is missing."

In actuality, it might not be missing at all. During the investigation at the bed and breakfast, a lone button was discovered behind a piece of drywall. It too bears the number 49. The investigators of DPI believe it to be the outstanding button.

Edwina Darke explains. "We have seen documents that detailed a secret engagement between Captain Kingston and Miss Ann Forbes of Newark. The Forbes family were the original inhabitants of the home, and the button was clearly in her possession. It is my belief that Ann kept this button as a reminder of her lost love."

Which leaves us with a mystery.

If Captain James Kingston was indeed cut down before the Battle of Queenston Heights, who killed him, and why?

History bloggers are already putting forth theories, and with a good measure of indignation.

"War hero murdered and dumped?" read one blog.

"Bring Captain Kingston home!" demanded another.

One can understand the concern when one considers that Brock's other aide, Lieutenant Colonel John Macdonell, received a hero's farewell, as well as entombment alongside Brock. The very thought that

Captain Kingston might not have been honored in the same way has turned up a few noses.

This startling discovery may also have an impact on Captain Kingston's legacy and military record. Because he went missing before the battle, he was listed as a deserter. A petition has now been started by a local troupe of War of 1812 reenactors, one in which they've demanded the word "deserter" be stricken from Captain Kingston's name in all official records.

There is also the matter of giving him a proper burial.

Bob Goodwin agrees. "If we can prove this is indeed Captain Kingston, we need to give him proper recognition. The man fought for us. He's part of our history."

The War of 1812, while a devastating loss for the United States, created a sense of nationhood in Upper Canada. It was the last time the United States would attempt to threaten a British colony in North America.

Authorities have attempted to contact any possible descendants of Captain Kingston. Although he had a brother in England, it appears neither of the men had children, and the family line died out. However, a descendant of Ann Forbes still resides in Niagara-on-the-Lake. Martha Cook, also an amateur historian, has asked that he be buried with his fiancée in the family plot on her property.

After two centuries below the ground, and weeks in a forensic laboratory at the Royal Ontario Museum in Toronto, it seems Captain James Kingston may finally be on his way home.

Chapter Twenty

"Ed-wiiiiiii-naaaaaa."

Just on the verge of falling asleep, Edwina was roused by the voice. It sounded so far away, and at first, she thought she'd imagined it. She rolled into the fetal position and hugged her extra pillow close to her chest. Once again, her eyelids fluttered shut.

She'd been in the middle of such a nice dream too, one of her and Simon traveling together, seeing all the amazing places they'd always wanted to see. Japan, when the cherry blossoms were in bloom. London at Christmas. Summer in Lake Louise. They were having so much fun exploring.

"Hello, Edwina."

The voice. It brought her to complete awareness.

She knew that voice, but it wasn't the one that normally tormented her dreams.

Without moving, without even wanting to breathe, she glanced at her bedside clock. The little digital light flashed midnight.

Maybe, if she closed her eyes, it would go away.

"I'm not going anywhere."

Shit. It was in her head. It could hear her thoughts.

It's a dream, just a dream. You know how this plays out. You need to sit up, face scary Grandma and soon it'll be over.

Even though she didn't trust her own logic, she sat up and turned on her bedside light. She trained her gaze on the closet opposite her bed and waited for all the familiar elements to unfold. The smell of sickly lavender. The preamble about snickerdoodles. Grandma in her embroidered giraffe sweater. Then, as always, she would see the creature that wasn't Grandma at all.

But none of those things happened.

Instead, the voice continued to speak as if its owner was right there in the room with her. "This isn't a dream, Edwina."

She clutched her covers, dragging them over her bare legs. "Who are you?"

"You know who I am." Her closet door opened slowly, but all that emerged was a shadow. A man-sized shadow that seemed to see everything, despite her attempts to shield her nearly nude body.

The image of the pale man on Simon's porch flashed before her eyes. "Are you Reginald Perry?"

The shadow shifted as it nodded its inky mass of a head.

"Show yourself."

"I cannot." Frustration crept into his sigh. "I am bound to that place."

So, was this the best he could do, then? "Sucks to be you, I guess. What do you want?"

"I am here because of what you want." His laughter sent a chill along the base of her spine, a tickle of darkness. "She's not free, you know."

Ann.

Edwina *knew* it. She clenched her fists. "Let her go, you arrogant fuck."

More laughter. "Such a dirty mouth you have. How I would have loved to shut those pretty lips of yours. Ann had a smart mouth too, much good it did her. It didn't help her when fire rained down on Newark. It didn't help her when she froze in the snow, heartbroken. Would you like to know something splendid, Edwina Darke? When I killed her sweet James Kingston, he cried out for her. It was pathetic. But I silenced him too."

"Listen, you rotting shithead. I realize you love the sound of your own voice, but let's cut to the chase. How can I free her?"

The shadow slithered toward her. "It's very simple. Just a little trade."

Edwina's stomach turned. "You want...me?"

He sniffed in disgust. "And listen to that harpy's mouth for all eternity? No. I want Adelaide. Or rather, I want what she can give me."

"And what's that, dickweed?"

"Life." From out of the darkness, two eyes blazed, lit by an inner viciousness.

"What the fuck does that mean?"

"Bring Adelaide to the house on King Street. She'll know what to do."

"And if I don't?"

"Then Ann Forbes will never find peace."

As Perry's wraith retreated back into her closet, or whatever hellhole from which he'd come, Edwina braced herself for his chilling laughter again.

But there was nothing. No sound. No humanity. No hope.

He'd left a void from which all good things were absent, and it terrified her more than any cruel laugh or noise ever could.

Ann was in that void too, stuck somewhere with that monstrous creature.

As he disappeared, the room seemed to brighten. Edwina squinted into the light coming from the lamp on her table. Her gaze landed on a framed photo on her bookshelf, one of her and her sisters when they were kids. It had been taken at one of their many family Christmas dinners. They were sitting around the kids' table, had just pulled their Christmas crackers, and they were all wearing colored paper hats. Susannah's broad smile lit up the photo, even though one of her front teeth was missing. Edwina was pretending to be a pouting model, but managed to look like a fish instead. And Adelaide had just stuck two straws up her nose.

My little group of weirdos.

Perry's words echoed in her mind. *Just a little trade.*

They had to free Ann. If they didn't, it would haunt them for the rest of their lives.

But if Reginald Perry, that unholy fuck, thought he was getting Addy out of the deal, he had another think coming.

* * * *

Simon was having a difficult time following the conversation. All he really understood for sure was that

Edwina had descended on the bed and breakfast with her sisters, like a bevy of modern warrior women, saying they needed to speak to him and Connie.

Connie was in the process of checking in their latest guest. She nodded at Simon, and mouthed, "*Go.*"

Not wanting to freak out any of their guests, they decided to speak outside. They all walked across the street to the site of Butler's Barracks. The old barracks were situated on a large plot of parkland, and it tended to be quiet there. Even now, just approaching six o'clock in the evening, the park was virtually deserted.

Simon didn't like it, though. Before meeting Edwina and the others, he'd never considered the possibility of ghosts when he walked around the barracks. However, after experiencing everything he had, the timbered buildings now seemed creepy. He could almost swear there were invisible eyes trained on them.

It didn't help that the Darkes were saying a lot of words that scared the shit out of him.

Words like, "attachment" and "possession" and "demonic."

Their conversation had verged into argument territory in the short time he'd been with them, and the women were talking over one another. He gestured at a couple of nearby park benches and suggested they sit for a while.

"Okay," he said. "Let's start over. I need you to explain this to me like I'm five."

Susannah spoke for the others. "As you know, I've had trouble figuring out what happened to Reginald Perry after Ann died. That didn't sit right with any of us."

"But does it even matter? I thought we were doing fine," said Simon. "There's been no paranormal activity."

"I was hoping that would be the case, but I think I was wrong." Adelaide leaned in, a sense of urgency to her movements. "It'll start up again."

"How do you know that?"

"I just know," said Adelaide. "Someone like Perry, or rather, the entity that he has become, can't help himself. He feeds on fear, so he needs to generate it."

"Hang on." His head was spinning. "What do you mean, the entity he's become? Isn't he just some dead guy?"

"Go on, Addy." Edwina's voice held a quaver of anger. "Tell him. Tell him about your private conversations with Mr. Perry."

Adelaide took a moment before answering. "I haven't been having *private conversations* with him. If anything, I sensed he was dangerous, so I never let him get too close. That doesn't mean he didn't try. You saw what happened when I reached out to Ann. But, after hearing about Ed's visitation last night—"

"Wait," said Simon, turning to Edwina. "What visitation?"

"I didn't want to call and stress you out," said Edwina. "I wanted to tell you in person. That's why we came as soon as we could." She took a deep breath. "Perry appeared to me in my home."

As Simon listened to her account of the ominous visit, his head felt ready to explode. "And this invisible bastard thinks he can claim one of you in exchange for Ann? How's that even possible?"

"Here's what I suspect," said Adelaide. "Reginald Perry was like me in life. He had abilities. A person like that, someone who was intimidating and mean at the best of times, would only think to use those abilities for evil. And that's what he did. I believe he welcomed in demonic forces, and he used his power to create a sort of attachment to Ann, in life and in death. This is a man who enjoyed watching people suffer."

"Good God." It all sounded like a wild movie script to Simon.

"Ann also had abilities," continued Adelaide. "Perry recognized that in her. It was part of the reason he wanted her so much. He thought he could influence her, that they could use their combined powers to wreak havoc. But Ann refused him until the end. She never let him get close, so he turned on her."

"Could we do an exorcism?" asked Susannah.

Adelaide shook her head. "I'm not convinced that won't hurt Ann. I need to sever the attachment between them first."

"What she means," said Edwina, "is that she needs to let him in. Addy's plan is to allow Perry to possess her. Which is totally fucked and I won't allow it."

"It's not your choice," admonished Adelaide.

"Yeah, well, I'm the big sister, and I'm making it my choice."

"Look, the reason he's been calling for me," said Adelaide, "is because he knows I'm a psychic medium. He thinks he can jump me, take over my body for good and have another shot at living. But, if I can toot my own horn for a second, I'm not easily influenced. In order to banish him, I need to let him in."

Simon was certain that he'd stumbled into some sort of dream world. Normal people didn't have these sorts of discussions.

Of course, he'd known going into his relationship with Edwina that life with the Darke sisters would never be normal.

Was he nervous? Sure.

Would he support them? Hell, yeah. "What do you need from me?"

"We'll need to do it at the B&B," said Adelaide. "So, we'll have to find a time when your guests are out."

"No," cried Edwina. "We came here so we could get together and talk some sense into you, Addy. This plan of yours is so beyond acceptable. It's one thing to communicate with people's sweet dead grannies. It's another thing altogether to allow a malicious spirit to possess you!" She turned to Susannah. "Help me out here."

Susannah sighed. "Addy knows best with these things. I don't like it either, but if she's willing to take the risk—"

"I can't believe this." Edwina's cheeks were blotchy and red. "Yes, Addy has the most experience with spirits, but you both know we've all seen some intense shit. I've seen enough to know this could go horribly wrong. Addy, what if something bad happens?" Her eyes teared up. "What then, huh? I'm just a baby medium. I won't know how to help you."

Adelaide reached for her sister's hands. "As it happens, I think you will know how to help me. You've always had the power. You just didn't know. Nothing's going to go wrong. I have faith that we can come through on the other side, and that we can send Ann into the light. But I need you to trust me. Can you do that?"

Edwina closed her eyes. Simon's heart went out to her. Trust was hard, even when one wasn't about to confront some villainous dead dude. He had half a mind to grab Edwina, and her sisters for that matter, and run away with them so he could tuck them away somewhere safe.

Unfortunately, it wasn't his choice either, and he knew fuck all about these things.

If anyone could do what Adelaide was talking about, it was the Darke sisters. Although, not knowing what exactly was involved, he was more than nervous.

"Fine." Edwina opened her eyes. "I trust you."

"Thank you," said Adelaide. "Simon, when would be a good time?"

"Our guests will have cleared out after the weekend. How does Monday sound? You can have the run of the place."

"Monday, it is." The muscles in Adelaide's jaw tensed.

"Just tell me this," said Edwina. "How can you be so sure we'll succeed?"

Adelaide sat back on the park bench. "You thought I was having private conversations with Perry, and he did try. But he wasn't the only one who made contact with me. Several others have reached out since we did our vigils. Simon, I hate to break it to you, but your property is crawling with dead people."

"What?" He had to clamp his jaw shut.

"Oh, they're all quite harmless. They just have some unfinished business, and it turns out that business involves Reginald Perry." Adelaide grinned. "We're going to have help banishing this motherfucker."

Chapter Twenty-One

As soon as Edwina crossed the threshold of the bed and breakfast on Monday evening, she stopped in her tracks.

The faces, they were everywhere.

They stared at her from the darkened doorways, out of unlit corners and from over the banister. There were old people and young adults, even children. Some were dressed in nineteenth-century finery, others in the more modest attire of farmers and servants. They were all connected to the area in some way, and all of them had passed over. In an instant, she knew these were not spirits who actively haunted Simon's house, but they too needed closure.

They'd been citizens of Newark during the War of 1812. Some had been friends of the Forbes family, some acquaintances from town. They'd all had their homes burned on the night of December 10, 1813, and they'd all come to bear witness.

Oblivious to the gallery of faces, Simon kissed her on the cheek. "Hey, you. Are you all right? You seem distracted."

"I guess I am." She made eye contact with several of the spirits, on the lookout for any malice, but she didn't sense any. Just curiosity and resolve. "It's beginning."

Although he did not look over his shoulder, his eyes darted around. "You're seeing ghosts, aren't you?"

"Oh, yeah. Big time."

"Excellent. Most reassuring." His smile was tight. "Let me take your jackets."

As Simon collected their things, the Newark spirits faded into the ether. Edwina knew they lingered, on a plane she couldn't see. Adelaide had told her not to worry about the preponderance of dead folks, but it still shook her confidence.

"I saw them too." Adelaide smoothed a hand over Edwina's hair. "It's all good, I promise."

"Geez, Addy, please tell me I'll get used to this one day."

"You will. You're stronger than you think."

Edwina wasn't convinced.

Susannah elbowed Adelaide. "So, now that you and Ed both have the gift, does that mean I have some undiscovered abilities too? Personally, I've always wanted to go back in time...you know, as long as I could bring a toiletry bag and be able to return unscathed."

Adelaide narrowed her eyes. "The jury's still out on you."

"That's not a no!" Susannah walked into the parlor, where Simon and Connie were waiting for them.

Adelaide pulled Edwina aside before heading in. "Are you ready?"

"Yeah." Edwina stopped chewing the inside of her lip. "I remember everything you told me. What about you?"

"Maria and I are ready. We've got this."

On entering the parlor, Edwina could see Simon had taken his instructions seriously. Adelaide has asked him and Connie to move the furniture to the far end of the room so that there was an open space in the middle of it. She'd also asked them to remove anything that could be regarded as clutter. They'd put any knick-knacks and pieces of art in other rooms for now. In the center of the parlor, there was a small table surrounded by a circle of chairs, one for each of them.

As per Adelaide's directions, they'd also opened all the windows and interior doors. This would allow spirits to leave when commanded.

Adelaide had brought a bundle of white sage with her. Before they got started, she lit it and trailed the smoke down her body before moving from room to room.

Connie leaned over to Edwina. "To remove the bad energy?"

"Yep. Addy uses it to cleanse the house, and we keep the windows open so that that the bad energy has no choice but to go out."

"Hmm." Connie tapped her chin. "I might have to buy some of that stuff. I know a few people that I'd like to toss out of the window."

Edwina didn't even bother to stifle her laugh. She needed it too much.

When Adelaide returned, she put the remnants of her sage down on a small plate. She invited them all to sit down in the circle and clasp hands on the table. "Thank you all for coming. I would like to begin by shielding those of us here tonight in a protective light. Imagine it as a bubble or sphere, surrounding you with white light. This aura of protection encircles your head and moves down your body, all the way to your toes. It will keep you safe from any who seek to harm you."

Edwina closed her eyes and envisioned an impenetrable dome, one that rose high above them, covering the entire house and its yard. She imagined Simon and the others right in the heart of the dome, where they were safest.

"As we continue," warned Adelaide, "you may feel discomfort and even pain. If it becomes too much, say so and we'll take a break. Is everyone ready?"

Simon, who was sitting on Edwina's right, raised her hand to his mouth for a quick kiss. "Ready."

Edwina would keep that love in her heart tonight, even if things got scary.

Adelaide began. "I am speaking to the spirit of Reginald Perry of Newark. Make yourself known to us."

The lights barely flickered. He was toying with them. Edwina kept her gaze locked on her sister.

"Come on, Reginald," coaxed Adelaide. "You've been trying to get my attention from the moment I set foot in this house. You have it now, but you won't have it forever. This is your chance to give us your side of things. Tell us exactly what you did when you lived in Newark. You know you want to share. I can feel your energy in this room."

As Adelaide paused, a few strands of her hair lifted away from her face, as if touched by an invisible hand. Her flinch was almost imperceptible, but Edwina saw it.

Maria saw it too. From somewhere behind Adelaide, a child's cough erupted as a pained bark.

"It's okay, Maria," said Adelaide, her voice strained. "I've welcomed him here. You see, I'm interested in what Mr. Perry has to say. I believe he feels misunderstood, even wronged by some of the people who knew him. After all, he was only doing what everyone else in Newark was doing. He was trying to survive. I believe Mr. Perry held a great deal of affection for Ann Forbes, in his own way. He offered his hand to her several times, and she refused him each time. Anyone in his position would have been insulted, and such an insult would not have been tolerated by a man like him. He had great plans, ones that were foiled when Ann turned him down. A twenty-one-year-old girl turned him into a laughingstock. Have I got it right, Reginald? *May* I call you Reginald?"

Edwina had to hand it to Adelaide. She'd turned the slight tremor in her voice into something coy and sweet, the sort of tone that would appeal to a narcissist like Perry.

And she was getting results.

Maria continued to cough in warning, so much so that Edwina could almost feel a tightening on her own lungs. As the coughs grew in volume, a shadow appeared at Adelaide's side.

"Holy shit," Simon whispered. "I see him."

Connie and Susannah, their eyes wide, clearly did too.

The shadow sharpened, and new details came into focus. Within seconds, a man stood before them. Edwina had to bite back a gasp. It was the same man that she had glimpsed on Simon's porch. He bore the same pale face, dirty hair and nondescript clothing. Everything on or about him was shades of mud, of dust and of resentment. Edwina tried not to judge people by appearance, but the man looked like a walking, talking grudge.

Nevertheless, there was an unholy fire in his eyes, and it was trained on Adelaide.

"Thank you, Reginald. You must be miserable, living this half life." Adelaide cleared her throat. "Come into me now. Use my body as your own and unburden yourself." She closed her eyes and let her head roll back.

Edwina braced herself as Perry's spirit turned into mist, seeping into Addy's open mouth.

Maria, so loud a few moments before, went silent.

Edwina never would have thought that she'd one day miss the sound of those creepy-ass coughs, but she did now.

For a few terrifying seconds, she worried that she wouldn't be able to do what Addy had asked of her. What if she wasn't strong enough?

Help me.

All at once, Edwina felt a delicate hand settle on her right shoulder. She glanced in that direction.

A young woman with dark eyes and hair stood there, her face full of compassion. She was dressed in a flowing gown of pale gold and wore a wreath of wildflowers in her black hair. Although she no longer resembled a sick child, there was no doubt who she was.

It was Maria, and she was there to help.

Thank you, Maria. This is my first rodeo, so I appreciate you thinking outside the box, so to speak. I know you're used to working with Addy.

Adelaide slowly faced them. She opened her eyes and Perry's wicked glare confronted them. Her lips, *his* lips, curled in what Edwina suspected was their normal aspect. When she spoke, an entitled man's voice emerged.

"That wasn't very smart of dear Adelaide, was it?"

It was Edwina's turn to take charge. Adelaide had coached her on what to do, and she wasn't about to let her down. Mustering up every ounce of bravado she had, the fierceness Simon so loved, she taunted him. "Oh, no. Whatever shall we do now? A douchebag has joined the conversation."

"Watch your mouth, bitch. I'm in control now." Perry cast a lascivious glance over Adelaide's body. "I think I might stay here for a while. I'll have fun playing with this pretty young thing."

A couple of seats down, Susannah grunted, ready to lash out.

Edwina caught her eye, silently reminding her to stay calm. This was all part of the plan. "Yeah, I hear you like that sort of thing, Reggie. By the way, how many girls did you assault in Newark anyway?"

"I haven't come here to trade insults with you." Perry glared. "You're nothing to me. You're weak, just like Ann was in the end."

"But she wasn't really, was she?" asked Edwina. "Otherwise, why would you pursue her for so long?"

"Ann was beautiful, it's true. When her doddering father first introduced us, I saw the potential for a pretty and docile wife. But there was something more to her. It wasn't long before I realized she had the gift of sight, as I did. I began to watch her very closely, and soon learned she had no wish to exploit her talents. I could have helped her develop her them, but she preferred that stupid Redcoat to me. She was content to live out a bland life, with her bland lover. Her rebuttals infuriated me. How could she choose him over me? I had no choice, you see. I had to kill him to make her forget him. Captain James Kingston, the brave soldier, felled by a couple of whacks to the back of the head."

Behind Adelaide's chair, the ghosts of Newark reappeared. They stood, two or thee rows deep, listening to the proceedings like a jury at a trial. Perry, lost in his memories, didn't seem to be aware of them.

Edwina continued to distract him. "And you buried Captain Kingston under the willow tree, didn't you?" She needed him to admit it.

"Of course." Perry snickered. "I had to move quickly too. I thought it rather poetic actually, burying Ann's lover in the place where they had their illicit meetings."

The Newark spirits looked at one another, expressions of shock and anger on their pale faces.

Simon jumped in. "But Ann didn't forget Captain Kingston at all. She loved him. You don't just forget a love like that."

"You weren't content." Edwina baited him. "It wasn't enough for you to destroy their love. You needed to punish her, to punish everyone. So you rode with Joseph Willcocks on the night they burned Newark to the ground."

"Joseph Willcocks." Perry scoffed. "They gave him credit for that idea, you know. They said he was the one who told General McClure to set fire to Newark. But who do you think gave Joseph the idea?" He sat back, smug.

"It was you," Edwina said on a breath. "You destroyed a whole town out of vengeance."

"Every single person in that town turned up their nose at me at one time or another. Those people meant nothing to me. Insignificant dogs, the lot of them. I took pleasure in watching their homes burn."

The spirit people of Newark raged silently behind him. Some raised their hands to the sky. The children cried. Others screamed, no doubt reliving the horror of that night. Although Edwina was unable to hear them, she felt their pain. It burrowed deep into her soul, and she knew she'd never forget that torment.

"People died," said Edwina. "Ann did too."

Something changed in Perry's face. She glimpsed a hint of remorse. "I didn't mean for Ann to die. I just wanted to teach her a lesson. In fact, I begged her to come with me, but once again, she refused. So I let her go. I thought she would seek shelter with the others. It's what anyone else would have done. It's what I would have done."

"Yeah, but she was better than you," said Simon. "She cared for others."

"I cared for her!" Perry railed. "In fact, later that night, I told Willcocks I needed to go back and find her, but he called me a fool for clinging to a memory. We needed to escape, he said. So I followed him. Only, as I ran near the river's edge, I slipped on a slab of ice, and plunged into the river."

Susannah leaned in. "That's why he had no death record."

"I tried to call out for help, but the frigid water filled my lungs. I slipped deeper into the river, and the water froze over me," said Perry. "My last thoughts turned to Ann. If it hadn't been for her stubbornness, we both could have lived. In anger, I called upon every being of darkness, and I cursed her. I condemned her to an eternity of misery, and I prayed that I'd be able to witness her anguish."

Connie huffed. "You're an evil sonaofabitch, aren't you?"

"I was a fool to think Ann could ever appreciate what I could offer her. All I wanted was to help her realize her powers. Instead, for two hundred years, I've been confined here with a shell of a woman, one who still pines for that useless Loyalist scum. But now I am one with the lovely Adelaide. Together, we'll leave this cursed house and have so much fun."

"No," countered Edwina. "Whatever crazed vision of power you have in your head, it ends here. It ends tonight."

"And how do you plan to achieve that? I'm *inside* Adelaide. You can't remove me."

"I can, with a bit of help." Edwina sat up straight. "We have come here today to banish the spirit of Reginald Perry. In doing so, we will sever his ties to Ann Forbes and remove him from Adelaide Darke forever. I call upon all good spirits of light to help banish this negative entity from the world."

Once again, the lights flickered in the room. Perry looked about nervously.

"I know what frightens you, Reginald Perry," said Edwina. "And it's a strong woman. Maria, now!"

Maria disappeared from the room. Even though she was only gone for seconds, it felt like an eternity to Edwina. The longer that creep stayed inside Addy, the harder it would become to force him out.

But Maria did return, and she wasn't alone.

She brought Ann with her.

Perry laughed. "Is this the best you can do? She won't do anything. She's still mourning her lover."

"Ann," said Edwina, "you were right to suspect Perry of killing James, and now he's admitted it. We found James' body. He's been removed from the place where Perry left him, and he's being treated with respect and care. We're going to make sure he receives a proper burial. He's not alone anymore, and neither are you."

"You found James," Ann repeated, in a daze.

Edwina nodded. "That's right, and there's no reason for you to linger here. Reginald Perry doesn't have any power over you, not really. You're stronger than any...*pathetic* curse he muttered two hundred years ago."

"I don't know." Ann turned up her hands in frustration.

"See? She can't help you." Commandeering Adelaide's body, Perry tried to stand.

"Hold him," cried Edwina to Susannah and Simon. "Don't let go of his hands."

"What are you doing? Let me go." Perry struggled, but the others held his hands on the table, keeping him in the circle.

Edwina implored Ann. "Ann, we need you to be brave again. I know he wanted to use your talents for evil, but you are a force of light. You have the power to resist him. Trust in your abilities, Ann!"

Maria touched Ann's shoulder, and a searing light passed between the two spirit women. In that moment, Ann's posture changed. She stood tall and her cheeks took on a preternatural glow. Her hair blew, as if in an invisible wind. She seized a breath, holding it for a time, and her face took on an expression of anguish. When she released her breath, it came out on a guttural cry. "You!"

In that moment, Perry shrank in his chair.

"That's it," said Edwina. "Look at him. He's terrified of you. He killed the man you love and laughed at your grief. He burned your house to the ground, signing your death warrant. But time has passed, and Reginald Perry no longer has a stranglehold on Newark. He has no more control over you than I do over the wind."

"B-but," Perry stammered, "she is bound to me!"

"Fuck your bond," shouted Edwina. "Do you see the people here? We have bonds too. We have the bonds of friendship, of family and of love. And those bonds are so much stronger than anything you might hold over Ann. You have no power here!"

Perry made eye contact with Ann. "Ann? I only wanted to love you."

"*Love*." She raised her arm and pointed at him. "You wanted to control me and take my father's business. You wanted to intimidate me, like you intimidated everyone in Newark. And yet, your sins didn't begin with me, Reginald. You hurt and abused anyone who ever came into contact with you."

Only then, did Perry notice the citizens of Newark gathered behind him. His gaze widened in terror as he realized they'd come for him.

"You tore my heart from my chest," said Ann. "Now, I will take yours. As you destroyed my spirit, so too will I destroy yours. You consigned me to fire then to ice. Now, I do the same to you!"

Together with Maria, Ann flew across the table, her arms outstretched. The spirit women reached inside Adelaide, in an attempt to pull the dark shadow out.

But Perry clearly wasn't going without a fight. As he struggled, Adelaide tugged on Simon and Susannah's hands. She kicked her legs under the table and her face twisted in agony.

For a terrible few seconds, Edwina wasn't sure it would work. Could they lose their sister to that fiend? What would happen then? *Fight, Addy! Push him out!*

Although Perry was strong, he was no match for the combined strength of Ann, Maria and Adelaide. The spirit women held on. With a mighty heave, they extricated the vile entity from Adelaide's body. It hung from their hands like a piece of wet clothing. A ghastly shriek emanated from the seething wraith.

Ann and Maria dragged Perry's spirit over to the people of Newark. As they swarmed him, his cries gurgled and died out. Then the townspeople disappeared, taking whatever remnants were left of him with them.

In the ensuing silence, Ann looked back at Edwina. Her head dipped in the slightest of nods. Then, on a sigh that filled the room, she faded away.

As for Maria, the spirit guide hurried back to Adelaide, who was now slumped over the table. She put her hands on Adelaide's shoulders and vanished.

"Addy?" Edwina raced around the table and knelt by her younger sister. Susannah was right behind her. "Are you okay?"

Slowly, Adelaide raised her head. It was her beautiful face again, her friendly eyes and kind smile. Not a trace of Perry remained.

"Is he really gone?" asked Edwina.

Adelaide reached out a hand and mussed her hair. "Yeah. You did good, kid."

The sisters embraced, letting Adelaide catch her breath for a few moments. But Addy wasn't done. "We need to salt the doorways and the corners of the rooms."

"I'm on it," said Susannah. "I've got a fresh box of salt standing by."

Connie went to help her. "Now that we've kicked that ghost's butt, let's make sure we keep him out."

Out of breath, with her head hurting, Edwina went to Simon. As soon as their hands touched, all her cares dissipated.

"You," he said, "were fucking fantastic. Remind me never to mess with you."

She nodded toward Adelaide. "I learned from the best."

Adelaide's voice cracked with fatigue, but a happy smile lit up her face. "Simon, I feel confident in saying this house is no longer haunted."

"Amazing. Thank you, all." He slung an arm around Edwina's shoulders. "You know what this calls for?"

"What?" asked Edwina.

He gave her a knowing grin. "Ice wine slushies."

Chapter Twenty-Two

"Blessed are they that mourn, for they shall be comforted."

The words of the Anglican minister resonated with Edwina, but as the service got underway, she listened in a state of numbness. She'd always been the sort to cry at funerals—unlike Susannah, who often had difficulty expressing emotion. Edwina appreciated a good blubber every so often, but this time around, she held back for fear of losing it altogether.

As for Adelaide, she was serene and pensive as usual, as she stared toward the line of trees in the distance.

Even though Edwina was managing to keep a lid on her emotions, she felt them all the same. As she let out a sigh, there was a wobble in her breath.

Ever attuned to her emotional state, Simon slid his arm around her waist, and drew her into his side. Kissing her forehead, he whispered, "It's okay."

And it really was okay, despite the rawness of the moment. Their adventure at the King Street Bed and Breakfast had come full circle.

It was Captain James Kingston's funeral, one of which he'd been deprived so long ago. Even though half of Niagara had wanted to witness the event, it was restricted to certain individuals. Edwina and Simon were there with her sisters. Connie had brought her wife, Margie. Of course, Martha had invited a dozen or so members of her family, and they had every right to be there. There was also some military brass in attendance, as well as representatives from the local government, Fort George and the historical society. Martha had insisted on an intimate group and didn't want the burial to turn into a media frenzy.

Kingston was being laid to rest in Martha's yard, in the plot next to Ann's. As the captain's nearest living connection, albeit via an engagement that wasn't so secret anymore, Martha had fought hard to have it that way.

The minister read some sweet words about waters of comfort and green pastures. Even though Edwina wasn't into organized religion, she hoped Ann and James were feeling some of that comfort now. She hadn't sensed either presence since the night they banished Reginald Perry, and sometimes the silence troubled her. However, as Adelaide had said not long ago, *"Communicating with the dead isn't an exact science. You won't always get the answer you want."*

Edwina still found solace in the fact that Ann had looked directly at her after they removed Perry. There was a sort of finality in that look, and somehow, Edwina knew she wasn't suffering anymore. She just wished she had some sort of proof that Ann had found

James on the other side. A part of her would probably always want tangible proof, wrapped in a nice, neat bow.

You just have to believe.

She was getting better at that. Life may have messed with her head for a while, but it had been pretty sweet lately. Her relationship with Simon was thriving. He made her truly happy, and in new ways everyday. In addition, she had some terrific new friends in Martha, Connie and Margie.

She had to have faith that Ann was at peace now. She'd wanted Perry punished for his crimes. Even though that hadn't happened in life, he'd certainly faced a preternatural jury of his peers.

The minister concluded the gravesite service with a few words of benediction. "May you be at ease. May you be free from suffering. May you dwell in comfort and compassion, and may you be a source of comfort and compassion for all you meet."

Edwina not only kept Ann and James in mind, she also said a silent prayer for the people of old Newark. She often wondered where they'd gone since that night, and her hope was that they were all at peace as well.

No more unfinished business.

When the service ended, Martha embraced Edwina and her sisters. "Thank you. I can't tell you what it means to know that Ann has her James back."

"It was absolutely our pleasure," said Edwina.

"I was chatting with General Ward earlier," said Susannah, indicating one of the army officers. "Thanks to his assistance, and that of the local member of parliament, James will no longer have the word 'deserter' attached to his name. Of course, we can't do anything about historical records, but going forward, he will only be remembered for his contributions."

Adelaide laughed. "Have you seen his Wikipedia page? Our friends from the War of 1812 reenactment society have already updated it. They've been relentless in restoring honor to his name."

"What a marvelous journey. Even though this is a funeral, I can't be sad. It feels more like a homecoming." Martha sighed. "And, speaking of homecomings, everyone please come into the house for some refreshments."

At her invitation, the group began to file in.

Edwina hung back. "Simon, call I talk to you for a minute?"

"You can talk to me for as long as you want, sugarcakes."

"So." Her heart was suddenly in her throat, even though she wasn't afraid to share her news with him. "I called Bernard Granger."

Simon's eyebrows rose in what she hoped was anticipation. "And?"

"He arranged a meeting between me and the Shaw Festival director. As it happens, their lighting tech just accepted a job in Stratford. The job's mine if I want it."

"You sneaky minx. I knew you were hiding something." He pulled her in for a hug. "But is this something you really want?"

"Yes. I want the job. I want to live in Niagara-on-the-Lake with you. I love it here. This place is full of hauntings! Besides, it's close enough to Toronto that I can still take on cases with my sisters."

"That's amazing. We can start looking for a place of our own."

"Oh, I've already started looking."

"Of course, you have," said Simon. "Let me guess. You found some excellent choices, and they're all old and creepy?"

"You know it."

"For you, I would live in a haunted house. I love you. All I really need in this life is for you to be happy."

"I'm happy, and I love you too. I don't want to do the long-distance thing anymore. I want to be with you."

Giggling like a couple of kids, they kissed. Edwina closed her eyes, loving the feel of his back muscles under her hands, and the way his smile felt against her cheek.

When she opened her eyes, she spied a movement over Simon's shoulder. "Oh my God."

He turned, and the same words spilled from his lips.

Just beyond James and Ann's graves stood two figures, ones she now knew well. And yet they'd changed, and the changes made her pulse skitter into a wild new beat.

One of the figures was a handsome man in the pristine uniform of a British officer. On this uniform, none of the 49th Regiment buttons were missing. His head bore no wounds, and there was no blood on his face.

As for the woman, her brown hair no longer hung loose, instead arranged in a pretty updo. She wasn't dressed in her worn nightgown anymore. She wore a fresh cotton muslin, and had a pink ribbon tied around her waist.

Ann and James looked unbelievably happy and at peace.

They clasped hands, smiled at Edwina and Simon, and faded away. In her mind, Edwina heard the words, *"Thank you."*

For a few moments, neither she nor Simon moved.

When he did, he cleared his throat. "Well, I don't know about you, but I'm about to inquire into the contents of Martha's liquor cabinet."

"I'm right there with you. I could use a little something to steady my nerves." Edwina grabbed his hand and they headed into the house. "We'll toast Ann and James while we're at it."

Against all odds, they'd helped a pair of star-crossed lovers finally achieve their happy ending. Now, it was time for Edwina and Simon to have one as well.

Want to see more from this author? Here's a taster for you to enjoy!

Darke Paranormal Investigations: Darke Music
Rosanna Leo

Excerpt

Noah: *Hey. I know it's last minute, but are you free for dinner tonight? My treat. There's something really important that I need to discuss with you.*

Susannah Darke sat at the Italian restaurant bar and read the text for the umpteenth time that day. It wasn't unusual for her to get texts from Noah Bellamy, her favorite hookup. It was just that most of them consisted of raunchy invitations to, well, hook up.

She wasn't opposed to the messages being raunchy either. God only knew she'd sent her share of eggplant emojis to Noah. It was their thing.

They'd met about a year ago at a soul-sucking group dating event. After ingesting a couple of limp spring rolls and some very cheap wine while dodging guys who wanted to regale her with their thoughts on cryptocurrency, she'd spotted Noah across the room. He was handsome and looked bored, and she'd recognized a kindred spirit of sorts in the way he'd clutched his wine glass as if it were a life preserver.

Feeling in need of her own lifeline just then, she'd cut through the crowd toward him.

A pleasant conversation had ensued, one in which they'd realized neither of them actually wanted to be there. Susannah had only agreed to attend the event because her sisters had egged her on, saying she worked too much and had no social life. Completely true, of course, but it didn't dispel her loathing of awkward group events. As for Noah, he'd attended with a friend who didn't want to be on his own.

She'd gone home with Noah for the first time that night, and they'd discovered they were really good in the sack together. Devastatingly good, in fact. Equally beneficial was the fact that neither of them wanted anything more than that.

As a result, their text conversations tended to be short, succinct and peppered with rude depictions of fruit, vegetables and little devil faces. She got a thrill every time she received one.

But this felt different.

She and Noah didn't "go out to dinner." They didn't "discuss important things." Heck, sometimes they barely had any conversation at all. They met when they had a particular need, one that involved an hour or two of mindless fornication.

What on earth could he want?

What if, after a year of happily messing up her sheets and ruining her best panties, he was no longer happy with their arrangement? She would hate to lose what they had. It worked so well.

Had he met someone else? It wasn't out of the realm of possibility that Noah might fall in love and want to settle down. He was a great catch. Although he'd always made it clear he was on the same page that she was, and that he guarded his single status.

Or was it the alternative? For a fleeting moment, Susannah teased herself into thinking Noah might want something more...with her. A tingle shot up her spine. What if Noah Bellamy, her hot hookup buddy, wanted her, *all* of her?

Surely not.

Would she even want that?

Surely not.

The bartender approached and took her order, returning shortly with a white wine. As he handed it to her, his fingers brushed against hers and he smiled. He was cute, and his attentions were not unwelcome, but Noah would be there shortly. Even though Susannah was nowhere near being exclusive with Noah, she wasn't in the mood to encourage anyone else. She thanked the bartender and concentrated on her phone.

Within minutes, Noah arrived. He stepped into her space, resting a hand on her lower back. Again, not unwelcome at all. "Hey, you." He leaned over and dropped a kiss on her cheek. Lingering there, he whispered, "Thanks for coming."

Susannah sucked in a breath. A flutter of delight rippled under her ribs. "Hey. I was surprised to get your message."

One side of his mouth quirked up. "I know, right? Not a single eggplant emoji in sight." His gaze dipped to take in her outfit, an intimate acknowledgment of all the sexy times they'd had together. "You look gorgeous, as always."

"Thank you." Confused and curious about his invitation, she'd made an effort to look nice, and had changed from her jeans and T-shirt into a slinky black dress that cinched at the waist. She checked out his perfectly tailored navy suit and impeccable dress shoes. Every time she saw him, he seemed to have a new pair.

These ones, gray Oxfords, shone as if a butler had spent half a day polishing them. Noah liked fancy shoes even more than she did. His style sense, combined with his short black curls and strong jaw, made for a devastating combination. "You're looking pretty good yourself."

"Thanks." He picked up her wine glass and grabbed her hand. "Come on. I've got a table."

As he led her through the restaurant, several heads turned his way. She understood his allure. It wasn't even that he was handsome in a high fashion model kind of way. He had what some might consider imperfections. His nose was crooked enough to make one think he liked a bit of mischief. He had some mild scarring on his cheeks, probably old acne scars. And his thick eyebrows tended to give him an air of severity, even anger sometimes.

But Susannah had seen him break into huge smiles, and she knew a cheeky sense of humor hid beneath his intimidating exterior. She'd seen him cursing at the arrival of a shattering orgasm and had witnessed the transformative beauty of that moment. She'd heard him talk about the students at his school with pride and awe, and nothing would ever convince her he was less than stunning.

Uh, Susannah. Remember your boundaries? He's your fuck buddy, not your soulmate.

Besides, she still didn't know the reason behind this unusual social call.

If only she'd gathered her thoughts a bit better. If Noah did indeed want to take their relationship to the next level, she would have to let him down gently but firmly. She wasn't interested in having a partner or a husband, or even a boyfriend. She was happy on her own. At thirty-four, she'd seen enough of the dating scene and its miseries to know it wasn't for her.

As for the marriage scene…well, she only needed to look at her circle of friends for a stark reminder at how badly that could go.

All Susannah needed was for someone to help her with her sexual needs every so often. If Noah was no longer up for the job, she'd find someone else. Although it would make her sad to lose him.

Really sad, come to think of it.

When they got to the table, a booth tucked into the far corner of the restaurant, he set down her wine glass and they sat across from one another. A server arrived, told them about the specials, and took Noah's drink order. As soon as the server was gone, Susannah turned to Noah in anticipation. "My curiosity is killing me."

"That's what I love about you, Susannah. You hate small talk as much as I do."

"It's not that I hate it." If anyone else were currently sitting across from her, she'd have no problem indulging in some chatter about the weather or what she'd had for lunch that day. But this was Noah, and they usually got straight to the point. "I don't want you to think I don't care about how your day went. I guess that's just never been our style."

He paused, mysteries swimming in his dark eyes. "I care too. I hope you know that." He reached for her hand. A hint of a smile tickled his lips again, and her heart swelled in response. "That being said, how was your day?"

"Fine, thanks. I'm about to finish writing a new article for *Ontario's History*. It's about the role of the rebel Canadian Volunteers during the War of 1812, and the impact their traitorous actions had on their communities."

"Sounds fascinating."

"I hope so. I was inspired to dig a little deeper when we had that case in Niagara." Susannah liked the eclectic nature of her work. She was a regular contributor to a couple of historical periodicals on Canadian history, which kept things fresh and exciting. She supplemented this work with some lecturing at centers for adult learning and even at different universities from time to time. "And, of course, things are busy as usual on the DPI front. My sisters and I are getting ready to debrief a couple of clients, and we're in the midst of scheduling the next ones."

As much as she loved her writing and teaching work, Darke Paranormal Investigations had become her true passion. Along with her sisters Edwina and Adelaide, Susannah investigated sites that were reputed to be haunted, and the three of them had made a name for themselves on their YouTube channel. Each investigation was the basis for a new episode. Their subscriptions had exploded about a year ago when they'd uploaded the footage from the King Street Bed and Breakfast in Niagara-on-the-Lake. Not only had they discovered the source of the paranormal activity, they'd unearthed the remains of an early Canadian military hero. Since then, the Darke sisters had been fielding calls from TV producers and people who wanted to take them to haunted locations around the world, but the sisters weren't interested in relinquishing control over their investigations. They agreed they wanted to retain the focus on Canadian sites and Canadian history.

"Actually," said Noah, "DPI is the reason I reached out to you today. Do you think you could squeeze me into your busy schedule? I need your help."

Icy shivers raced down her spine. Susannah leaned in. Knowing what Noah did for a living, she'd been wondering if this day might come.

Noah was the dean of the Asch Institute of Opera, a prestigious school that coached young singers who were destined for careers in operatic performance. Some of them had already attended the nearby University of Toronto's Faculty of Music, and they went on to do an intensive performance-driven program at the Asch. It had nurtured many young stars, and its list of alumni was impressive.

Susannah had been inside the building before, but not for many years. The place had made an indelible impression on her, and not necessarily in a good way. Even though a part of her never wanted to revisit the Asch Institute, a more significant part of her wanted to investigate it and debunk its stories. Debunking her own experiences there would be even better. "Tell me everything."

The server returned to the table with Noah's beer and asked to take their orders. They both realized neither of them had even looked at the menu yet, so they just ordered two of the pasta specials.

Once they were alone again, Susannah pulled a small notebook and a pen out of her bag. "Do you mind if I take notes?"

"I figured you would. Things have been…unsettled at the Asch for a long time now. But lately, I've seen it affect my students in a big way."

"To be clear, you believe the Asch Institute of Opera is haunted?"

"I was a student there. I know it's haunted, but it feels like it's escalated. In the past, I wasn't in a position to do anything about it. Now I am."

"What kind of phenomena are we talking about?"

"Items are thrown around the classrooms, things like chalk and sheet music. Music stands are knocked over when no one is nearby. There are footsteps in empty hallways, disembodied voices, doors slamming, that kind of thing. Worst of all, some students claim they've been locked in rooms from the outside."

"Any apparitions?"

"I've never seen any, but there are plenty of accounts. People have seen a man in a top hat and cane. Dr. Victor Asch, presumably. There have been lots of shadow figures too. Oh, and there's one everyone calls the Gray Lady."

"Right." Susannah scrawled those details down as quickly as she could. "I'm familiar with the story of Dr. Asch. His wife died on the school property. I understand she fell down the stairs. I always used to hear that he haunted the building, searching for his lost love."

"Well, if that's the case, it's not as romantic as it sounds. It's become very distracting. I'm worried about one of our students, actually. She's our star mezzo-soprano. Her name's Ava Choi. When you look into her eyes lately, she's just not there. She began the school year with so much promise, and now she seems to be wasting away."

"I don't like the sound of that."

"No. I've talked to her several times, to see if she's having problems in other areas of her life, but she swears she isn't. She has lots of friends, but I haven't seen her with them for some time. She spends hours in the basement practice rooms. We can't seem to pry her away from them. She's even missed a few classes. I just can't shake the sensation that something is wrong, and it's something I can't see."

"My sister Edwina would say we should look at the most reasonable conclusion first. Ava could be dealing with stress. She's chosen a demanding career. Maybe she's not cut out for the opera."

Noah shook his head. "You should see her perform. She was born for this. Besides, it doesn't change the fact that the other students are freaked out too. These aren't little kids, either. They're young adults. The conversations in the hallways are wild. All they do is talk about the haunting."

"It is one of Toronto's famous urban legends."

"I get it, and I'm sure every creaky Victorian building has its stories. But this is my old school, and these are my students. I want them to be safe."

The server returned with two steaming pasta specials. Susannah and Noah tucked in, and he shared a couple of the accounts of students getting locked in the practice rooms, despite the fact that there were no locks on the doors. Because those rooms were located in the basement of the Asch Institute, it had to be a scary experience for them. Whether or not the phenomenon was truly paranormal, Susannah didn't like the idea that Noah's students felt uncomfortable in their place of learning.

She understood that feeling, and all too well. When Susannah had been about ten years old, she'd taken some private piano lessons at the Asch. At the time, it had housed a different music school that offered Saturday lessons for beginners. She'd studied there for about a year, until she'd had her own brush with the paranormal within its walls. The experience had changed her, and in ways that still haunted her.

"What do you think?" Noah twirled a length of fettucine around his fork. "Does it sound like the kind of case that might interest you and your sisters?"

Susannah didn't even need to consult with Edwina and Adelaide to know they'd be interested. In fact, ever since she'd spilled the beans about sleeping with Noah, they'd been asking her to finagle an invitation to investigate the Asch Institute.

What she really needed to decide was whether or not *she* could take on this case. As a kid, she'd tucked her frightening moments at the Asch into a deep pocket of her soul. Even now, she didn't like thinking about them.

Perhaps it was time to face the beast. If she took the case, there would hardly be a choice. She knew how these things worked. If she started exploring the building, even for someone else, those disturbing memories would resurface whether she wanted them to or not.

Could she turn Noah down? Sure. They had plenty of cases awaiting their attention.

It just didn't feel right, though. She considered his students, in particular his star mezzo-soprano. It sounded as if Ava had a bright future in opera. She didn't deserve to lose it because some faded wraiths insisted on clinging to a structure they knew in life.

If anything, Susannah and her sisters were in the best position to help. "I can speak for my sisters. We'll take the case."

"Great. How soon can you come?"

"Oh gosh. That bad, huh?"

He nodded.

"Noah, I haven't done any prep. I mean, I know a bit about the history, but not enough for the purposes of a full-scale investigation. I don't like going in unarmed."

"We have a library at the school. I can get you access to whatever you need. Would that help?"

His eager expression caused a wibble-wobble in her stomach. She couldn't disappoint him. "Tell you what. I'll book a time for a walk-through, so we can get the lay of the land. I just need to check with Edwina. She's the one with the theater job in Niagara-on-the-Lake, so we have to work around her schedule. In the meantime, I'll start gathering some information."

"That would be awesome."

"Of course." Susannah's face heated upon seeing him brighten. "I don't want to leave you in a lurch. Paranormal activity can be upsetting, even at the best of times."

"You're the greatest, Susannah. Thank you." He glanced down the hallway leading toward the restrooms. "Excuse me. I'll be right back."

While Noah visited the restroom, Susannah called her sister Edwina.

Edwina picked up right away. "Hey, Suz."

"Hey. You won't believe the case I just snagged for us. Noah wants us to come to the Asch Institute."

"Get out!" A muffled shriek of excitement accompanied Edwina's exclamation. "We finally get to dig through the scary place where you took piano lessons as a kid?"

"Yup."

"Wait. Are you okay to go back there?"

"Sure. The place always creeped me out, but this is a paranormal investigator's dream. It's an iconic example of old Toronto architecture, and it's bound to have all sorts of dark corners and secrets." Another series of shivers assaulted her backbone, but she rolled her shoulders to ease them. If only a good stretch could eliminate the sudden ache in her stomach. "This is a chance to uncover the truth behind the Asch. I'd be foolish not to take it."

"As long as you're sure. Wow. I have to tell Addy right away."

"Addy's there with you?"

"Yeah. I had some questions about the whole mediumship thing, so she came out to Niagara-on-the-Lake to have dinner with Simon and me."

"Oh." The tenderness in her stomach turned into full-on cramps.

"She's just the only one I can talk to about this stuff. Hang on. I'll be a sec."

Stricken by a sudden case of FOMO, Susannah cleared her throat. She knew her sisters wouldn't purposely try to exclude her. They just had things to talk about, things to which she couldn't relate.

A couple of important developments had happened during their investigation at the King Street Bed and Breakfast. Firstly, Edwina had fallen in love with Simon, one of the property owners. Secondly, Edwina had learned she was a medium, a gift she shared with their younger sister, Adelaide. Because Adelaide had been talking to dead people all her life, she was able to help Edwina with the strange transition.

Susannah didn't have any unusual gifts, unless one counted the ability to talk for hours on end about early Canadian social history. Now, after months of conversations to which she couldn't really contribute, she was feeling left out. Suddenly, after a lifetime of being especially close to her sisters, it seemed she had less in common with them. Twinges of jealousy tore through her whenever one of them brought up their unique bond.

Susannah listened as Edwina shared the news with Adelaide. When Edwina got back on the phone, Susannah didn't really feel like chatting anymore. "Listen, Noah's on his way back. Could you just text me your availability for the next few weeks? I'll talk to you later."

"Okay." She could almost hear Edwina leering over the phone. "Have fun with Noah." She made a bunch of kissy noises.

Susannah disconnected the call. *See? You're being silly. It wasn't as if they set out to exclude you.*

And yet, this wasn't the first time they'd hung out without her. It had been happening a lot, and despite her best efforts to let it go, the knowledge triggered the worst of her insecurities.

Noah returned and sat down. "Feel like some dessert? They have amazing cannoli here."

A conversation from Susannah's childhood suddenly popped into her head. When she and her sisters were little, they'd all had to grapple with Adelaide's strange talent. Whenever she would communicate with dead people, Susannah and Edwina had had to deal with the comments and the stares. One of their aunts had tried to console them by saying, *People just don't understand that Addy's special.*

Of course, that hadn't been any consolation at all. And now Edwina was "special" too.

What did that make Susannah?

Don't be childish.

"Did I lose you," asked Noah, "or are you just distracted by the idea of those cannoli?"

"Dessert, right." Feeling untethered after her quick conversation with Edwina and the news that the Asch Institute was still a source of concern, Susannah was consumed by the need to hold onto something.

Someone.

"Hmm." She grabbed Noah's hand and pulled it toward her. Leaning forward on the table, she pressed her breast against his knuckles. "What if I told you I don't want dessert tonight?"

"Oh, yeah?"

"Yeah. I just want you."

Their corner of the restaurant was dimly lit, and no one was looking their way. Noah discreetly brushed his thumbnail across her nipple, over her dress bodice. When he spoke, his voice was hoarse. "That can be arranged." He sat back, hailed the server, and quickly paid for their meals. He stood and held out his hand. "Your place or mine?"

They both lived downtown, but Susannah's condo was only a block away. "Mine."

They exited the restaurant, and marched down Bloor Street West. Neither of them said a word as they walked north on Bedford Road, toward Prince Arthur Avenue. They remained silent as they entered Susannah's condo building. When they got on the elevator, they had to ride up with a couple of other residents, so they didn't say anything then either.

They arrived on her floor and hurried down the hall to her unit. It was only as she stuck her key into the lock that she noticed the tension in Noah's jaw and the heat in his eyes.

Good. That was how she liked him. Focused, hard and hot. As they shoved her unit door open, his thick eyebrows became a slash of concentrated desire.

Noah closed and locked the unit door for her, then moved her up against her foyer wall. "You're a naughty girl, aren't you?"

In response, Susannah reached under her dress, and tugged on her panties. Still in her heels, she slid the silky scrap of fabric down her legs and over her shoes. "I have my moments."

She was about to toss the panties on the floor, but he took them from her hand. His gaze never leaving hers, he shoved the panties in his suit jacket pocket.

"I happen to like those, you know," murmured Susannah, even though she didn't mind him taking them in the slightest.

"You'll get them back. Eventually."

"Looks like you're the one being naughty now."

"Oh, yeah? My behavior's about to get much, much worse." His breath coming hard, Noah dropped to his knees, and pushed the bottom half of her dress up toward her waist. With one hand, he urged her thighs apart and then slid his fingers between them. "Already wet, huh?" He brought a finger to his mouth and sucked. "Delicious."

He moved one of her legs over his shoulder, buried his face between her legs and licked.

Susannah closed her eyes and dug her fingers into his thick curls. *Yes, this.*

She was already out of sorts after hearing about the phenomena at the Asch Institute, and the weird situation with her sisters just amplified it. This was all she needed. A sexual recalibration. When Noah was between her legs, she forgot everything else. He was her perfect distraction.

They would have a lovely fuck, hopefully up against this very wall, and her emotional slate would be wiped clean.

Perfection.

Only, as her orgasm began to build with wave after wave of heady sensation, Susannah remembered her earlier questions. At the start of the evening, she'd wondered if Noah might ask to take their relationship to the next level, but he hadn't.

He didn't want her, after all.

When the first noises ripped from her throat, they sounded like her usual cries of ecstasy. But something else propelled them, something unsettling and mysterious.

Something that felt an awful lot like of disappointment.

About the Author

Rosanna Leo writes contemporary and paranormal romance. She is the First Place Winner of the 2018 Northern Hearts Contest (Contemporary Romance) for *A Good Man*.

From Toronto, Canada, Rosanna occupies a house in the suburbs with her husband and their two sons, and spends most of her time being tolerated by their cat Sweetie. When not writing, Rosanna works for her local library, where she is busy laying the groundwork to become a library ghost one day.

Rosanna loves to hear from readers. You can find her contact information, website details and author profile page at https://www.totallybound.com

Home of Erotic Romance

Sign up for our newsletter and find out about all our romance book releases, eBook sales and promotions, sneak peeks and FREE romance books!